KILL FOR ME

REBECCA BRADLEY

Text copyright © 2019 Rebecca Bradley
All Rights Reserved

This book is a work of fiction and any resemblance to actual persons living or dead, is purely coincidental.

Cover art by Design for Writers.

1

Lucy looked at the clock on her dashboard. She only had ten minutes to get to the school to collect Faith and the journey took just under fifteen minutes in the best conditions, but today, today was horrendous. She looked at the queued traffic in front of her, the red brake lights that glared angrily at her to match her mood, her stomach twisting in knots. She would be late. Faith would worry and probably start to cry. She was four years old and the morning visits to nursery were enough for her at the minute until she started full-time school next year.

Faith was an easy-going child, but she liked routine. If she didn't know what was happening, she would stress. Lucy hoped one of the teachers would say the right thing to keep her calm.

Lucy had no idea what had happened to build up the traffic like this but she had been pushing it anyway. She had left the doctors' surgery she worked at a couple of minutes late as she had picked up the phone instead of walking away and leaving it to one of her colleagues. She should have known better. Old Mr Jones had been on the other end of the line and no amount of cajoling would get him off until he had said all he wanted to say. When asked the reason he needed an appointment he thought this was an ideal time to give the whole medical history. Lucy had tried to get him to jump ahead, to curtail him and tell him she had it, but he had ignored her and kept on and she couldn't cut him off. She'd be in big trouble if she hung up on a patient.

The cars crawled forward and she could finally see there were new roadworks ahead of her. Her fingers tapped on the steering wheel, impatience skittering through her veins.

After ten minutes she pushed past the temporary traffic lights as they changed to red and put her foot down to be the last car through. The last couple of miles went by in a blur as her mind raced with the possibilities of her daughter's state. Her gorgeous beautiful daughter. She was so very proud of her and hated to let her down, but it happened sometimes, being a single mum. She couldn't be everything to her all the time, no matter how hard she tried. And she did. She tried to be it all. The good parent and the bad parent who disciplined. It was hard to strike that balance. To find a middle ground where Faith knew she was loved and secure, but where rules were in place, like bed times and eating at the table together.

The school was in sight.

Lucy let out a breath of relief and bowed her head to thank whoever needed thanking that she wasn't any later. Her phone pinged in her pocket but she ignored it.

She reversed into a parking spot, climbed out the car and closed the door behind her with a slam.

Her phone pinged again.

She ran into the school playground where children were playing. Those children who were either brave enough to stay all day or were waiting to start the afternoon session. She recognised Faith's teacher on playground duty, Mr Hughes, and ran up to him. She wished it wasn't him. Not after what had happened with him. It shouldn't matter anymore, but Lucy still felt a tingle of... what? Embarrassment? Even though they were trying to sweep it under the carpet.

'Oh gosh, I'm so sorry I'm late,' she gushed at him. 'It was one of our older patients on the phone and then there were roadworks. It's been a nightmare.' She looked at the teacher who wore a confused look. 'But I'm here now,' she finished, looking around for Faith, who she had expected to be clinging to Mr Hughes for grim death while she waited for her mum. She must be inside, too upset to be outside with everyone else. Poor mite. 'Is she inside?'

''Ms Anderson?' Mr Hughes looked concerned, gone was the hurt look he usually tried to hide, now there was a furrow of eyebrows over his dark eyes. 'Why are you here?'

'To collect—'

Her phone pinged again. There was an insistence to it.

'To collect Faith of course.'

'But, you texted us, you told us a friend was picking her up early for a dentist appointment and you couldn't get out of work on time. He came by and took her. We only let him because the text came from your number.'

The ground shifted under her. The grey flat concrete moved like an escalator, tilting upwards. Lucy pushed her hands outwards to steady herself.

'It said what?' Her voice was little more than a dry croak.

'That Faith had a dental appointment and your friend was to pick her up ten minutes early.' Concern flashed across Mr Hughes' face. 'Do we have a problem, Ms Anderson?'

Lucy pulled her phone from her pocket. It had come from her phone? The phone that had been beeping her the last ten minutes. There were four text messages. All from the same unknown number. They all said the same thing.

I have Faith. Do not go to the school. Await further instructions. Do not alert the police or you will never see her again.

2

'Ms Anderson?' The teacher was ignoring a child that was hanging on to his leg as Lucy clung to her phone, fingers tight around the device, brain screaming incoherently at her. White noise that she couldn't make sense of.

The children in the playground blurred in front of her eyes. Her breath caught in her chest and was pressing down into her diaphragm. She couldn't breathe. The tips of her fingers on the phone tingled. It was as though she didn't belong in this body. The ground tilted, Lucy bent over, placed a hand on her knee in an attempt to stay upright. She sucked in air hard.

'Is everything alright, Ms Anderson, with Faith?' The teacher's concern was seeping through the sound in her brain.

You will never see her again.

The pressure built up in her chest, Lucy gasped hard for air.

Mr Hughes placed a hand on Lucy's arm, gentle and guiding. 'Come inside, we'll call the police.' A quiet whisper to the child at the side of him, 'Go and find Mrs Grainger and she'll sort you out.' He started to herd Lucy towards the school building. Police. He'd said police.

This jolted Lucy enough to be able to speak, to make some kind of decision, if only that she needed time to make a decision. She needed to get away from the eyes of Mr Hughes and find some space for herself. Call the number back. Talk to Faith. Know she was okay.

'No. No. It's fine. I sent that message then managed to get away, but then got tied up and in the mess forgot I sent my friend.' She turned to walk away. Away from the grip of Mr Hughes. 'I'm sorry to do this to you.' She was taking big strides. Trying not to run, which would look suspicious after her behaviour just now. But her legs were itching to get back to her car so she could read the message again and then phone the number. It was as if there was electricity running through her.

'If you're sure?' Mr Hughes voice was uncertain. 'Ms Anderson?' he shouted out as Lucy moved further away.

Lucy couldn't stop herself. As she neared the gate she made a run for it. Her legs pumping hard as she flew towards her car, parked down the road. It seemed as though it was moving away from her as she bolted towards it. Then she was there and she ran into it with a body slam. Her breath hot and heavy, her throat dry, her tongue sticking to the roof of her mouth. She opened her bag.

'Fuck.' Her keys were in her bag somewhere, tossed carelessly inside when she thought she'd be able to stand at the side of the road a minute searching for them with Faith at her side chattering about her morning, not like this, not in fear for Faith's life. Her hands shook as she moved bits of paper, her purse, a lipstick, her phone, a bag of sweets.

'Fuck, fuck, fuck!'

A woman on the other side of the road looked across at her with disdain. This would have upset Lucy on any other day, but this was not any other day. This was the day a madman had picked up her daughter from school and was threatening to kill her.

'Fuck.' She cursed again, just before she wrapped her hands around her keys. Her fingers were numb, like they weren't her own, as though someone else were controlling them. She fumbled with the lock on the car. Failing to push the key into the lock then unable to twist it. Eventually she was in. She pulled the door, threw herself inside and grabbed her phone and pulled the car door behind her at the same time.

She needed to speak to this man. She needed her daughter back. Whatever he wanted she would give him. She didn't have much but she would give him it all to get Faith back. She pawed at the screen, opened up the messages and read them again. *No police. Never see her again.*

Lucy opened the car door and vomited onto the pavement, splattering sour liquid back up into her hair. The smell foul and acrid. She didn't care. She wiped her mouth with the back of her hand, sticky and yellow, closed the door with a slam, the violent scent of vomit in the enclosed space barely registering as she dialled the number that had sent the text message.

She was going to get her daughter back and she would do anything to make sure that happened.

3

The phone rang. Lucy waited, vibrating with shock and fear. Had she done the right thing to run away from the school, from Mr Hughes. He had wanted to help her, to shepherd her into the safety of the school building, but Lucy had bolted. She had taken heed of the words on the screen. Her first instinct was to protect her daughter and that meant following the orders that were directed at her. But now, as she listened to the familiar tone of a ringing phone, she wasn't so sure of herself or her actions. Surely the police were best placed when a child had been taken? What the hell had she done? Would they really hurt her baby? How was she supposed to know? She had no idea who *they* or *he* or even *she* was. All Lucy knew was that Faith must be terrified and she had to get her back home safe.

The phone rang off. There was no answer. Lucy pulled it away from her ear and stared at the screen. No answer. How could they do this to her? They must have demands. Instructions. Something they needed so that she could get Faith back. They didn't just want Faith. In fact they had implied if she went along with them that she would see her again. So they must want something in exchange for her.

Suddenly Lucy had something to cling onto. She clicked into the text message again to confirm what she had figured out.

Do not alert the police or you will never see her again.

Or you will never see her again. Yes. This implied that if she didn't go to the police that she would see Faith again. Her heart lifted in her chest. She was going to see Faith again. It would be okay. All she had to do was what they said and Faith would be home.

Lucy scrubbed a hand over her face, frustration driving her every movement. She needed them to answer the phone so she knew what she had to do.

She dialled the number again.

A woman walked down the street, at the side of the car, hand-in-hand with a young boy. He looked to be about the same age as Faith. Probably in the same nursery and had been collected on time. He was skipping, his mum's arm waving along with him as he jolted her about with each little jump.

Oh Faith, Mummy is coming to get you. I will give them anything for you, sweetheart.

The dialling tone ended again.

Lucy screamed into the steering wheel. Why wouldn't they answer? How could she give them what they wanted if they wouldn't answer?

She screamed again.

There was a knock at her window.

She jumped in her seat.

An elderly gentleman was stooped over peering into the car. Lines ran out from his eyes and underneath them. His skin soft looking, like fine dough she would be able to knead if she reached out and touched him. She pressed the button and the window moved down an inch.

'You okay, love?' he asked with kindness in his voice. 'Can I do anything?'

She so wished he could do something to help her.

'Love?'

Lucy realised she hadn't answered him as his face pushed to the window. She placed her palm against the glass. The coolness seeped into her skin. Grounded her a little, reminded her of where she was and what she was doing.

'I'm fine, thank you. A little frustrated with life, that's all.'

The old gentleman laughed, the small lines running from his eyes deepened. 'Oh I understand that one alright. But don't let it get you in that state, love. You need to laugh in its face, don't let it drag you down.' He paused, looked down the street as though an answer would appear there for him. 'Can I do anything to help?'

'No. No, thank you.' She was so grateful for his thoughtfulness, but she needed for him to go so she could call the number again.

The phone pinged in her hand. Lucy jumped. Her heart flew into her mouth. She scrabbled about, nearly dropping the phone in the eagerness to get the screen to face her.

It was the same unknown number.

'Are you sure you're okay?' The old man sounded concerned.

'Yes, yes, thank you.' She pushed the button and the window back up. The old man pursed his lips at her and scratched his head. He muttered something under his breath and turned and walked away.

She was alone again.

She pressed through to the message.

Go home and await instructions.

That was it. Go home and await instructions. They expected her to just wait? In this state? She was expected to wait?

She pressed the dial button again and listened, but instead of it ringing out the call was rejected. She pressed through again, and again the call was rejected.

Another text came through.

Go home and await instructions.

She wanted to scream again but she would draw attention to herself and she had no idea how this was going to play out or what she was going to do. She was still parked outside the school. She could still go inside and call the police.

Another text came.

Do not call the police or you will never see her again. And I will know, trust me on that.

What, did they have a scanner in her head?!

She couldn't risk Faith's life. She had to do as they said for now and maybe change her mind later on, depending on what their demands were.

Why were they even doing this? It wasn't as though she had any money to speak of. She worked part-time in a doctors' surgery.

Lucy looked back at the school. The bell had been rung, the kids were queuing with their teachers to go back inside. Parents were dropping the afternoon children off. Safety was back there. But not safety for her. Not safety for Faith. Safety for Faith was back at home.

Lucy started the engine.

4

The three-bedroom semi that Lucy and Faith shared on Peter's Close, Arnold, felt as though it had no soul when Lucy pushed the front door open. Faith added the soul to the house and right now Faith was supposed to be running about asking what she could have for her lunch. Lucy's scalp prickled as she closed the door behind her and she was left alone in the hallway. The silence was oppressive, like being under a winter quilt when the sun was shining. She just wanted to get out from under it, but there was no escape from this. Nowhere to go. She had been told to go home and that's where she was. This was supposed to be her safe space but that had been torn away from her. It was as though the walls were watching her. Her every move stilted and foreign because she was sure they knew what she was doing.

She walked through to the kitchen and dropped her bag onto the counter, fished out her phone and texted the number back.

I'm home. Now what?

She couldn't simply wait for demands. She needed to push this along.

The silence continued. She wanted to claw the hair right out of her head. She wanted to run from the house and not come back. But where would she run to and why was she running? She scratched at her arms as she paced around the small kitchen.

The complete silence and lack of Faith in the house was unbearable.

Faith, oh Faith sweetie. What is happening to you? This thought slammed into her brain like a speeding train and whipped the breath out of her. Tears flooded her eyes. She hadn't had time to process what all this meant until she got in the house and time had at last slowed for her to think. Now she had to consider what they had her for and what they were doing to her. It felt as though her insides were being carved in half. She wrapped her arms around herself, bent over and the tears spilled.

'Faith,' she wailed. 'Faith, oh Faith.' The pain was immense. She was alone and she had no idea who or what was happening to her darling daughter. She had to get her back. Lucy stepped backwards as she cried and she hit the wall with a thud where she allowed herself to slide down to the floor. The tears came relentlessly. Her baby was with strangers and would want her mummy. How could this have happened?

Was she cold? Had they hurt her? Where were they keeping her? Did she know she had been abducted or were they still pretending they had picked her up on the say-so of her mummy. Oh sweet, sweet girl. Please be okay and think that Mummy is on her way. Be eating too many sweets and sugary drinks. Be kicking your feet on a sofa and watching a cartoon. Be talking too much about lions and zebras and giraffes. Feel safe and unconcerned.

The pain ripped through Lucy like a physical blade tearing her apart. She needed some answers. She couldn't wait.

She wouldn't wait.

She picked up the phone again.

Swiped at her face. Pushing the tears out of her eyes so she could see the screen. Tapped through to the last call dialled and dialled again. Again it was rejected.

She went to the text message and sent another.

I'm home. What do you want?

Lucy clutched the phone hard, staring at it, willing it to respond to her. To tell her what it wanted from her.

It pinged in her hand. She couldn't open the screen fast enough.

What would you do for your daughter?

She was fast.

Anything.

How far would you go?

She didn't even need to think about it.

As far as was needed.

There was silence. Lucy had the urge to throw the phone across the room and into the wall but it was her only communication with the person or people who had Faith. She had to keep it close.

They were talking to her now. They wanted something. She just had to get it out of them what it was they wanted. She would do it. She would do anything.

The text message came. Relief swept through her. This must be it. This must be what they wanted. This was her chance to get Faith back. She would do what they wanted and she would get her daughter back.

She opened the message.

You have to kill someone.

5

'Happy birthday to you, happy birthday to you, happy birthday dear Aaron, happy birthday to you.' The noise in the incident room was raucous. My detective sergeant, Aaron Stone, was sitting at his desk looking uncomfortable with the noise surrounding him and the fact that the noise was aimed at him. He lived with Asperger's and no one in the office knew this other than me which was why there was this much fuss directed at him. I hadn't been able to deter the team, no matter how much I had tried. And I had. I warned them that he wouldn't appreciate it, that he hated fuss, that he didn't want to celebrate his birthday, that he wanted it to pass unnoticed. But, this was happening. No one paid me any attention. They adored Aaron and wanted to show him that.

Pasha Lal, the newest member of the team, was standing in front of him wielding a chocolate caterpillar cake with five candles down his back to denote Aaron's forty-fifth birthday.

'Blow them out then?' she insisted. 'And don't forget to make a wish.'

'Yeah, that we get a decent job in the office,' said Ross.

I raised my eyebrows at him. 'Really?'

'Not that I want anyone to die, Boss, but... you know what I mean.'

I did. He was fed up dealing with the more mundane cases we had been given in lieu of a murder.

Pasha pushed the caterpillar closer to Aaron who leaned back a little. Not much but I noticed.

'Blow,' she said.

He gave me a pleading look. I smiled at him apologetically. He was struggling but he knew the team and had worked with them long enough to be able to cope with them. He would do what he needed to after this to calm himself.

With a feeble breath he blew on the candles. They flickered and went out and he breathed a sigh of relief that it was all over. Then they relit themselves. The room roared with laughter.

Damn, they'd bought those stupid candles that you can't blow out.

Pasha looked at Aaron's face. She must have seen something because she took a step back. 'Okay, I'm going to cut this delicious looking creature up. Who wants some?'

Several shouts of 'Me!' went up and Pasha walked to her desk where there was a pile of paper plates and a large knife. She had come in prepared. It was usual practice for the birthday boy or girl to buy the cakes but today Pasha had thrown that habit out of the window and had brought the cake in for Aaron herself.

'Want to cut—' she started, but Aaron glared at her. 'I'll do it, shall I?' she laughed.

'Dibs on the end piece,' said Ross from his desk.

I shook my head. 'Dibs?'

'Yeah, it's a real thing where cake is concerned, Boss.'

Pasha handed it out to the team. It was gratefully received.

I sidled up to Aaron. 'Did you have a good morning with Lisa and the kids?'

'Yeah, she made a healthy breakfast before work and I opened my presents.'

Aaron had changed his diet since he he'd had a heart attack about four months ago and this was enforced by his wife.

The incident room doors opened and our DCI, Kevin Baxter,

walked in. 'Looks like I'm missing something interesting.' His eyes landed on Pasha cutting up the caterpillar cake. 'I have good timing though.'

Pasha stood in front of him with a piece of cake on a plate. 'Like a piece, Sir? It's Aaron's birthday.'

'Is it now?' He turned to Aaron. 'Happy birthday, Aaron.'

Aaron nodded mutely.

Baxter turned his attention back to Pasha. 'It'd be rude to say no.'

She held out the plate.

'Am I taking this from someone's starving mouth?' he asked.

Pasha laughed. 'There's plenty to go around.'

'Was there something you needed?' I asked him.

He looked to Aaron. 'No, no, it'll wait. I'll catch up with you later.'

I didn't like the sound of this. Baxter was trying to get rid of Aaron out of the Major Crime Unit. He had offered him a position in the Training Department a couple of months ago but Aaron had turned him down. I knew Baxter still wanted him gone. Aaron and I were determined Baxter was not going to win this battle. We would do whatever was necessary even if that meant going over his head and talking to Superintendent Catherine Walker.

Aaron pulled his earphones out of his desk drawer and plugged them into his ears. Baxter gritted his teeth. This was one of the issues. He had no understanding of Aaron's sensitivity to noise and presumed he wanted to listen to music during his work day and was slacking when he should be working. He didn't realise it actually helped Aaron and kept his productivity levels up.

Baxter looked at me, a what-are-you-going-to-do-about-it look on his face.

We needed to resolve this sooner rather than later.

6

Lucy stared at the phone screen.

She had to kill someone?

If Faith wasn't genuinely missing she would think someone was trying to wind her up. In fact, maybe that was what was happening. Maybe someone she knew had collected Faith from school and this was all a wind-up. No one would suggest she kill a person in reality.

Not if they knew her.

She was the person who caught spiders and let them go outside. Her last ex, Faith's father, he had laughed at her for this. He told her to stand on them, that there were plenty more of them willing to rampage through the house, but she refused to listen and had saved every one. Though he didn't know he was a father, and the guilt at times ate away at Lucy, she was adamant she had done the right thing. She had thought she was in love with him, and he had doted on her but he had shown a different side on occasion, a streak she wasn't willing to bring a child into the world with. A mean and nasty streak. So she had ended the relationship when she found out she was pregnant and had walked away.

Her head didn't feel as though it belonged to her. What was this ridiculous game and how was Faith involved with it?

Just send Faith back now, or tell me where to pick her up. Enough is enough. She sent the message.

The phone vibrated in her hand.

If you want to see your daughter again you will kill someone.

There was no ambiguity about the message. No one was laughing.

I won't. She sent.

Say goodbye to Faith.

Lucy whimpered. Pushed her back into the wall and pulled her knees up to her chest. Was this real?

Please tell me she's okay.

There was silence. Why wouldn't they answer? Lucy closed her eyes tight shut. Pleaded for them to respond. To let her know that Faith was fine and was waiting to come home.

The phone vibrated in her hand again. She pressed at the screen with jagged movements. It wasn't them. It was her best friend Sophie.

Hey, thought I'd check, see if you're still up for movie night on Saturday? I'm fetching the wine! Yummm.

Lucy started to cry again. The tears streamed down her face. Life was going on around her and she wasn't interested. All she wanted was Faith and someone was holding Faith. Against her will. The phone slid out of her hand and onto the floor. She couldn't go on like this if they didn't answer. If the silence continued then she would have to go to the police. She would have no choice.

Her phone vibrated and shimmied across the floor tiles. Lucy grabbed for it, snatching it up. It had to be them. They had to text back.

It was them.

It was a photograph message.

Faith was sitting on a sofa watching television. There was nothing to say where she was or who she was with, just that she was alive and well and hadn't been hurt. It was even possible she didn't know she had been taken away from her mummy without permission.

Lucy cried even harder, holding the phone close to her chest before bringing it back in front of her face to stare at the image of Faith mesmerised by the television again. She was oblivious and Lucy was grateful for that. She couldn't be more grateful for anything. Grateful that she was the only one who was suffering.

The phone vibrated again.

You've seen her.

Lucy let out a deep breath.

Now if you want to see her again you will kill someone.

Her hand holding the phone started to shake. She couldn't read the words on the screen. Her body was trembling. Her foot was tapping on the floor.

Were they serious about this? Was this the price to get her daughter back? She had to kill someone? But who? Who did they want her to kill? And why?

She sent a message. Who? And why?

It doesn't matter why. The who doesn't matter. The choice is yours. You kill someone, anyone. Take a photograph, send it to this number and you will get your daughter back.

She would get her daughter back. She would get her daughter back. Six words that drummed a beat in her chest. She would get her daughter back.

Yes, she would do anything to get Faith back.

Did that include killing an innocent person?

7

How on earth would she kill someone?
And was she actually sitting on the freezing floor considering this?
She was.

If this was the only way to get Faith home then yes, yes she was. He had said he would know if she called the police or if they were involved. She didn't know how, if it was because he had someone in the police or... she looked around her kitchen... did they have devices in her home? She had no idea how well planned this had been. How far in advance they had prepared this. How technologically advanced they were. They had managed to clone her phone number to text the school so they were somewhat tech savvy. She couldn't take any risks. Not with Faith's life. With her own, yes, but not with Faith's.

Once she had Faith to safety she could hand herself in to the police. Do her time. Make it all right. But first she had to get Faith back. Make sure she was safe and secure.

Her phone vibrated. It was Sophie again. Three question marks graced the screen. She was impatient. Oh how she wished she could talk to Sophie. Tell her about the mess she was in and about what she was contemplating. Sophie had a good head on her shoulders and would know what to do, the right move to make. Though Lucy couldn't see any move other than to do as she was told.

She texted Sophie back that she thought she was coming down with something and she would let her know nearer the time if they needed to cancel. Sophie sent big virtual hugs back. Lucy loved Sophie to bits.

Maybe Sophie could help her kill someone? Come up with a quick and painless way that would be bearable. It needed to be as painless for Lucy as it did for the unsuspecting victim. This was going to psychologically kill her as much as it was going to physically kill them. And how the hell was she going to choose a victim? What was she supposed to do, roll a dice? Get people to pick a card? What the hell!

And how would she do it? Scenarios ran through her head but they were all too violent or too bloody or would take more strength than she possessed. She had to think of not having witnesses, because even though she was going to hand herself in, she didn't want the police to come for her, she wanted to go to them in her own time. When she had sorted Faith out. Made sure she was back and secure.

Her head was spinning so much that thought was barely possible. She realised just how ill she felt. How she was supposed to be in any state to do this she didn't know. She wasn't in much state to stand up at this rate.

Back to what she had to do and her head spun even more. It wasn't even as though she read crime novels. She was a romance reader. People fell in love and ended happily ever after. She couldn't pick up one of her books and figure out a way to do it from there. The most she could figure out from her books was how to learn to love herself, enjoy life and be worthy of being loved. Not that she had been loved since she had had Faith. She had concentrated on being a mum. The best mum she could be. Relationships hadn't come into the equation, though Sophie had been talking about it recently. Trying to nudge her into that direction. Talking about starting an online dating profile or even setting her up on a blind date with some bloke or other that she knew. But she couldn't go there. Faith was her world and she couldn't imagine bringing a man into it. And what man was interested in a woman who had a ready-made family?

Her bones started to stiffen. How long had she been on the kitchen floor? She looked at the phone at the side of her. Two hours had passed. She had been crying and wailing and thinking and texting with them, for the past two hours. It would start to get dark in another couple of hours. She needed to decide what she was doing because she couldn't sit here all night and the longer Faith was out, the more concerned she would become about why she was not at home. She would wonder where her mummy was and why she hadn't collected her. Lucy had to get her back which meant she had to come up with a plan.

She started by dragging herself up off the cold tiled floor. Her joints screamed in protest as she climbed up the wall, one slow movement at a time. Once she was upright she looked around her, as though the room had the answer. She looked out of the window and there it was on the driveway. An answer of some description. A way she could do this without feeling it as such, without seeing much of anything happening and without getting any evidence on her person.

Outside on the drive was the car. If she drove at someone hard enough she could knock them over and kill them. If she did it in the dark on a quiet street, there would be no witnesses and no CCTV. There would be no blood on her clothes. She would take the car straight to a car wash.

She moved closer to the window and stared out at her car.

Yes, this was the way she could do it. She was going to kill someone with her car.

8

He looked at the little girl on the sofa and let out a sigh. It had been easy enough to do and it was all going to plan. Faith was a pleasant child and was trusting and generous. She had taken food from him and was now sitting on the sofa watching a cartoon he had found on one of the many networks.

All he'd had to do was clone her mother's phone number. He had been surprised she still had the same number as when he was with her but she obviously had. He sent a text message from his computer to the school as though it was coming from her number and they had given the girl to him. Any old hacker could pull this trick. Just because he was good with a computer shouldn't mean he could walk away with a child this way.

He looked across at her again. She wore a bright smile and was relaxed enough. He didn't want to scare her, all he wanted was to hurt Lucy. Taking Faith wasn't enough. It was too easy to take her – as he had found. No, he had to make Lucy pay in a much more brutal way. He would make her very, very sorry she had ever crossed him even if she never knew why this was happening to her. That wasn't important. In fact, it made it all the more sweet.

He would keep his word though. He would return the child if she carried out his demand. But he wanted evidence that she had done it. He didn't trust her. Not one bit.

And thinking about evidence. He then had to worry about Lucy being evidence of the crime. Of it all leading back to him when she did as he asked. If he knew her she wouldn't be able to live with herself. She might even tell someone, even if it was just her best friend. He couldn't have anything lead back to him. He knew full well that he would be as liable, legally, for this murder, as she was. And he had no intention of going to prison for something she did. That she deserved.

He would have to think of a solution when it came to it. For now, he kept checking his phone. She had to do it soon because she'd be desperate to get her daughter back.

He was, however, prepared to hold on to the child for as long as it took her to carry out the task, he'd rented the AirBnB for the night so he was covered, None of his neighbours would see him with the child. And he was serious when he said he would know that she had been to the police. He was currently tapped into her phone camera and could see the ceiling of her kitchen. He would know if the police came and she showed them her text messages.

9

Lucy watched the clock tick down. Her body alive as her nerve endings screamed in frustration. They wanted to get this over and done with, but she needed for it to go dark first and for there to be fewer people around to witness it. It wouldn't be dark until six pm. It was a hell of a long time for Faith to be with a stranger, but she looked happy enough in the photo. She wasn't being held in a shed or any other dingy place. It looked like she didn't even realise she was not supposed to be there. Lucy hoped whoever had her remembered to feed her.

The street was turning grey as the light dimmed. It was early February and the overcast sky looked even more dull when the night crept in. She would do something nice with Faith when the days were brighter. She would help her forget all this. Even if she would never forget it.

Eventually the darkness rolled in and Lucy decided she was safe enough to go out.

She was about to head out the door and kill someone. Would she actually do this?

She picked up her phone from the kitchen counter and sent a text message.

Please, let me have Faith back. You can have everything I own. Please don't make me do this.

She waited for a response. Her arms jangling by her sides.

The phone buzzed across the counter. She snatched it up.

Kill or don't see her again.

She had no choice.

What if she went to the police? Was it too late? Would he know if she went? Did she have the balls to risk it? She ran her hands through her hair. It was Faith's life she was risking. It was nothing to do with her having balls. Was she prepared to risk Faith's life that way? It was a fifty-fifty chance he would or wouldn't know. Fifty per cent was a large amount to bet against. She checked the time again. Six fifteen.

Lucy picked up her car keys from the bowl on the end of the kitchen counter. It was filled with loose change and her house key, car key and the key to the garden shed. The rattle from the bowl was loud in the silence of the house. The house without Faith.

Again her stomach was roiling. She told herself this was for Faith and most people would give their life to save that of a child. She would. But, being the one to make the decision to take a life, it was another matter altogether.

She grabbed her coat, buttoned it up and pulled on her woolly hat, pushing all her hair up into it to give herself some disguise, and stepped out of the house. The temperature had dropped considerably from earlier in the day when she had been happy with the world and oblivious to what Faith was going through. It was mild for February this morning but now there was the sharp bite of the winter month, brought in by the darkness. She hoped that wherever Faith was had warmth, heating. And again, that they had fed her, that Faith still didn't realise she wasn't allowed to come home to her mummy. It wasn't too late yet but it had been several hours and it was a long time for a small child.

Lucy looked at the car, the vehicle that was about to turn into her killing machine. An innocuous looking thing, standing on the driveway without its engine running or anyone behind the wheel, but very capable of killing with a slip of concentration or alcohol in your system, and here she was about to get inside it and use it to hurt someone.

I'm coming, Faith, was the only thought she could allow herself. The street light spread its dim white glow across the car and Lucy noticed the number plate. She needed to do something to prevent people taking her details if they saw her. She needed to obscure her details in case anyone was quick enough to log her vehicle registration.

She ran back to the house, unlocked the door and went straight to the kitchen cupboard where she pulled out her boot polish. Locking up behind her again she rubbed the boot polish over the rear number plate, obscuring the registration. She climbed into the car, turned it on and cranked up the heat. She was freezing now she'd been stood outside for a good ten minutes.

She needed to drive out of her area so that no one recognised her or the car. Not that she knew loads of people here, but, being a mum at the school gates and a receptionist at the local doctors' surgery, it did make her more recognisable. She would drive and find a quiet street then wait for someone to walk by.

The radio in the car burbled away but the DJ's cheeriness made Lucy clench her jaw and created a pain behind her eye. She switched it off. Filled the small space with the loudest sound of all – silence. It was suffocating. Leaving her with her own thoughts and fears. She contemplated putting the radio back on but she couldn't bear to hear the happy voices of the DJs or the tunes made for dancing or heartbreak. Whichever they played, they would grate on her. She was in a no man's land where whatever she did was not the right thing.

She drove out of Arnold towards Carlton, up Carlton Hill and right onto one road. It was too busy, too many houses. She cursed, turned around in the road and went back onto Carlton Hill, tried another right turn and again the same thing. It was going to have to be a populated street so there would be a person to knock over, but there had to be some odds in her favour of not getting caught straight away.

Her fingers gripped the steering wheel, the knuckles white as she tightened her grip in frustration. Eventually she turned down Manor Crescent. It was a street with homes on, houses facing out, but it was a quieter than the others. They were detached homes, set wide apart, and if she was quick and didn't make a lot of noise about it, then she could get it done and over before anyone looked out. After all, people tended to hibernate in the winter, didn't they? Who could be bothered to drag themselves away from the television on a dark night to see what the noise outside was? It was the best she was going to be able to do without driving around all night. She didn't have the time to plan this properly. She wouldn't allow Faith to stay with whomever had her overnight. Who knew what kind of sicko they were? And thinking that made her want to vomit again. She put a hand to her mouth and gritted her teeth. Please no, don't let her be hurt by this animal. Let her come home safe and unaware.

Lucy pulled up at the side of the road and turned the engine off. She didn't want to draw attention to herself if she stayed here ticking over for a long time. Quiet was the way to play it.

Lucy could hear her heartbeat pounding in her ears. This was it. She was here to kill someone. There was no backing down. She'd driven here with the intention to do it and she would, but her legs shook and every intake of breath hurt her chest. She had to fight it and ignore it.

This was for Faith. Tonight she would kill to save her daughter.

10

Lucy pulled her phone out of her pocket and put it on the passenger seat so she would be able to grab it easily when she needed it to take a photograph. Urgh, that was so grim – as though doing the act itself wasn't. But stopping to photograph what she had done, there was something even more disgusting about that. She supposed it was the only way she could prove she had done it without him waiting for the news cycle to pick it up, which meant she could get Faith back.

Sitting in the car waiting for someone to walk by was hideous. Sweat ran down her back even though the interior of the car was cooling. Her chest was tight and every gasp for breath felt as though it was her last. The car was a tomb. The air was being sucked out and she would die inside it. She rubbed at her chest but it made her cough and gasp even more.

Then he was there. A man, walking out of his gate, alone. His hands in his pockets. His shoulders hunched up against the cold.

Did she start the engine now or wait until she was ready? If she waited would it be too late? But if she started her engine now would she draw attention to herself? She decided to stay silent until the last minute. She would start the car and put her foot down as soon as she needed to. All she had to do was wait for him to cross the road.

Her eyes blurred as she stared at him. Her legs shook.

He was picking up pace but he was staying on the pavement. If he didn't cross soon he would be out of sight and she would miss this chance.

Come on, she needed to do this for Faith.

He stopped, fumbled about in his jeans pocket, pulled out a phone that was flashing in the dark. Someone was calling him. He put the phone to his ear and started to move again. Still he stayed on the same side of the road. Was she supposed to mount the kerb to do this? She hadn't thought about that. She had only thought about being on the road. It would be bumpy for the car if she mounted the kerb. Could the car take the kerb at speed, without breaking down and getting stuck there? She had no idea what a bump like that would do to it. She had always looked after her car.

She decided not to risk it. And then it was too late. He was gone and out of sight. Her chance to get Faith back had rounded the corner and she was still sitting in the dark, alone, with no Faith and no way of getting Faith back. She hammered on the steering wheel with her fists, mindful not to hit the horn and alert the neighbourhood to her sitting here waiting to kill one of them. It was as she was throwing a tantrum in the car that she caught sight of someone in her peripheral vision, behind her, coming up on her, also on the phone, not paying attention to anything around them. A young male, looked to be in his early twenties.

This was it. She wasn't going to let this one walk away. He was too young to have a child at home, she could console herself with that.

Her hand went to the key, ready to turn it. Her foot hovered over the accelerator pedal.

He was moving in front of the car. A laugh, loud in the quiet night, rang out. He rubbed the tip of his nose then laughed at the person on the other end of the line, again.

This boy had his whole life in front of him and she was about to rip it out from under him. But, so did Faith. Faith was only four and she had the world at her feet. This boy had more years that he'd been able to enjoy.

Lucy was sure she was going to be sick. She swallowed. Tried to gird herself. This was for Faith. She willed the boy to cross the road. Checked her rear-view mirror. There was no one about. The street was empty. Curtains were drawn.

He moved to the edge of the pavement. Lucy's hand tensed over the key.

And then he did it. He stepped out into the road.

11

Lucy sucked in a breath. Shit, this was it. This was really it. Panic welled up inside her. Her legs shook uncontrollably and black spots danced in front of her eyes. She took another breath in. Held it then let it out slowly. Nausea swept up her gullet and her head spun. She swallowed hard.

He was halfway across the road and walking diagonally away from her, creating more distance, which was good because it gave her more time to accelerate.

This was it. Time to move. To act.

She turned the key in the ignition and the car revved into life.

The boy didn't even turn. He was waving his free arm around to describe something the listener had no chance of seeing. He laughed again.

Lucy put her foot on the accelerator, pushed down a couple of times, felt the power of the car beneath her foot.

Her leg was barely her own and her vision was tunnelling fast. She took in a deep breath and tried to hold it, but it made her cough and gasp.

She had to get this over with.

I'm coming for you, Faith.

She planted an image of Faith in her mind and clung to it, pulled the handbrake off, closed her eyes, pleaded with God, if there was one, to forgive her for what she was about to do, though murder was not a sin that could be forgiven, then she opened her eyes and pushed her foot down hard.

The car lurched forward and she jolted in her seat, her wobbly leg slipping sideways off the pedal. She straightened it up and kept the pressure down. The lad was some way in front of her but still wandering about in the road. His conversation taking all his attention.

She started to pick up speed. Ten, fifteen, twenty, she pushed down harder, but her foot was to the floor, thirty-five miles-per-hour, tipping close to forty when she slammed into him. The car took his legs right from under him. Both his arms flew upwards and his phone flew into the air and crashed to the pavement. The young lad shot up onto the bonnet, his head smashing into the windscreen. It cracked but stayed intact. He slid back down and onto the ground.

Lucy braked. Her heart was pounding as though it was attempting to force an escape out of her ribcage. Blood rushed in her ears.

Her whole body shaking she looked out of the rear-view mirror. The lad was a tangled mess. One leg was laying at a really odd angle. Had she done enough to kill him though? She needed to get out and take a photograph and get out of here before anyone came out to have a look. He hadn't screamed and she hadn't made a big deal out of braking, so there hadn't been a huge amount of noise.

Her eyes widened in horror as an arm lifted from the ground and reached for his head. He was alive.

No.

Faith.

She'd done the worst bit. She had to finish it now.

She swivelled back in her seat, pushed the gearstick into reverse, put her foot on the pedal and pressed down. Her eyes were half closed as she felt the bu-bump, as she reversed over him. Now he was in front of her with the headlights picking out the mess. There was no way he had survived.

Lucy went to grab her phone, but it wasn't there.

The band around her chest tightened. She needed to get out of here.

It must have slid off as she... she didn't want to think about it.

She leaned forward and grasped around in the darkness of the footwell. Her hand reaching out, searching, needing, desperate. Her fingertips touched something solid and it slid away from her. 'Fuck.' She leaned further forward and stretched under the seat scrabbling, rummaging around on the floor until it was in her hand.

Lucy clambered out of the car, the cold night air brittle against her face, like Bambi on her legs, as though they were new to her and she were only now learning to walk on them. She checked around her. There was still no one on the street, but a light had come on behind a front door. She didn't have long. She ran, as much as her legs allowed, to where the boy lay, swallowed the acrid vomit that lurched up into her mouth, then took two photographs with her phone and ran back to the car. She thought she heard a front door open and voices within. She threw the phone back on the passenger seat with a dull thud, grabbed the gear stick in her stiff hands, did a three-point turn and drove out the way she had come as fast as she could, as fast as her shaking legs would allow her, the car lurching under her body.

A couple of streets away from the scene and she could hold it in no more. She steered into the side of the road with a sudden jerky movement, causing the driver behind her to berate her with their horn. A dull loud blast in the night air. Lucy pushed her door open, leaning out and emptying her insides into the road and hoping a car didn't drive past and take off her head, but she couldn't stop. She'd killed a man in cold blood and she had to live with it. Why anyone wanted her to do this she had no idea. It was evil. She had never heard of anything so evil as what had happened this evening.

When she had vomited herself dry she wiped at her mouth with her sleeve, smearing the off-yellow fluid onto her coat, the smell finding its way into her nostrils. They twitched in complaint but she wiped again and tried to tidy herself up; she shut the door then stayed where she was, still and silent in the car for a minute, taking in what had happened. She might get Faith back but she didn't know if she could ever live with herself.

She ran a hand through her hair as tears formed in her eyes. She needed to finish this.

She picked up the phone, went to the photo app and stared in horror at the two images that she'd taken of the boy. They were horrific. He was so clearly dead, his body distorted, limbs at wrong angles and his eyes staring ahead, blind, and she had done this to him. With slow sluggish movements she sent one of the photographs to the number that had been texting her.

Please let me have Faith now, I have done as you've asked.

Her stomach was sore. Her body ached.

She wanted to wait for a response but emergency vehicles would be here soon and she needed to get out of the area. She needed to go home. She'd be able to sort everything out with Faith from there.

He would give her back. He had said as much. She was getting her daughter back.

12

The text message came through to his phone sooner than he had imagined it would.

Please let me have Faith now, I have done as you've asked.

It was accompanied by the image of a young male on a road, crumpled and broken. Blood all over his face. What you could make out of his face anyway. It was smashed in and indecipherable from a human form. He knew he had asked her to kill, but hell, he hadn't expected her to do such a job of it.

This would damage her.

Payback was a bitch.

He looked to the child asleep on the sofa. There had been some tears when she had been told Mummy was still working late today but it shouldn't be too long. She was used to being with Mummy most of the time, and the tears had worn her out.

He looked back at the image. It really was rough. He wanted her to kill, but fuck, what a mess. Could he trust her to keep this to herself? To allow this to haunt her for the rest of her life? Or was she going to do something stupid and get the cops looking for him? Yes, she'd be up shit creek, but if they took her story seriously – which was debateable, because, come on, it was a little far-fetched – then they would look for him to hang this murder on as well. He had directed her to do it. Just the same as someone hiring a hitman being liable.

Maybe he should clean up his mess. If only he could clean it up with as much ease as he had carried out today's little experiment. Get someone else to do it for him. There would be no trace of him near the murder. No DNA on the scene and an alibi for the time of the murder. He'd make sure of it. Not that he should come up in inquiries, but, if the impossible happened, then he was safe because he was nowhere near it.

He just needed to find a willing volunteer.

13

There was a small knock at the door. Lucy was in the kitchen, pacing the tiny room in a couple of short strides before turning around and pacing back again. She jumped with the sound. Her nerves stretched to their very limit. She hadn't heard back from the person who had Faith and she had killed a man this evening. Two things that alone, separately, could undo her, but together they had her in a complete and utter tangled mess. She didn't know which way was up at the moment.

Was this the police? Did they know it was her already? Had one of the neighbours seen her, even with her obscured number plate had they somehow been able to identify her? Was there someone living up there who took a child to Faith's school or went to the doctors' surgery she worked at?

Her empty stomach told her it was on the brink of attempting to void itself again, but there was nothing left to bring back up. She had vomited twice and she was hollowed out.

Lucy walked to the door at a crawl, reluctant to face the person standing on the other side. She had to get Faith back first, she didn't want to endanger that. If it was the police would the abductor think she had called them? How would he know, either way? She rubbed her sore stomach and then raised her hand to the door handle. Bit her bottom lip then, slowly, she opened the door. At first she thought there was no one there, then...

'Mummy?'

Lucy looked down.

She dropped to her knees, grabbed Faith and dragged her into the house, into her arms and a bone-crushing embrace. 'Oh my God, Faith!'

The little girl allowed herself to be dragged into her mother's arms. Stood still while her mummy pushed her face into her neck and inhaled hard. She didn't flinch when tears started to slip from her mummy's face onto her own.

'Oh Faith, sweetheart. You're home. You're safe. Are you okay? Are you hurt?'

Faith shook her head, took a step back to look at Lucy, confused. 'You were working late. I had to wait with that man. I don't like you working this late, Mummy.'

Lucy dragged her back into her bear hug. Faith didn't know anything about what had occurred. Nothing bad had happened to her child at all. It had been an horrendous day for her, but not to Faith. She had to be thankful for that. She ran her hands down Faith's arms, then down her legs. Faith looked annoyed. She had never seen her mummy behave like this before and she didn't understand it.

Lucy's body flooded with gratitude. There were no injuries, no signs of harm. She had to try to get a grip of herself otherwise she would be the one who would scare Faith.

She leaned forward and pushed the front door to.

'How did you get home, sweetheart?' she asked.

Faith's confusion continued. Her brows furrowed over her eyes. 'The man dropped me off like you asked him to.'

With that Lucy was up, nearly knocking Faith over in her desperation to get out of the door she had just closed. She scrabbled for the handle and yanked the door open, stepping into the cold night air. There was no car outside. She looked left and right, but nothing was moving.

'Faith, where is he? Where did he go, Faith?'

There was no response.

'Faith!' she shouted.

Still nothing.

Lucy turned around and Faith was still standing in the same spot, now turned around to face Lucy, a single tear working its way loose over her bottom eyelashes. Her lower lip trembling.

'Oh, Faith.' For the second time, Lucy found herself dropping to her knees in front of her daughter. 'Don't cry. I'm so sorry. I didn't mean to upset you. You've had a long day. You must be ready for bed. Shall we run you a nice warm bath and get you in your PJs?'

Faith nodded. 'He went as soon as I got out the car.'

Lucy nodded. 'It's okay, it doesn't matter, sweetie. What matters is me and you and we're both okay, so let's go and start that bath.' She scooped Faith up into her arms and trudged up the stairs with her cradled close.

That was brave of him to drop her off right at her door. She had to forget about him for tonight. He had done what he had said he was going to do and he had given her Faith back. Now she had to settle Faith down and finish the day for her as though it was any ordinary day and hope against all hope that the police didn't knock on her door tonight and take her away.

14

It was easy once he had decided what he wanted, to do what he needed. People who collected indecent images all gathered in the same places online and once they thought they were safe they tended to talk quite freely. He found a group of them and watched as they talked while they exchanged their filth. It took several different attempts with several different groups to find one who said he was a teacher and not only a teacher but from his IP address he could see he was local.

His next step was to infiltrate this man's computer and see what his life was like. It couldn't have been more perfect. He was a teacher and he was married with adult grown children, two young grandchildren, and he had a penchant for indecent images. This was one man who would not want this part of his life exposed to his wife, his children or his employer.

He laughed out loud. It nearly too easy. The thrill of this, of what he was doing, of what he was able to do, it excited him. He almost wished he could be there to see what he was setting in motion. But that was the whole point, so he didn't have to be there. Someone else was going to be there. Someone else was going to do his dirty work for him.

And he was going to get all the fun out of it.

15

The night was dark, as nights tended to be, but Lucy had a pair of blackout curtains up at her window because when summer came around she had been waking at four in the morning when the sun came up. Now her room was pitch dark no matter the time or season.

She had no idea if she would sleep. She didn't imagine she would. Her brain was playing the image of the boy in the road on a loop. Lucy wanted it to stop. She wanted to sleep to escape what she had done, for just a few hours. She knew she didn't deserve the peace. After all, she had ended his life and ruined the life of those who loved him. Her stomach lurched again as she thought of those left behind. But she desperately wanted a little respite. Just so she could face it all again tomorrow. Please, if she could sleep now, she would look at it head-on tomorrow. She'd deal with all the emotions that came with it, no matter how terrible they were.

Lucy looked at the sleeping outline of Faith in the bed at the side of her. Her long mousey hair splayed out around her like a halo. A thumb in her mouth to replace the dummy she had taken off her a couple of years ago. Lucy had never been able to wean her off her thumb though. Faith was curled up in a small ball, barely taking up any space, but she was sleeping diagonally across the bed. Her head on the pillow near the edge of the bed and her back curled against the rest of the pillow. Feet ready to uncurl right into Lucy's kidneys at any moment.

Faith had been surprised when Lucy had told her she could sleep with her tonight as Lucy had always been adamant about that one thing, keeping her out of her bed. She knew friends who had made rods for their own backs by allowing their children into their beds at a young age and were now unable to get them out without lots of screaming and tantrums. She explained that it was a special treat and a one-off. Because Mummy wasn't well and wanted the company.

Faith looked perplexed. 'Well, I don't want to be poorly, Mummy.'

'It's not that kind of poorly, sweetie. You'll be fine.'

Faith had grabbed her pillow, because it was covered with Frozen and Elsa, and settled down quickly.

Lucy closed her eyes and tried to relax. Her body was exhausted. She ached. Every bone complained. But her mind was fighting sleep. She rolled over and looked at her daughter. Took deep breaths and tried to relax. What she had done today she had done for Faith and now Faith was home safe and sound. Who knew what kind of night she would be having if she hadn't have taken the action she took? She could be in a police station or a hospital grieving over the murder of her daughter.

Tears slipped from her eyes. She couldn't bear to lose her daughter. She tried to keep the crying quiet, but she fell into a proper sobbing session. Whether she was crying for Faith and what could have been, or crying for what was, she couldn't tell. But she was releasing it all anyway.

Faith slept on.

And with the released tears, the energy in Lucy's mind was released and she closed her eyes. Damp cheeks drying as she drifted into sleep.

Her sleep was filled with darkness, with shadowy shapes and then a screaming figure she couldn't make out. Loud piercing shrieks in the pitch-black space, blood and broken bones. She was mesmerised and stepped closer and closer to the shrouded figure and as she got up close the screaming bloody figure turned into Faith. The blood was dripping down her face which was cracked and contorted in pain. The sound emanating from her was splitting Lucy's brain in two. This was her child and it was horrific. She reached out a hand and, the moment her fingertips touched her, Faith burst into flames.

Lucy screamed, waking herself up, jerking upright in the bed. She was hot and sweating, her breathing ragged. She turned to Faith who simply groaned and rolled over, unperturbed.

She tried to steady her breath, placing a hand on her chest, but she was shaken up. She looked down again at Faith, reassuring herself that she was safe and secure in the bed at the side of her. She reached out a hand to touch her, yet afraid to do so at the same time. With gentle fingertips she stroked Faith's shoulder, relieved that her child was sturdy beneath her touch. Shuffling back down into the bed, Lucy curled awkwardly around Faith and drifted back into sleep.

Back into the darkness, into the shadowy place with the shrouded figure with the piercing scream. She didn't want to but she found herself moving towards the figure and seeing, yet again, that the figure was a bloody and broken Faith, who screamed and writhed and once again, burst into flames as she tried to help her.

Lucy's heart was hammering in her chest when she woke again. She clicked the bedside light on and sat up. She couldn't do this, she couldn't sleep and keep going through this. She would avoid sleep and avoid the nightmares of the night. The day had been bad, but the distortion the night brought was a whole other affair. It wasn't as though she would ever forget the day, the loss of Faith and the young lad in the road, but she couldn't handle the horror of it in her sleep.

When morning finally came around and the alarm clock called time for the day to start, Lucy got them both out of bed and they went downstairs.

The daytime brought clarity and Faith was bouncing around, excited for another school day.

'There's no school today, sweetie,' Lucy said from her place on the sofa. Legs tucked under her. A steaming mug of coffee wrapped in her hands.

'Why not? They said see you tomorrow when I left yesterday.' Her bottom lip jutted out.

'Come here a minute.'

Faith stepped up to Lucy with a confused expression.

Lucy reached out a hand and pressed the back of her hand to Faith's forehead. 'Yes, I thought so, you're a bit warm, sweetie, we don't want to give your friends anything poorly. So better to stay off and go back tomorrow when we know you're okay.'

Faith put her own hand on her head. Her brows furrowed. 'I'm not, am I?'

'Just a little bit,' said Lucy, 'that's why I think you'll be okay tomorrow.'

'But I like school.'

Lucy patted the seat at the side of her. 'I know you do. But we'll have a good day at home today. We'll watch *Frozen* and some other stuff you like. That's what we do when you're poorly. Curl up on the sofa together.'

Faith jumped up next to her mother. 'What about work?'

'Well, I'll have to let them know I can't go in because I have to stay off to look after you.' She didn't want to let Faith out of her sight. Who knew what would happen today? Maybe they could get back to some level of normality tomorrow. She couldn't keep them both off work and school indefinitely. But neither could she tell anyone what had happened to them. Faith had been so easy to kidnap once. Lucy was terrified she would be taken again if she got the authorities involved. Though she wasn't sure she could live with herself and what she had done. Perhaps she needed to be honest about her actions and face up to the consequences. Her mum could look after Faith when she was sent to prison. Faith loved her gran and the feeling was mutual.

'Are you okay, Mummy? You look sad.' Faith was looking up at her.

Lucy's stomach was in knots and it was hard to fill her lungs properly. She was clammy and shaky but she forced a smile down at Faith.

'I'm fine, sweetie, though I do think I might have a little bit of what you've got. I don't feel at all well.'

Again Faith looked puzzled and put a hand back up to her own head then twisted her lips. 'Go back to bed, Mummy.'

Bed was the last place she wanted to be. She might slip into sleep if she went to bed. She couldn't bear that. It was hard enough to hold up under the scrutiny of her daylight analysis of the previous day. 'I'm okay here with you. Let's get you some breakfast, shall we?'

Faith leapt up. 'Yay, snap, crackle and pop!'

'Snap, crackle and pop it is then.'

They walked into the kitchen and Lucy served Faith her cereal and poured the milk on.

'Are you having some, Mummy?'

'I'm not hungry this morning.' She didn't know if she would be able to eat again. She didn't deserve to eat. That young man wouldn't be eating again, would he? She pulled her phone out of her pocket and went to the news app. This was going to hurt but she needed to do it. She needed to know what they had so far.

It didn't take long to search out the article.

Carlton man killed in hit and run.

The article didn't name him yet, but said the police were appealing for witnesses.

The police hadn't come knocking on her door. That had to be a good sign. This would go the way she wanted it to go. She could hand herself in when she was ready and when she felt it was safe to do so, when she thought it was safe for Faith. Because she couldn't live the rest of her life like this. She would walk into a police station and tell them she killed that man. She wouldn't live her life as if nothing had happened. She wasn't like that. She looked at Faith. Maybe she hadn't done the right thing yesterday, but she sure as hell would do the right thing now.

16

I finished checking the emails that had come in overnight, then picked up my green tea and carried it through to the incident room for the morning briefing. We didn't have a lot on at the moment so it was just a matter of seeing what everyone had planned for their day and to see what had come in overnight. If there was anything we needed to be aware of.

'Morning, Boss.' Ross was the first to greet me as I walked through the door.

'Morning, Ross. How are you this morning?'

'I'm good thanks.'

'Apparently we're going to get snow this week,' Martin piped up. The oldest member of our team.

'Crap. I do hope not. I bloody hate snow,' Ross grumbled.

'No snow angels from you then?' asked Pasha, laughing at him.

'We could always throw the boss in the snow and make a snow angel out of her?'

'If you like using both of your legs I'd suggest it's not something you try and do.' I put my mug down on the table I had perched on and glared at him.

Martin and Pasha laughed at him.

'You're not a fan of the snow either then, Boss?' He was laughing as well now.

'Let's just say I don't like getting up close and personal with it.'

'Got it. Martin it is.'

Martin threw a paper ball at Ross and it landed squarely on his head before bouncing off and rolling under a desk.

At that point DCI Kevin Baxter walked in. 'I've not missed the briefing have I?'

'No, we're just about to get on with it,' I said.

Baxter looked at Aaron who was sitting at his desk working on his computer with his headphones in. He wasn't needed up until this point and was tuning out the noise. Typical that Baxter would walk in as Aaron had them on.

'Care to join us, DS Stone?' His voice was hard and clipped.

Pasha gave a short nod at Aaron to indicate his attention was required.

'You're here for the briefing?' Baxter snarked again.

Aaron gave a curt nod. I really did need to do something about this. I couldn't allow Baxter to continue treating Aaron in this way, especially in front of the other members of the team. Aaron did not want me to disclose his Asperger's diagnosis, but we had to do something to resolve the issue. It couldn't carry on.

I picked up my tea and took a drink. It was nearly cold.

'So, we'll see what everyone has on today before we go through the morning briefing shall we?' I started. 'Martin?'

He leaned back in his chair, relaxed. 'I have a couple of extra statements to obtain in relation to the Denning case that the coroner has asked for.'

'That file must be close to completed?'

'Yeah, I thought it was, but the request came through yesterday. These are mopping up. Making sure she has every piece of the picture she might need. Especially with it being such a high profile case.'

'Okay, get those done and that finalised. I turned to Pasha, asked her what she had on for the day.

'Ross and I are tied up with the post office robbery still.'

I nodded and went round the rest of the staff.

'Okay, who has done the morning briefing sheet today?' I asked the room.

Ross lifted his chin. 'That'll be me, Boss. Not a lot happened late yesterday or overnight. It was a quiet day, all in all. A higher rate of phone thefts and robberies in the city centre than usual for this time of year. A domestic that nearly turned into a homicide. The wife had enough of being beaten and hit him around the head with the kettle while it was full of boiling water. He has some nasty burns and she hit him in such a place that he's still out for the count. There's a history of calls to the address though, it's all recorded that he was beating her. And last but not least of all, we have a hit and run. The Roads Policing guys are saying it looks like whoever did it ran over the victim twice. Once might have been an accident, but they reversed and killed the young lad. Only twenty-two.'

'Ouch,' said Martin from his relaxed position.

'Reversed over?' Pasha screwed her face up.

'Yeah, so it says on the incident log.'

'Why are we not getting it?' Pasha asked.

'Traffic deaths are their remit. They can do all the measurements etc. If we took it off them we would still need their help so they just keep it and deal with it.' Even the pragmatist Pasha wanted a job to come into the office.

'So, we're all sorted for the day and the briefing is done, let's get on with our tasks.' I stood from the desk I was perched on. 'If anyone wants to make a fresh brew then feel free, mine is freezing.'

Pasha rose. 'I could do with another. And I'd rather do it than have one made by Ross, if I'm honest.'

'It's a ploy, you know,' said Martin. 'So you never ask him to make the drinks.'

Ross laughed. 'Ha, you will never know, will you?'

'I'm going to run out of paper to throw at you at this rate, Ross, if you keep coming out with little gems like that.' Martin whipped a sheet off his desk, screwed it into a ball and again managed to hit Ross square on the head.

'Can I speak to you and DS Stone in my office please?' This wasn't a request from Baxter. He didn't look amused by the joviality in the office. His mood was serious. What was this about?

17

We followed Baxter into his office and took the two seats in front of his desk. His office was immaculate, which was a vast difference to mine, which had paperwork all over the desk, though I knew where to find everything. Nothing was out of place here. It was a sterile place, you'd be hard pressed to know anyone worked in here.

I waited in silence while Baxter settled himself, wondering what the hell was wrong with him now and hoping it was just a meeting about crime statistics or some other such managerial crap that I hated. But usually these things are scheduled in advance.

He looked to Aaron then to me.

'I'm afraid to say this is a performance review meeting, Aaron.'

Damn. This was the first I was hearing about it. I was glad I had thought to bring my notebook and opened it to the next blank page and dated and timed the top. I was going to make sure I logged everything he said in here.

Aaron didn't flinch. He didn't even look to me. He waited for Baxter to impart more information. He wasn't one for jumping in until he had all the facts. If it were me, I'd be getting emotional already and having my say before Baxter had even got started.

Baxter's notes were open in front of him. It looked as though he had been keeping a log of items to bring up. I should have known he was going to go for something like this after he failed to get Aaron to agree to move to the Training Department. That would have been the best way to get him out but Aaron had turned him down. He wanted to stay and work with me and the rest of the team.

'You're unfocused at work, regularly choosing to plug into earphones instead of getting on with the workload you have on. This is to the detriment of your job and your team.'

I'd like to see the evidence of that. I suspected he was making it up to suit his agenda.

'Just this morning I walked in and you had your earphones in, Aaron.'

I made notes that he'd declared Aaron was letting the earphones affect his work, because as his direct supervisor, I knew damn well they weren't and I imagined it was why I was in here, because I was Aaron's line manager.

Baxter turned to me. 'I presume you have noticed the earphones, DI Robbins?'

Of course I'd noticed them, what did he think I was, blind? But what should I say? How should I answer this? I couldn't break a confidence, but we were now at the point where we had to address it. 'Yes, I'm aware of DS Stone's use of his earphones.'

'And you agree that they affect his work?'

Ahh, he expected me to agree with him because he had made his feelings on this matter clear to me in the past. 'No, I'm sorry. I don't think they affect his work at all.'

Baxter glared at me. The pen that had been underlining words or adding a couple of sentences on his notepad was still in his hand. 'I'm sorry? You don't think something you do out of work, enjoyed in work time, is detrimental to the work environment?'

'I'm saying there is no change in DS Stone's work at all. In fact, I rely on him a lot and this meeting has come as somewhat of a surprise.'

All this time Aaron had not said anything but he was rubbing his thumb and forefinger gently together on his leg.

Baxter decided to turn to Aaron. 'DS Stone?'

'Sir.'

'Do you have any comment on the use of earphones in the workplace?'

Aaron took a deep breath. 'As DI Robbins said, I don't believe they detract from my work at all, Sir.'

'Do you think they're appropriate?' Baxter asked.

How would he answer the appropriateness of them without saying why he wore them? Aaron was going to have to make a decision. This was make or break for him.

18

I looked across at Aaron who was staring out of the window.

'DS Stone?' Baxter was pushing Aaron for an answer.

My mouth went dry at the thought of answering this question. I licked my lips. Come on, Aaron, you can do this. I willed my thoughts into his head. Willed for him to pick up on my support. Stared hard at him so he could see I was there for him.

Aaron continued to stare out of the window.

'Sir...' My tongue was sticking to the roof of my mouth. I was uncomfortable. Who knew how Aaron was feeling?

'What is it, DI Robbins?'

I leaned forward. 'I think for this kind of conversation, DS Stone is entitled to have his Fed rep with him, is he not?'

Baxter shot me a look of pure anger. Did he think he could bully his way through this?

'Yes, of course, you are right. Though,' he looked directly at me, 'I presumed by having his direct line manager in with him, he was covered.'

How shit must Aaron feel to have us speaking about him as though he wasn't here? I would detest it. I'd be furious.

'Shall we rearrange this meeting then until we can get hold of one?' I suggested.

Baxter nearly growled at me. 'I shall get Kirsty to sort it out and let you both know when to attend.'

Kirsty was Baxter's poor long-suffering PA.

I nodded. 'Is there anything else, while we're here?'

'No, that will be all, thank you.'

We both rose from our seats.

'But, Aaron.' Baxter hadn't finished.

Aaron turned to face him.

'I do expect an answer next time we see each other in here.'

Aaron gave him a curt nod. I ushered him out of the door.

'My office,' I said, leaving him little choice.

Baxter's office was on the floor above ours and once we were downstairs and in my office I found a steaming mug of green tea on my desk waiting for me. Obviously made by Pasha. 'Do you want to go to your desk and get your coffee?' I asked Aaron.

He shook his head. He looked deflated. Defeated.

'We need to sort this out, Aaron, and sort it out now, we can't put it off any longer. What were you going to say to Baxter in there?'

He slumped into the chair opposite me. 'I was going with the truth.'

'You were going to tell him?' I was surprised. He had insisted he didn't want to disclose it to him.

'If he asks me outright I can't lie to him. There's a difference between not telling him something and lying to him.'

I picked up my tea. 'And how do you feel about that?'

He shrugged.

'Aaron.'

'He's arrogant, he's not the kind of manager I want to give that kind of information to.'

'So, what are we going to do?'

He looked at me, frustration oozing from him.

'I'm sorry, Aaron. I'm sorry that it has come to this.'

'It's not your fault, but I think we're at the point where I have to talk to Walker.'

Catherine Walker was our Detective Superintendent. She was happy if the unit was running smoothly and now Baxter was here, she had taken more of a back seat than she had when Grey was the DCI. It seemed she trusted him to run things more.

'You want to do that now?'

He rubbed his face. 'I don't want to do it at all, Hannah. I'm sick at being pushed into this position.'

'Do you want me to do it? I don't mind. You can get on with the job and I'll deal with this for you. Walker can then get Baxter off your back and hopefully without even having to tell him the whole truth, though I can't promise you anything on that count. She'll deal with it the best way she sees fit.'

Even with my caveat he looked relieved. 'If there's no other way around it. Are you sure you wouldn't mind? I'm not sure I'm up to going through this after this morning.'

'I don't mind at all. It's what I'm here for.' And I was. If it was going to make Aaron's life easier then I would do it for him.

'Thank you, Hannah.' He stood to leave.

'Just promise you won't let him get to you, Aaron. You won't let him affect how you do the job. You're an integral part of the team and I need you.'

He gave another nod. I could see he was fatigued with it all. I wished I could take the stress away from him.

'What can I do for you, Aaron? To make this easier?'

He straightened his tie. Which was not uneven in the first place. I could see he was desperate to leave, he'd had enough of talking about this.

'Aaron?'

He was closing down.

'You're doing it. If you can talk to Walker, that would be the most helpful and useful thing that could happen. There's no getting out of this any longer. I don't know if she's going to be annoyed that I didn't tell her sooner or that I'm not telling her myself, but I can't do it, Hannah.' He started to rub his finger and thumb together.

I needed for him to calm down. He'd had a heart attack in the middle of last year. The doctors had said it wasn't stress-related, but we all knew that stress could be a factor. Having had one attack, he was prone to another and he was a very dear friend and colleague. I'd been terrified that I would lose him back then, I certainly wouldn't lose him now. And that was part of the reason Baxter had held off so long in playing this hand. He didn't want to come across as heartless. He obviously presumed enough time had passed to go the route of poor performance to kick Aaron off the unit.

Bastard.

'Walker will be fine, Aaron. I'll explain everything to her. She's a level-headed person. You have nothing to worry about. Let me deal with it and I'll let you know when it's done and then we shouldn't have to deal with Baxter anymore.'

I for one would be glad to have this over and done with.

Aaron turned for the door.

'Do you need to take a break, Aaron?' I asked as he reached for the handle.

He turned to me, his hand in his hair, rubbing the back of his head. 'No, Hannah, I don't need a break. What I need is to go back to work and do the job I'm capable of doing, if people would just allow me to get on with it.' And with that he was out the door.

I needed to sort this out before he became even more stressed.

19

Catherine Walker's PA, Brett Howe, waved me through. Catherine was sitting behind her desk tapping away at her keyboard. I stood before her, waiting for her to notice my arrival and to finish up what she was doing.

'Have a seat, Hannah, I won't be a moment,' she said without lifting her head.

I took one of the three seats in front of her desk and waited. It was a lovely corner office. Two walls of windows behind where she was sitting. Though I couldn't say the view of St Ann's was particularly beautiful. It was a dreary estate, but the people cared for it deeply and were loyal to the area, desperate for regeneration and love. They lived with hope. It drove them forward and helped them thrive. They fought against the bad image and the gangs that attempted to bring the area down. The renewal in gun culture, the shootings that had been taking place. They were a proud people.

As I looked out of the windows, Catherine stopped typing and lifted her head and took me in. 'What's brought you to my office this morning, Hannah? You don't tend to pop in for a chat.'

She was right, Baxter was usually my first port of call.

'Not that it's not a pleasure to see you, you understand.' She smiled. 'But, I'm imagining you have an issue you want to talk about that you can't discuss with Kev. Am I close?'

I shifted in my chair.

'Spit it out, Hannah.' She tapped a finger on her desk.

'It's a delicate subject, Ma'am.'

She leaned back in her chair. 'I'm listening.' Her sleek dark bob glistened in the winter sun that shone through the windows.

'It's about Aaron.'

She leaned forward in her seat now, alert. 'Is he okay?' Like everyone here, she had been upset when he had his heart attack last year. 'Do we need an ambulance, have you called one? Is he at the hospital?' She barely took breath.

I held up a hand to calm her down. 'No, it's fine. His health is fine. It's not his heart anyway.'

She let out a sigh of relief. 'Don't scare me like that, Hannah.'

'I'm sorry.'

'It's okay. If you mention Aaron everyone leaps to the conclusion that something is wrong again. He gave us all a pretty good scare, didn't he?'

'He did that. But, he seems to be doing okay. He's sticking to his diet and exercise regime. I think he's doing well, to be honest.'

'Okay, so if it's not that?'

This was it, I had to do this for him. No matter how much he hated it, this had to come out now. The only reason I knew was because I had been shouting at him about the death of a colleague, about how well he seemed to be taking it and he'd disclosed that he was dealing with it in his own way and he told me why. I'd felt like such a bitch, but that had slid off Aaron's back and we had grown closer for me knowing. I think he was ultimately grateful that someone on the team was aware. Much as he hated it. It was cushioning for him.

'He has a...'

I didn't know the correct terminology, how to describe it, was it a condition? It wasn't a disease. Hell, why hadn't I researched this before I came in here? I had researched it after Aaron told me, and I understood it in terms of how to interact with Aaron better, but this basic task, telling someone else, I was about to fail and I was glad Aaron wasn't here to hear me make such a mess of it.

Catherine looked concerned still. I was doing nothing to allay her fears.

'Like I said, it's delicate and he doesn't want the office to know. He would rather not have DCI Baxter be made aware, which is why I have come to you. There is an issue that has arisen with the DCI but it can be resolved with you knowing about Aaron.'

'You're talking gibberish, Hannah. Just spit it out will you? I can't do anything about this until you tell me what's happening.' She was curt. Her words clipped.

'Aaron is living with Asperger's, Ma'am.'

I'd said it and I left it out there to settle. To be taken in and assimilated.

Catherine pursed her lips, her brain ticking over. A slow nod started. You could practically see the cogs digesting the information. 'Okay. I can't say it was something I would have identified, but is there a reason I need to know now? I'm presuming there is, because he's functioned this long within the team without the need to tell anyone and yet here you are, informing me.'

This next part was as difficult as telling her about Aaron, because I was about to complain about Baxter and his treatment of him. I needed to be tactful and try to explain it as sensibly as I could. As though Baxter was not the bully he so obviously was. 'It's DCI Baxter, Ma'am.'

She rolled her eyes. 'I thought it might be. What has he done?'

I wasn't expecting that response.

'We didn't have any of this with DCI Grey did we?' she continued. 'Anthony never had any run-ins with Aaron. And I'm presuming that's what's happened.'

I wanted to be tactful. 'Aaron wears earphones when he's working sometimes. The noise in the incident room can be a little overwhelming for him so he tunes it out and wears his earphones. I have no idea if they're noise cancelling or if he's listening to something, but they keep him on a level and he gets on with his work. It doesn't detract from anything he's doing and if he's needed he takes them off and is present and fully with us.'

She nodded. 'Okay. I get that.'

I was over-heating. The heating was on and the sun was shining through the windows. I was getting uncomfortable but I continued anyway. 'DCI Baxter, he sees Aaron with his headphones on and he doesn't like it. He had us both in his office this morning to... well, he was doing a poor performance review of Aaron specifically because of the earphones.'

Catherine let out another sigh. 'How is Aaron?'

'He wasn't great when I last saw him. He agreed that I could talk to you, but he isn't keen on the DCI being made aware. He doesn't want to aggravate the situation with him.'

'And he thinks that if DCI Baxter knows about the Asperger's he will become even more difficult to deal with?' She didn't sound surprised but she was asking the question around Aaron's thought processes.

'Yes, Ma'am. He does and he just wants to come to work and get on with his job. And if I can say so, he is an integral part of the team. I couldn't do what I do without him as my second. He's invaluable. He definitely does not need a poor performance review. My take on the situation is that DCI Baxter is aiming to remove Aaron from the team, which is why he had him in the office this morning.' I'd well and truly laid my cards on the table. But I said I was going to bat for Aaron and I meant it. I was not going to stand by and watch as he was manhandled out of the job he loved.

'First things first, Hannah. We need to make sure Aaron is okay. I need you to reassure him that his job within the team is secure and he will not be going anywhere.'

I nodded. If I felt this relieved, I could only imagine how Aaron would feel. I was so grateful to Catherine. She was an exacting Superintendent, but she was also fair.

She rummaged in a drawer and pulled out a notepad and scribbled in it. 'I will speak to Kev. There will be no more of this silliness in relation to Aaron wearing earphones. I see no reason why he can't wear them if they help him and they're not preventing him from working.' She looked at me. 'They're not preventing him from working, are they, Hannah?'

'Absolutely not. He works well at his desk with them on. A lot better than if he was distracted by the noise in the office without them, to be honest. Every time we have a briefing or need his attention for something he takes them off. It's not an issue.'

She gave me a curt nod and made another note in her book.

'Is there anything else Kev has taken against for some reason?'

'Not that he's told me, I just don't think he likes the way Aaron can be sometimes. When he's a little blunt.'

She laughed. 'If only everyone was as refreshingly honest as Aaron was. I'll talk to Kev. There will be no more issues.'

I looked at her.

'No, Hannah, neither will there be any blowback for you for going over his head.'

'What will you tell him?'

She put her pen down on the desk. 'Now, there's a question. It would be fairly easy to resolve if I could tell him the truth. As it is, because Aaron doesn't want him to know it's going to be more difficult. Are you sure we can't tell him?'

'Aaron did say if there was no other way around it then you could tell him, but he doesn't want to hear anything about it from the DCI. It has nothing to do with him and it's none of his business. He does his job and he does it well.' I grimaced. 'I'm sorry, these are Aaron's words. He was quite upset by it all at this point.'

'It's fine, Hannah. I understand. I'll make his point very clear when I speak to Kev and I'll get this cleared up and Aaron can get back to enjoying the job.'

'Thank you, Ma'am.' I stood to leave.

'Oh, Hannah.'

I looked at her.

'Thank you for bringing this to me and trusting me with this information. I hope Aaron does feel more settled here very soon.'

20

Scott Rhodes was an average man, or so he believed as he ruminated on his situation in the car. It was late, he was usually at home at this hour, sitting watching television with Wendy, but he'd told her he was in need of some chocolate so had come out to the shop and now found himself sitting here contemplating his life.

He was a happily married man. They'd been married for thirty-one years. Yes, they'd had some ups and downs in that time, but nothing they had not been able to get through.

Once they had had to seek the help of a marriage counsellor. A quietly spoken woman who had nothing but questions and answered every question they had with another question. She'd frustrated Scott because she didn't have the answers he so desperately needed. Like why could they no longer communicate? Why was their home so quiet? It had gone on like this for several weeks and eventually they had figured out that it was because the last of their two children had left home and they had empty nest syndrome. Or more specifically, Wendy had empty nest syndrome. She wasn't dealing well with the kids moving out to live their lives and not needing her.

He had accepted it as part of life and this, it seemed, had annoyed

Wendy even more. She wanted him to share in her grief. So what they had to do was to spend more time together. To rekindle their own love. Recognise that there was still life beyond the children and to find activities to do as a couple.

It had worked. They had become stronger. Started to enjoy life. Found new friends. Started talking to each other again. It was good.

Their children had gone on to produce grandchildren. Wendy's new focus as a grandparent took over her life. He adored his grandkids, of course he did. But Wendy, she took it to a whole new level. She was always buying them something. She would see a new cute outfit and she'd have to buy it; a pair of booties, or a snuggly teddy. As they started to toddle, she'd buy them toys they could walk around with; push-alongs. She didn't care that these things were supposed to wait until Christmas.

So, he had a happy marriage and three wonderful grandkids. He was also a teacher. A job where he felt a little put-upon, but also felt like he was doing something worthwhile. Though as he was getting older, he had started to feel the appeal of retirement.

He turned the heater in the car up a notch.

If his life was so good, how was it he found himself here, sitting in his car, pondering his life this way? How did he find himself in this predicament, convincing himself that he was an average man?

Would an average man be sitting here with the information he had been given?

Would an average man be sitting outside the house of a woman called Lucy Anderson, with a plastic bag in his hand, planning to do something not so average with that plastic bag?

21

Lucy was sitting in front of the television staring at it but not seeing anything. In fact the set wasn't even on. She had been in this state for most of the day. She'd phoned school and told them Faith had a temperature. She couldn't bear to let Faith out of her sight yet. Tomorrow was another day and she hoped to be able to return to a more normal routine, but for today, she wanted Faith with her. They had spent the day curled up on the sofa watching their favourite programmes and movies. They'd watched *Frozen* three times, but Lucy didn't mind. So long as she was with Faith they could be doing anything.

This silence, now Faith was in bed, was excruciating. It gave her room to think about the previous day. Not just the kidnapping of Faith, but what she had done to the boy, the young man, the lad with his whole life in front of him. Someone else's child. Someone's mother would be sitting at home right now. They would feel as though their own life was over. Lucy knew that it could easily have been her sitting in that position, but it didn't help that it wasn't, that she had put someone else in that seat. No one should have to bear this, not her, not the other mother, no one.

Whoever was at the other end of the phone organising all of this was evil and deserved anything bad that came his way. She hadn't dared ask Faith too much about him because that would have alerted her to the fact that Lucy hadn't sent him for her and that Lucy didn't know who he was or who had had Faith and that would have scared her. Lucy was scared enough for the two of them.

She decided she should take a cup of tea up to bed, not that she planned on sleeping much again tonight, not if last night was anything to go by. She didn't want a repeat performance of that. And she'd put Faith back in her own bed tonight. Anything out of the ordinary was cause for concern and Lucy wanted to keep life ticking over the same as it always was, as much as she could.

Flicking the kettle on she poured milk into her cup and rubbed at her face. How much longer would she leave it before going to speak to the police? How much longer before she felt safe enough to do so?

A knock at the door jolted her from her thoughts.

Her heart jumped into her throat. She wasn't expecting anyone. Would he come for Faith again even though Lucy was here with her?

She was letting her imagination get away from her. Of course he wouldn't try to take Faith from her in the house. It was probably someone trying to sell something. It could even be the police. They could have found her already. Oh God, she wasn't ready. She really wasn't ready. She hadn't had enough time with Faith yet, not after only just getting her back. She wanted another couple of days. Maybe she could hide and pretend she wasn't in?

But she looked around at the house, all the lights were on, it was like Blackpool illuminations in here. She was so scared to be in the dark and alone, unprepared for what might happen that she had every light on that she could. There was no way she could pretend she wasn't in.

Who would look after Faith if the police took her in tonight? There was no way they would agree to wait until tomorrow when she could get her mum to look after her, not for murder. It wasn't as though she had nicked a jar of coffee from the supermarket.

Shit. What was she going to do?

She had to answer the door. She couldn't hide from the cops.

Lucy rubbed at her face again, frustrated with herself, with her situation. This man had turned her into a gibbering wreck. She walked to the front door. Beyond the glass she could make out a shape and nothing else, no gender or age or weight or most importantly, what they wanted.

She turned the key in the lock. The figure waited. Cops would come in pairs wouldn't they? If they had come to arrest her anyway? Maybe if it was just one of them they were just here to ask her if she had seen anything because someone had spotted her car near the scene. She could lie for tonight. Say she didn't see anything. Just for tonight. She was planning to give herself in. But she wanted another day or two with Faith. Time to settle down and make Faith feel safe again. Help her feel safe again. It would only be a temporary lie. She had killed a man and she would own up to it. She would pay her dues. Every single second of what she owed.

She turned the handle and opened the door.

The quick glimpse she got of him was that he was middle-aged.

But that was all she had time to think because before she could consider him any further or open her mouth to ask him what he wanted he was upon her, pushing her backwards, back into her own home, pushing hard with his hand over her mouth preventing her from screaming out for help, kicking out behind him to close the door as he stepped over the threshold into her home. Her home where she lived with Faith. Faith who was upstairs.

Faith.

She had to fight back. She had to get him out.

His momentum continued and she was pushed right up against the hallway wall. His hand over her mouth. Nothing but muffled grunts escaping from her, he had such a tight grasp on her. He smelled of hand wash, something floral, something a woman would buy. Lucy's head was pushed back, her chin jutting out. She couldn't see him well with the position he had her in. He was breathing hard, seemingly as panicked as she was. They were both panting. Lucy brought her hands up between their bodies and pushed, tried to get him away. Tried to put some distance between them.

'No, no, no, no, no,' he said, as much to himself as he did to her.

She lifted her knee and aimed for his groin but they were so close together it barely impacted. She wriggled to try to get out of his grip swishing her head around so he couldn't keep his womanly smelling hands around her face. The feel of them was making her insides crawl.

He grappled to keep hold of her and they spun in a circle where they stood until they fell down to the floor and Lucy had her back to him, but he still had a tight hold of her. She still could not see him, but she didn't need to see him to be terrified of what he was about to do.

22

Scott Rhodes could never have imagined he would be in this position with a woman in his life. How did he get here? How had he managed to get in a position where he could be forced to be on the hallway floor of a house with a woman in his arms, and with that woman rightly terrified of what he was about to do to her? And he didn't know if what she was scared of was more or less terrifying than what he was going to do.

Because what he was actually going to do was pull the plastic bag out of his pocket while they were in this position. It crinkled and you could just hear it under the ragged breathing of the pair of them. He wasn't even sure if she had heard it because she was breathing so hard. Putting up a fight against him.

'Not Faith, please not Faith again,' she said between struggles for breath.

Who the hell was Faith? What was she talking about? The man hadn't mentioned anyone else at the address. Shit.

'Who's Faith?' he barked out at her. Angry at everyone, himself included. His body slick with sweat at the effort of trying to hold her in position. His legs were wrapped around her lower body and his arms around her upper body. Carrier bag still screwed up in one of his hands.

She sounded equally confused. 'Faith's my daughter.' She tried to twist her head to look at him but he stopped her. 'She's asleep upstairs in her bedroom.'

What the hell?!

He had to do this as quickly as possible and with as little noise as possible. But that would mean the little girl would be the one to find her mother in the morning. What kind of monster did that make him? All so he could protect himself and his life. He was prepared to do this to a little girl?

He clung on to Lucy Anderson as he considered his options. The man had him over a barrel, but it really was his choice on whether he went through with it or not. He was a teacher for fuck's sake, and here he was contemplating allowing a young child find her mother's cold dead body when she wakes. That would destroy the rest of her life. Any prospects she may have had up until this point would be flushed away the moment he carried this act out and Lucy Anderson waited to be found by her daughter. Once Faith Anderson found her murdered mother, her mind would never be the same again. The grief and shock would destroy her and it would eat away at her into her adulthood and it would all be his fault.

Lucy Anderson took the quiet moment to take another chance against him and tried to break the lock his arms had on her by forcing her own arms apart as hard as she could. At the same time she tried to force her head back into his nose. There wasn't the momentum, but she was trying, there was no stopping her. There was no walking out of here without a continued fight and he needed to escape with as little injury to explain to Wendy as was possible in the circumstances.

He shook the bag out and, with one hand clamped around her and his legs squeezed even tighter, he lifted it over her head. She looked up and saw it hovering above her. Comprehension dawned on her and she struggled for all she was worth but Scott was a big bloke and he had her contained pretty well.

With a huge amount of effort the bag was over her head and he had rolled onto her, so her back was on the floor and he was above her, pinning her down. It was the only way he could control the situation and get this done. He sat on her stomach and his feet stretched out behind him to control her legs but they kicked out as best they could. There was little harm she could cause but she continued to kick out. He had both her hands locked over her head in one of his and he held the bag in place with his other hand. She was attempting to rock from side to side from under him. Lucy Anderson was trying anything to get out of his grip, to get out of the bag. Her mouth was wide and taking in deep sucking breaths but she was not getting any air. The bag was being sucked in and out of her mouth and the motion started to slow.

Scott Rhodes was overcome with tiredness watching Lucy Anderson as she slipped away behind the carrier bag. She'd put up one hell of a fight, but he was bigger and heavier than she was and she hadn't stood a chance.

Now his life was safe. He would destroy his computer. Not just what was on it, but his actual computer. They were bad for you anyway. They sucked you in to places you didn't want to go. He'd destroy it and tell Wendy it had broken and that they were going to live a better life, technology free. And hopefully this would be the end of the matter.

He stood, his bones tired, and looked down at the woman on the floor, face hidden behind the bag. Her arms and legs listless, no fight left in them.

He should get out of here. There was a young child upstairs.

He should go. He pulled out his phone from his pocket, opened up the camera app and aimed it at Lucy Anderson. Was he expected to take the bag off her for the photograph? He didn't know. But he didn't want to touch her again. She was dead and he didn't want to touch her now she was dead. That was too hideous for words. He took several shots. Tried to get a shot up the carrier bag, a partial of her face, but it was grim, her face was contorted into a scream-like position. He was leaving her like that.

He'd had enough. He sent a couple of the images where he was supposed to then put his phone away then remembered he had to find and destroy her phone. A shiver went up his spine. He couldn't get out of here fast enough. What if the child woke and came downstairs? He would terrify her being in the house still. Other than her mother being dead he really didn't want that. He rushed into the living room and looked around. He couldn't see it. Didn't people usually have it close to them? The panic he was feeling consumed his whole body. His heart felt as though it was about to stop in his chest and his stomach was rising with each passing minute.

He moved to one of the chairs and pushed his hands down the back of the cushion. It wasn't there. He moved to the other chair and did the same. His hand was shaking. It wasn't there. He moved to the sofa. He pushed his hand down. It wasn't there either. Bile rose in his throat. This was ridiculous. He needed to get out of there, but the instructions had been clear. He needed to get this done properly.

He found the kitchen and looked around. Sitting on the counter plugged into the wall was a mobile phone. He could have wept he was so relieved. He pulled it free from the cord and pushed it in his pocket. He would destroy it and get rid of it as soon as he could but first he had to get out of the house. He walked past Lucy who was still laid on the floor with the bag over her head and he crept out of the house, checking there were no neighbours in view. It was clear. He stepped outside. The cold fresh air hit him and calmed his body a little.

Scott Rhodes was back in his car wondering how an upstanding member of the community like him could end up in the position he had found himself in tonight. It would never happen again.

23

He knew he wanted to punish her, and he had, he had punished her, in making her kill someone, going against everything good in her soul, he had punished her badly. And now, he had killed her and she would never know that the things that had happened to her over the last couple of days had been down to him. He wasn't sure how he felt about that.

It was one thing to get others to do his dirty work so that his DNA was never left at any scene, but it meant that he never got to look her in the face and tell her it was him, that this was him paying her back. She who had thought she could do nothing harmful, had hurt him more than anyone had ever hurt him and he had ripped her apart and she had never known.

He clenched his fists until his stubby fingernails started to dig into his palms, then he pushed even harder until his palms were damp. He released his grip and crossed his arms over his chest, wiping the damp on his jumper.

He didn't regret what he had done but he did wish, with everything he had, that he had been able to tell her it was him, that he was the one who had destroyed her life and then ultimately took it. He would have loved to have seen her face. The realisation of who had stepped into her life and destroyed it.

That couldn't be though, it had happened the way he planned it and there was no use crying over a perfect plan. The one surprise was how well it had all gone. How easy it had been to manipulate people. Like pieces on a chess board they had done as he told them to. They'd moved where he told them to move and done as he'd told them to do. He felt powerful and it was a feeling he liked and could get used to.

Maybe he should clear up the next mess in the same way?

He could create a vicious circle where the police could never catch up because the killer was always killed by the next one and he was pulling the strings but not a single strand of his DNA was left at the scene. It was priceless. Pure genius.

He was a genius.

There were enough people in the world who were more interested in saving themselves than anything else that they would do as he told them to.

There were some fun times ahead.

24

The white Tyvek suit crinkled around me as I stood over the body of a young woman in her hallway. Her arms and legs were splayed around her and a plastic bag was pulled down over her head. Bruising had formed on her arms indicating she had put up a struggle.

'No forced entry,' said Aaron at the side of me.

'No. Looks like she either knew her attacker or they knocked at the door and pushed their way in when she answered.' I looked from the young woman on the ground, to the door and back again. The distance wasn't great.

'Time of death?' I asked Jack Kidner, our Home Office registered forensic pathologist who was bent over the woman taking some tapings from her body.

He paused what he was doing and sat on his haunches. 'I'd say sometime late last night. Between nine and midnight. Best estimate. I don't know what her heating is set to do, when it's set to turn off at night and come back on in the morning and what temperature it's set for. I'll need someone to check the thermostat and timer for me before I do the PM.'

I nodded and Aaron made a note in his notebook.

'Where's the young girl who found her?' he asked, signing an exhibit label for one of the tapings he had done.

'Faith Anderson.' I sighed. 'Poor thing. She's going to live with this for the rest of her life. Social care have taken her and we're helping them track down her gran. We couldn't get much out of her about next of kin, but we did find out that she has a gran, so we're on that. She was hysterical when uniform got here. She'd gone next door to the neighbour who called us and she hadn't calmed down much by the time we got here. Though it's going to be difficult for her gran to ease her granddaughter's pain while at the same time dealing with her own grief.'

Jack pulled a couple of small bags out of his worn medical bag and a couple of pieces of brown paper. He placed the paper shiny side up, under Lucy Anderson's hands and then gently placed her hands in the bags. The paper was to catch any debris that may fall while he was bagging up her hands. Once he had secured her hands he bagged up each piece of paper individually and labelled the bag, signing the exhibit label, with time, date, location and his details.

There was a CSI around us taking video, keeping a running record account of events. Crime scenes inside an address were so much easier to contain because you didn't have to worry about keeping the public back and prying eyes away from your scene, neither did you have to worry about the weather washing away particles that might prove important. Outside crime scenes were so difficult and often time sensitive.

Once Lucy had been processed *in situ* she would be removed and the rest of the house would be searched for anything that would give us a clue as to what had happened here. As Aaron had said, there had been no forced entry, she may have known her attacker and evidence of that and her life would help immensely.

I wandered into the kitchen and left Jack to his work, Aaron followed.

'There's only one mug on the side,' I pointed out the dirty mug left next to the kettle.

'So, it's not likely someone who was here visiting,' Aaron replied.

'I feel for the daughter. To find her when she wakes up, that has to be devastating. It's going to have a huge effect on her life, Hannah.'

Aaron had a couple of kids. A boy and girl. Both had been devastated when Aaron had his heart attack and that had been a natural event and they'd had their mum's support and Aaron had been whisked to hospital and had survived. This was something else altogether.

'How do you grow up after this?' I shook my head.

'She's going to need a hell of a lot of support.'

'What about a father, Faith only mentioned a gran, but what about her dad? Are there signs of a man in the house?' A kitchen wasn't the ideal place to know who was living in a house.

Aaron put voice to my thoughts, 'We need to check the rest of the house. I'll do a Voters check.' He pulled his radio out of his pocket and checked the house with the control room. He shook his head. 'There's only Lucy Anderson registered at this address. So, if there is a father he isn't living with them.'

'Thanks, Aaron. We need to identify him. First, to eliminate him from our inquiries and then to see if he is a suitable carer for Faith, though that is a decision for social care to make. I wonder if they've had any dealings with the family.'

'It's a place to start.' He put his radio away and made a call to the office and requested contact be made with social care and the relevant inquiries be made. We needed to locate Faith's father as soon as possible. It was always the first port of call in a case like this.

We walked upstairs and into the little girl's bedroom. It looked like any other little girl's bedroom I'd ever been in. Very pink and girly with lots of teddies around the room as well as an overflowing toy box and a chalk board in the corner with stick men and stick animals drawn all over it.

Next we checked the main bedroom. This was Lucy's room. There was no sign of a male presence. Aaron opened the wardrobe.

'Only female clothes in here.'

I opened the bedside drawers. 'Yeah, this is a lady's drawer.' I walked to the other side. 'This is more like a spare drawer, but what it's not is a male's drawer. Looks like she lives alone. Unless there's a male in a spare room.'

We walked to the third bedroom and found a single bed covered in a pile of ironing waiting to be done. Female clothes. Clothes that would now not get ironed by Lucy.

A proper search would be done shortly. We'd get a full search team inside and take everything that could possibly be of help. Her life up until this point had led to her death.

Aaron's radio crackled. He picked it up. Listened to the transmission. 'The search team is outside and ready to go when you are.'

'Let's go and brief them. They can't come in until Jack is done and Lucy has been removed. Doug will have to let us know when they can come through.'

Doug was the crime scene manager. A job he took extremely seriously.

As we walked downstairs I found Jack standing talking to Doug at the bottom of the stairs.

'I'm going to talk to the search team. Do you know how long you will be?'

Jack turned to Doug. 'What do you think, old chap? Are we nearly done?'

Doug wasn't that old but his mass of grey hair had given rise to Jack's friendly turn of phrase. Doug didn't mind. No one could mind Jack. He would do anything to help anyone and often had. He would be there for you in a heartbeat and had supported me when I needed him and his medical knowledge when Aaron had been taken to the hospital last year.

Doug rubbed an eye which was nearly the only part of him showing in his protective gear. 'Give us twenty minutes and I think we'll remove the body and be out of your way.'

'Great, we'll let the search teams know they can cool their heels till then.'

'I'm sure they'll be fine about that. It's not as cold as it has been, out there. But they're sensible lads and lasses, they'll be wrapped up.' Jack smiled at me.

We left them to it.

The search team were gathered on the drive, each with a mug of something steaming in their hands.

'What've you got there?' I asked the nearest one, I recognised her but didn't know her by name.

'Tea and coffee. A couple of the neighbours saw us standing around out here, bouncing on our feet pretty cold, so offered to make us some drinks. We weren't going to be rude and turn them down.'

'I missed that one. Did anyone organise one for the DI on duty?' I asked.

She had the sense to blush. 'Sorry, Ma'am. Do you want me to go and organise you one? I'm sure they won't mind making one more, they've been ever so amenable.'

I laughed. 'No, it's fine. I don't need one really. I've had the easier task of spending the last hour inside the house while you've been waiting out here. You deserve a cuppa. Aaron wouldn't have had one anyway, would you, Sergeant?' I smiled at Aaron knowing full well he didn't drink coffee from other people's houses.

'Nope. I don't want a drink.'

The PC looked relieved. 'Do you know how much longer it's going to be, Ma'am?'

'Yes, the pathologist said about another twenty minutes.'

She nodded.

I looked at the car she was standing beside. A dark blue Ford Focus.

'Is this Lucy Anderson's car?'

The PC looked at it, as though she had just realised it was there. 'I presume so, it's on her driveway.'

I started to walk around the vehicle taking it in as I did so. 'Can you check with the control room that it is hers please?'

She got onto her radio and did a vehicle check.

This car had been involved in an accident recently. There was damage to the front end and the rear end as well. Though the majority of the damage was at the front. It was crumpled like it had been in a head-on collision and the damage at the rear was lower as though it had been hit by something low or hit a low wall. I couldn't think what could have caused the rear-end damage.

'What kind of accident causes this kind of damage?' I asked Aaron who was bent down at the rear end.

'I don't know, but this doesn't look like it's been rear-ended. I'm not sure what it looks like.' He got on his hands and knees and rubbed his fingers together. 'Something has been smeared over the rear number plate.' He put his fingers to his nose and sniffed. 'It's shoe polish. Someone has hidden the rear VRM on purpose.' He took a tissue out of his pocket and cleaned his gloved hand off and then crouched further down and looked underneath the car.

'Ma'am.' The PC came back to me. 'The vehicle is registered to Lucy Anderson. No other drivers on the insurance.'

'Hannah, you need to come and look at this,' Aaron shouted me over.

I thanked the PC and walked to where Aaron was bent looking under the car.

'What is it, Aaron?'

'You need to see this. Our victim isn't as innocent as we might believe she is.'

'What do you mean?' I crouched down beside him.

'I was interested in how low the damage was on the back-end compared to the front-end. The front was as you'd expect from a run-in of some description, but the rear, it was too low for someone to have run in to her. It was as though she had driven over a log or small brick wall in reverse. So I looked how far underneath the damage went.'

'And what did you find?'

'Have a look for yourself.'

I got onto my hands and knees, the concrete of the driveway cold on my knees through the thin Tyvek suit. I twisted my head sideways to look under the car. 'What am I looking for, Aaron?'

'You'll know when you see it.'

I pushed myself underneath slightly and strained my eyes under the darkness of the undercarriage. Then I saw it. I saw what Aaron had pushed for me to see for myself.

There was a huge swatch of what appeared to be human skin and a small section of bones, like a partial section of a hand. There was part of a person underneath Lucy Anderson's car. If anything was motive for murder I think what we had found under the car might just be.

25

A buzz was building back in the incident room. It was always the same when a new job came in.

'I know I wanted some action, but I never wanted a kid to be traumatised,' moaned Ross to Pasha.

'Do you want me to throw more paper at your head, youngster?' Martin leaned back in his chair and folded his arms behind his own head. Always relaxed no matter what was going on around him.

Ross grunted at him in response.

'We know you don't want anyone to get hurt at all, never mind any kids in whatever way, but you just want to be busy, it's part of the job. Take it easy and get on with your job now it's here.'

Ross rolled his eyes.

'Martin has a point,' I said.

Ross looked at me in query.

'About getting on with your job.'

Martin laughed.

'And you.' I directed at Martin.

Ross laughed even louder and Pasha smirked at them both.

'Right, let's get this briefing under way. Is everyone ready? We all have a drink, ready to go?'

There were murmurings of yes from around the room. A few raised mugs of coffee and tea to show they were organised. I had a steaming mug of green tea at the side of me. I couldn't work unless I was being powered by green tea. Though the way the turn this job had taken I think I could have worked on adrenalin alone.

'Theresa, is there a new HOLMES job up and running for Lucy Anderson?'

Theresa, our HOLMES inputter, tapped a few keys and looked at the screen. 'Yes, Ma'am. All ready for you.'

'Great.' I looked round the room at the expectant faces. 'As you are all aware, we have a new job in the office. Those of you who were attached to other tasks are now freed up from them and are assigned to this. This murder takes priority. Martin, you can manage to run with this and fill in the bits and pieces you need for the coroner, can't you?'

'Absolutely.'

'Glad to hear it. Everyone make sure you let your loved ones know it's the start of a new job and to expect long hours for the first few days. This looks to be a complicated job from the start so I want all hands on deck and every avenue explored and I don't care how many hours that takes or how much overtime is used.'

I shuffled backwards onto the table I had been leaning against and made myself comfortable on it. 'Lucy Anderson was killed in her own home last night between the hours of nine and midnight. There is no sign of forced entry and the door was closed behind the killer when they left. She was found by her four-year-old daughter, Faith Anderson, this morning when she woke up and came downstairs after first looking for her mum in her bedroom. As you can imagine, Faith is pretty distraught and we are looking to identify both her father and her grandmother to see if one of them can take her in. She is with social care at the moment while those inquiries are ongoing. As far as we're concerned, we're interested in the father. We want to know who he is, what the relationship was like and where he was last night. There are no signs of a male living at the address with Lucy and Faith so we need to identify him.

'Lucy was killed by suffocation with a carrier bag. She will have had to have been overpowered to keep the bag on her head and there's bruising on her arms to show she put up a pretty good fight. We'll know more when Jack does the PM this afternoon.'

Heads were down and notes were being made.

'Ross, Pasha and Martin, you were responsible for doing the house-to-house inquiries. Did any of the neighbours see or hear anything last night?'

Ross spoke first, flicking back a couple of pages in his notebook. 'I went to the house on the left of Lucy's as you look at it. Mrs Anne Carlyle. An older lady with a walking stick. She was the neighbour Faith went to this morning. The little girl was hysterical and a huge mess. Mrs Carlyle went around to Faith's house. She wanted to know what had got Faith into such a mess then came back home to where her husband was trying to calm Faith down, which wasn't working, as you can expect, and called us. She was pretty upset herself after seeing Lucy's body. She didn't hear anything last night. Her living room is at the back of the property. She said they were both watching the television and didn't hear anything strange. She said Lucy is a great neighbour, never any trouble. And Faith is a good little girl. Always polite. She never hears her throwing any tantrums and says the walls are fairly thin and is sure she would hear if she did.'

I butted in. 'The walls are thin but she didn't hear the struggle last night?'

'She reiterated that she had the television on and was watching some action film with her husband and he has it turned up quite loud.'

I nodded.

'She did say that she never sees a bloke coming to pick up Faith. She's of the opinion that Faith doesn't see her father.'

'So, she's nosey enough to have this kind of opinion and notice those comings and goings, but doesn't notice a killer walking into the house or hear the struggle of a murder? That's helpful.'

'Yeah, sorry, Boss.'

'Not your fault, Ross. What about other neighbours?'

He flicked over another page. 'Pretty much the same thing at the houses I attended. No one heard or saw anything. There was no answer at a couple of the addresses, they must have already left for work, so I need to go back later, after work hours.'

'Okay, thanks, Ross. Martin?'

Martin didn't need to rely on his notebook. His response was easy enough. 'No one saw or heard anything last night but they want to know if they should be worried that a killer is entering homes to kill them.'

I rolled my eyes. 'Great, the first thing they worry about is themselves? Though I do suppose we'll have to reassure the public that they're safe, that we don't believe a killer is doing that. That this was a personal and deliberate attack and not a random one at any old house. But let's get to that conclusion first, shall we? Pasha?'

Pasha also picked up her pocket notebook and peeled back a couple of pages and read what she'd written.

'The same as Martin, other than one gentleman who noticed a car parked over the road that he'd never seen before. He's a bit of a nosey neighbour, in his own words and he wondered who the owner of the vehicle was visiting, because the car was parked outside the old couple, Mr and Mrs Dean, and their lights were off. They tend to go to bed early. So it wasn't likely that the owner of the car was seeing them.'

This was something interesting. 'And did he get the details of the car?'

'Ah, that's where it's a let-down, I'm afraid. We don't have a VRM, just that it's a dark-coloured five-door Ford Focus.'

'Damn. That's a shame, but it's a start and if we get an offender we can tie them in with the vehicle. Let's action that on HOLMES, Theresa, check anyone we're interested in with that vehicle.'

Theresa nodded and tapped away at her keyboard.

I looked at the team, ready and willing to get going on what we had. 'We found something useful at the address this morning.'

All faces looked my way.

'I don't know if you noticed, but Lucy's car on her driveway was damaged. There was front-end damage and also some at the rear.'

'I saw the front but didn't notice it at the back,' said Martin.

'You needed to be closer at the back-end to see it,' said Aaron.

'Yes,' I continued, 'the front was rather obvious, but the rear was more subtle. Anyway, Aaron got down and had a look at it and spotted human remains stuck to the undercarriage of the car.'

'Urgh, what?!' said Pasha.

'Exactly that, Pasha. Skin where it had been dragged from a body and a partial hand.'

'Just, urgh again,' she said.

'So what do we think our victim has been up to?' Ross asked.

'Nothing good by the sound of it.' Pasha was definitely disturbed by recent developments.

'Nothing good indeed and that's what we need to find out. What exactly she has been getting up to. If ever there was a reason to kill her I think we found it underneath her car this morning. It's been lifted to CSU for a full forensic examination where I'm told the body parts will be recovered and they'll try to obtain a fingerprint if that is at all possible, and if not, then they'll take a DNA sample. They'll examine the car and see what they can tell us about what it has impacted, if it has had contact with anything other than a person. But the main source of help from this will be the ID of the victim. From there we talk to people who may have known what happened. I think we'll find our killer amongst them.'

Pasha looked to Ross. 'That poor little girl. Not only has she lost her mum, but she will one day learn that her mum was a killer. Adults, they never remember what effect they are having on the children in their lives, do they?'

Ross shook his head. 'I've worked in here long enough to realise that people don't think things through very well at all. If they did, there wouldn't be much need for our department, would there?'

Pasha shrugged in resignation.

I picked up my tea which had cooled a little and drank some before continuing. 'Our main priority today is to identify and locate

Faith's father. First of all for our inquiry, and at the same time, provide his details to social care so they can see if he's suitable for Faith to be homed with. Martin, I want you on that please.'

Martin nodded and jotted a note down in his book. It would be one of only a few notes in his book. He was not known for keeping his paperwork up-to-date, which was the only problem I had with him on the team. Though it was a pretty important problem and one that could come back and bite him on the arse one day. Paperwork tended to be one of the more important parts of the job, unfortunately.

'Also, I want you to go back through Lucy's last couple of days. See if there is anything in there that can tell us why this happened. As we know, the odds are that the victim knows the killer, especially in a case where the murder happened in the victim's home. I'm putting all my money on Lucy knowing her killer in some way, through some interaction. You don't just enter a stranger's house and kill them. Something in Lucy's life will lead us to what happened. And bearing in mind what we know of her life because of the car, I specifically want to know when and where that happened and who the person is under the car. And following on from that, who knows about the accident, who could know Lucy was responsible. There's a lot of work here for us. Don't forget to take some breaks, feed yourselves. You can feed me as well if you feel like it.' There was laughter around the room.

The door to the incident room opened and Baxter walked in. 'Have I missed the briefing?'

I looked at the team and then back at Baxter. 'I'm afraid so, Sir. I didn't realise you planned on being here or I would have waited for you.'

He gave me a curt nod and turned around on his heel and left the room without another word. It looked as though Catherine had spoken to him.

26

He looked at his laptop, at the cursor flashing on the empty search bar. He had no idea what he should even look for this time. He couldn't search for the same thing, it would be too easy. Though did he really think there would be another teacher in the area with that kind of stuff on his laptop? He needed something to hold over a person that they would be willing to kill for. He liked that he could kill but not be present. Not have his DNA at the scene. He was the puppet master. Like God. Present but not present.

But he needed to get his head into gear. What would people die or kill for to protect?

He had an idea. It would take some clever photoshop skills so he could put the pressure on, but it would be worth it. And he had the next killer nearly lined up. The thrill of other people killing for him was immense.

27

We located Lucy's mother easily enough. She came to us when she'd heard about the murder on that estate and couldn't get in touch with her daughter that morning. She wanted to know if it was Lucy or Faith and we said we would check and get straight back to her.

It wasn't a message you wanted to give over the telephone so Aaron and I went around to see her straight away. It took us fifteen minutes to get back to Arnold where Cheryl Anderson also lived and by the time she answered the door she was in a state. Her face was drained of colour and her hair looked like hands had run through it multiple times. Her cardigan was on inside out and she had odd socks on.

The minute she saw us standing on the doorstep she crumpled to the floor, her knees giving way beneath her.

'No, no, no, no, nooooooo.' Aaron caught her arms before she reached the ground.

'Shall we go inside?' he said gently and manoeuvred her around and into the house. We stepped over the threshold behind her.

It was a clean and tidy home and smelled sweet, floral. There was an air freshener on the windowsill, pumping out sweet-smelling liquid drops into the air.

Cheryl Anderson struggled to hold herself upright, even with the help of Aaron who held both her arms as he supported her from behind. The loss of a child before you go is not the natural order of the world. You always leave your child behind. You never expect to see your child go before you do. And not in violent circumstances. Not in any circumstances.

We shuffled into the living room. It was like the hallway, neat and clean. There was a box of toys in the corner. For Faith I presumed. Unless she had other grandchildren as well. But they looked to be girls' toys and for a child of about Faith's age.

Aaron helped Cheryl into one of the chairs. She fell in on herself.

'It really is Lucy?' she asked.

'I'm sorry, Mrs Anderson. I was at the house this morning. It is Lucy. We'll need you to come to the hospital to do the official ID, but we're certain it's her. The identification is purely protocol.'

Tears flooded her eyes. 'When I heard on the news this morning...' Her voice cracked. 'She didn't answer the phone.'

'Is your husband around? Do you need us to call him for you? We can collect him if you need us to?'

She shook her head. 'No. Thank you. I'm a single parent. Always have been. That's why Lucy felt strong enough to do it herself. She'd seen me do it. Said I was both a mother and a father to her and she never felt she missed out on anything so if I could do it, so could she.' The tears fell freely now. I spotted a box of tissues on a sideboard next to the fireplace and collected a couple of them for her. She took them and stuffed them into her face as she collapsed into herself. She sobbed and sobbed, breaking her heart for the daughter she had lost. I still needed to ask her some questions but it was impossible right now. She was lost in her grief.

She continued to sob and then bolted upright as though someone had shot an electric current up through her. 'What about Faith? Where is she? I presume she will be coming here to me? I will be taking the poor wee girl in. She'll need me, she'll be scared witless. What on earth have you done with her?'

I held out a hand to calm her. 'Social care are taking care of her at the moment—'

She looked horrified. 'No, she must come here. Not one of those dreadful homes.'

'It's okay. They have no intention of keeping her. They are just taking care of her until we found you or her father.'

Cheryl grunted at the use of Faith's father. We hadn't discussed him yet, it was something we needed to cover.

'Once we let them know we've found you they'll get in touch, come round to talk to you and organise bringing Faith round to you and let you know what happens from here on in.'

The tears were still flowing. 'That poor, poor child. She's lost her mother and she's all alone. I have so much love for her, but it's not a mother's love, I'm not her mother. She knows I'm not her mother. How will she ever get over this?'

Loss like this was traumatic for all the families left behind. Murder rippled out and hurt those left behind for a long time to come.

I tried to get Cheryl back on to the subject we needed her on. She was obviously focused on her family. We were focused on the investigation.

'I'll put the kettle on,' I said quietly to Aaron.

He nodded, not looking comfortable at being left with the sobbing parent. He was usually the one to go and put the kettle on, he didn't do sobbing relatives well. He didn't know the right thing to say to them. The truth was no one knew the right thing to say to them. There was no right thing. Words would never ease the pain. That wasn't the point of the words. You wouldn't and couldn't stop their pain, but you could offer support, just by being there, letting them know they weren't alone. Sitting silently with them was support. Because grief is a lonely isolating place.

I found the kitchen and put the kettle on. Took time to have a bit of a look around. Like the rest of the house it was clean and smart.

Lucy had come from a nice home. How did someone like Lucy, with a parent like Cheryl, end up doing what Lucy had done? And end up on Jack's slab because of it. It was a big mess. It must have been a traumatic last few days for Lucy.

The kettle boiled and I made a tea with three sugars in for Cheryl and a coffee for myself. I drank black coffee if there was no green tea.

I handed the tea to Mrs Anderson and she took it with shaking hands. While I had made the tea and looked around the rest of the downstairs, her sobbing had eased. She would cry a lot, not continually, but on and off all day for days.

'I need to ask you some questions if you feel up to it,' I said.

She nodded, her hands clasped around the mug. 'It's about Faith's father. Do you know who he is?'

A sigh escaped and she nodded again. 'I do. Lucy never told her husband at the time that she was pregnant, she just left him. What she did do though is put his name on the birth certificate because she thought it was only right that his name was there. She didn't want Faith to grow up with *Unknown*, listed where Father should be.'

She wiped her face as more tears started to trickle down her cheeks. 'Lucy said Faith could search him out when she was older if she wanted to. But she didn't want him in Faith's life in her early years. It was those early years that Lucy didn't want him impacting on her, imprinting on her. She wanted the best possible start for her child. She divorced him as soon as Faith was born.'

I nodded, Lucy sounded like a strong woman. 'Why didn't she want Faith's father in her life? What was wrong with him?'

Cheryl took a slurp of her tea before answering. She considered this one before she spoke. 'He was a little volatile. Initially I thought they made a good couple and then the arguments started. He never beat her, but he was controlling. He wanted to know where she was every minute of the day and who she'd been talking to on social media, especially if he didn't know them. Lucy knew it was because he cared, he loved her but she started to feel suffocated by it. She didn't tell him she was pregnant, but said she was ill and needed to spend the weekend in bed alone, to give herself some time to think about her future and what she wanted to do. He took himself off out with his friends. He was afraid of catching whatever it was she had. He texted her relentlessly, but that cemented Lucy's fears of her future with him. After that she broke things off.'

'And it ended just like that?' asked Aaron, echoing my thoughts.

Mrs Anderson barked out a brittle laugh. 'No, of course it didn't. He moved out but he hounded her for weeks. Eventually told her he didn't need her and that he'd found someone else. Now I wonder if it would have been better had she stayed with him, at least she would have still been alive. She wouldn't have been alone in that house with Faith. He wouldn't have let this happen to her. He loved her too much and would have protected her to the ends of the earth.'

'Do you remember his name? Lucy's husband?'

'Yes, of course. Mark Wallace.'

'Thank you. We are so sorry for your loss,' I said as I stood with my mug in my hand. 'Thank you for all the information you've given us. It should help us track down Mark. We'll keep you informed of how the investigation progresses.'

Cheryl stood with us.

'Can I ask?' I said as we moved towards the front of the house. 'When did you last see Lucy?'

Mrs Anderson stopped still as she thought this question through. Her head bobbed slightly as she counted back the... what, days, weeks?

'It was about four days ago, I think. She brought Faith round and we had some cake with our tea.' Her eyes filled with tears again.

We didn't know how long ago Lucy had been involved in the accident. 'Did she mention being involved in a car accident when you saw her?'

'Gosh, no. Why? Do you think she was?'

'Well, her car was damaged on the driveway and we're wondering what happened. There's no police report of an accident for that vehicle. So whatever happened, she didn't report it.'

'That's strange, she always follows the rules. If something

happened and she needed to report it to the police then she would have done.'

'You didn't notice anything worrying her? Anything off at all?'

'No, she was her usual self. And I would have noticed. We have a very good relationship.'

I nodded.

'Had,' she whispered. 'We had a very good relationship. I'm going to have to get used to saying that, aren't I?'

'Again, I really am sorry for your loss.' I pulled a card from my pocket and handed it to her. 'If you think of anything that might be of help, please do call, or if you want an update, if you haven't heard from me, get in touch. If I'm not available, if I'm out or dealing with something, leave a message and I'll call you straight back.'

She took the card. 'You'll speak to social care and get me my little Faith?' she asked.

'Yes, I'll do it as soon as I get back to the office.'

She stared down at her hands, the tissue crumpled up.

'And you'll call if you think of anything that might help, anything you remember about Lucy in the last few days? Anything she might have said or an impression you got from her behaviour. The slightest thing might help. Nothing is too small.'

Her chin trembled, she wrapped her arms around her body and nodded, her shoulders quaking.

'Can you come to the hospital now to identify Lucy?' I asked.

Cheryl's face crumpled.

I placed a hand on her arm. 'We'll be with you every step of the way.'

She nodded and wiped away the tears that were falling down her face. 'However hard this is, I want to see my daughter.'

28

That was another family we had decimated with a death message and ID procedure. It was one of the hardest parts of the job, delivering the news to a loved one.

'You think she really didn't know about the accident?' I asked Aaron as we walked into the incident room.

'It's easy enough to believe. If the accident,' he wrapped air quotes around the word, 'didn't happen until after she last saw Lucy then the daughter she saw will have been the normal young woman she was used to seeing.'

He was right. We needed to know what had happened in Lucy's life in the last couple of days.

It didn't take us long to locate Mark Wallace using the voters register.

I picked the car keys back up. 'I suppose we'd better go back out and find out when he last saw Lucy and what he was doing last night. Oh and let him know he's father to a four-year-old little girl.'

'If he's interested in taking her in he's going to have a fight on his hands from Mrs Anderson,' said Aaron.

Having stood in the cold this morning, my arm was throbbing. I needed some painkillers before we went into the cold again. I had been stabbed during a job nearly eighteen months ago and it still played up sometimes.

'Give me a minute before we head out,' I headed to my office.

In the hallway I saw Baxter walking towards the incident room. Shit, I hadn't seen him alone since my chat with Catherine and I didn't know how he was going to take it. If he was going to have more of a problem or if he was going to be an adult about it.

'How's it going, Hannah?'

So far so good. He sounded fine.

'We've identified Lucy's family. Her mother. We've spoken with her, she doesn't know anything about the car and didn't notice anything different about Lucy the last time she saw her about four days ago. We've also identified Faith's father and we're going out to see him in a minute. I just need something from my office. We're going to tell him he's a father and see what his movements were last night. It'll be a lot to take in.'

Baxter nodded. There was a smell of cigarettes about him. He had obviously been outside to have a smoke. 'It's an interesting job. You'll get further ahead when you get the results from the body parts under the car. Very strange case. She gets murdered, but she's already killed someone herself by the looks of it.'

I admitted it was one of the strangest jobs we'd had in the office, and we'd had a few over the years.

His eyes softened towards me, as though he knew where I was headed. 'Yes, I know about the basement and what happened there, what happened to you and to your colleague. I'm so sorry about what you went through, Hannah.' His voice was quiet.

I didn't know what to say. I had never spoken of this with him. He had arrived after that job, he had arrived precisely because that job had gone wrong and had never mentioned it. I wasn't sure why he was discussing it right now. I felt wrong-footed.

'Thank you, Sir. I'm just... I'm going to, I'm...' I pointed aimlessly down the corridor where my office was amongst the others down this bland corridor.

'Yes, yes, go and do what you need to and I'll catch up with you at the next briefing. If you can let me know before you start it, I'd like to be present. This case has piqued my interest and I'd like to be involved as much as I can. Whatever help I can be to you.'

'Yes, Sir. Of course. I'll let you know. Thank you, Sir. I'll just...' Again I pointed towards my office.

He smiled and strode off towards the incident room.

I was so perturbed by the interaction it took me a moment to realise that he was headed straight into Aaron's path and that they hadn't yet run into each other since I had spoken to Catherine. Though this was a different Baxter to the one we were used to dealing with. I was confused by his perception, how he seemed to realise my mind was on those events. How he had allowed me to fumble and had left me rather than question the ramblings.

I walked into my office and grabbed a strip of painkillers out of my top drawer. Threw them into my mouth and downed them with the cold green tea sitting on top of my desk. I screwed up my face at the taste of it at this temperature and slammed the mug back down on the desk.

It was time to go and see Mark Wallace and let him know he had a four-year-old child. This was certainly a day of surprises.

The heater in the car was slow to warm the space. I turned it up to full as Aaron directed the vehicle through the lunchtime traffic. We needed to make decent time as we had the PM this afternoon.

'So, what was Baxter like when you saw him?' I asked as Aaron focused on the road, his hands in the ten two position.

'He was fine. He said he'd spoken with you and you'd updated him on seeing Mrs Anderson and he knew we were on our way to see Lucy's ex. He told me he was fascinated by the job and hoped he could be some help during the investigation.'

There was silence.

'And that's it?' I pushed.

'That's it.'

'He didn't say anything personal?'

'Nothing.'

I wasn't going to get much more from Aaron.

'You're okay?' I asked instead.

'I'm fine.'

And he was, because if he wasn't he would have told me. I had learned that much about Aaron. He was brutally honest.

Fifteen minutes later we were standing outside Mark Wallace's house in Beeston. I used the doorbell and waited. There was no response. I tried again.

'Okay, I'm coming.' The shout through the door sounded impatient.

'Okay, okay, I'm here.' Wallace was flustered when he opened the door and glared at me and Aaron. He was an average man in every way, average height, weight, nothing about him stood out other than the brace on his teeth I could see peeking out through his lips. 'Can I help you? I'm trying to get organised to go to work. I'm on afters today.'

He was a shift worker. At least we hadn't woke him up after a night shift.

I showed him my warrant card and introduced myself and Aaron. He looked surprised and ushered us into the house.

'Is this going to take long? I need to get ready for work.'

'You might want to give them a call and let them know you won't be in today,' Aaron said.

'What do you mean I won't be in today?' Mark furrowed his eyebrows, his eyes darkening underneath them. He was confused. Worried. The police only turned up if they had bad news.

'Is there somewhere we can go and sit?' I asked.

'Why do we need to sit? Tell me why you're here.'

'Can you tell me where you were last night? Between the hours of nine and midnight,' I asked, even though we were still standing in the hall and had not moved any closer to the living room.

'I was at work. What's this about?'

I looked at Aaron. There was no good way to break this kind of news. It was not the same as a death message, though there was a death message wrapped up in there, but we were about to bring a man's life crashing down around him. It would never look the same, no matter what he decided to do once he knew.

'It would be more helpful if we could have a seat to discuss this,' I pushed.

Wallace glared at me and didn't move an inch. He folded his arms across his chest and Aaron pushed his hands into his pockets. It looked like we were going to have to have the discussion here, standing in the tiny space that was his entrance hallway at the bottom of the stairs.

'Do you know someone by the name of Lucy Anderson?' I asked.

He frowned. 'Yeah, I knew her a few years ago, but by a different name. She had my name then. I presume she's changed it back to her maiden name? I haven't seen her for about...' He stopped his eyes taking a faraway look as he figured it out. 'For about five years now. Why, what is this?'

'Lucy was murdered last night.'

His body seemed to shrink before us. 'Damn.' He staggered back a little and reached a hand out for the wall, feeling it and leaning back against it.

'Shall we go into the living room?' Aaron asked.

'Yeah, maybe we should.' He nodded. A little unsteady on his legs, he led us into his living room.

It was a nice space, not quite what I was expecting for him. Soft furnishings and photographs on the wall.

I looked closer at the photos. They were of him and a woman. I checked Mark's left hand. I hadn't noticed it before but he wore a wedding ring. Mark was married. This was going to not only change his world, but change the world of a woman who also had no idea he had a child. He couldn't be blamed for keeping it a secret from her though, not when Lucy had hidden it from him all this time. She hadn't even gone after him for child support. She had raised Faith on her own.

'I see you're married,' I said as we all seated ourselves on the sofa and chairs.

'Yeah, it's been three years. Kate is lovely. We never row, not like me and Lucy used to.' His eyes were glassy. He still had residual feelings for her. Or he was a pretty good actor.

'Where is your wife now?' Aaron asked.

'She's at work. She's a vet. So much smarter than I am.' He laughed, a bit of a forced laugh in the circumstances. 'Do you need her here?' he asked suddenly. He looked at his watch. 'In fact, she should be here now. She doesn't work conventional hours as a vet. She's either working long hours into the evening or she's got a morning off.' He tried to crack a smile while he talked about his wife but it was obvious his thoughts were still elsewhere.

'No, no, it's fine, not at the moment anyway.'

He looked from me to Aaron. 'Why are you here? Like I said, I haven't seen Lucy for about five years. What does this have to do with me?' He rose from his seat. 'Do I need to be worried? Why did you ask me where I was last night? Why the hell would you be looking at an ex from over five years ago?!' He ran his hands through his hair. 'Shit, what the hell is happening? I'm supposed to be going to work and now this. Of course it's horrific that Lucy is dead, that she was murdered, but I had nothing to do with it.'

I held out my hand and asked him to sit back down. 'We will of course need to check with your place of work that you were there, but we're also here for another reason, Mark. Lucy had a daughter.'

Mark sank back into his seat, all the anger seeping out of him. 'Oh poor kid. I presume Lucy's mum has her.'

I nodded. 'There is another option, someone else who may be interested in having Faith though.'

I didn't know if it was starting to dawn on him but he didn't look as though he had any idea. I was just going to have to say it. I looked around the room again.

'Do you and Kate have any children?' I asked, pointing towards the photographs on the wall.

'Not yet, it's something we've discussed, but we've not been in any rush.'

'The thing is, Mark, Faith Anderson is your daughter.' That was it, it was out there.

I wasn't sure he heard me. I was still looking at the photographs on the wall, of him and Kate, of their lives together.

'What did you say?'

'You're the father of Lucy Anderson's daughter. She's four years old. Her name is Faith.'

Mark's hand went up to his mouth. 'Is this some kind of joke? If it is, I don't understand it. Why would the police do this? What is it you're saying?'

I leaned forward in my chair. 'Look, I'm sorry, Mark, but when Lucy got pregnant she broke up with you. I heard from her mum that you didn't take it well but eventually you left her alone, before she started to show. She had the baby alone, with her mum's help and put your name on the birth certificate because she wanted Faith to know she did have a father. But she brought her up alone, which was the way she wanted to do it. But she's gone and Faith is alone in the world and you are her only living parent.'

There was no other way to put it other than to go with the blunt truth.

'I have a daughter?' His voice was high-pitched. His hand went up to his mouth.

The front door opened and I heard someone step through it and stop to take off a coat. His wife was home. 'Honey, is someone here?' she shouted through to the room. 'I saw a car parked outside. Is it here?' She walked through into the room where we were all seated. Mark still with his hand up to his mouth looking shaken.

'Oh.' She stopped in the doorway. 'I didn't realise you had people here. I'm sorry.' She looked from Wallace, to Aaron, to me and back to Wallace for some kind of response. Some explanation for who these people were in her house.

Mark stayed where he was. 'Hi, love. These are police officers.' He waved a hand towards us. 'I'm sorry, I can't remember your names.'

'It's fine,' I said. He had too much on his mind now to remember the names he'd been told when we first entered. I stood and walked over to Kate Wallace. 'I'm DI Hannah Robbins and this is my colleague, DS Aaron Stone.' I held out my hand. She took it and we shook hands.

'Is there a problem?' she asked looking at her husband.

Mark looked to me. 'I'm not sure I know where to start.'

'Would you like me to fill Kate in on some of it?' I asked him.

'Mark?' she stared at him. 'Please? What the hell is going on? Why can't you tell me?'

He scrubbed his face with his hands. 'Remember my ex-wife, Lucy?'

She nodded.

'She's dead. She was killed.'

Kate walked to the sofa and sat down next to Mark. 'That's awful, Mark, but what's it got to do with you?'

He looked at me and then looked Kate in the face. 'She had a daughter, Kate. My daughter.'

This time it was Kate's turn to put her hand up to her mouth. She turned to me. 'Is she hurt?'

'No. No, she's fine. She found her mother so she's traumatised but she's physically unhurt.'

There was a sharp intake of breath when I said that she found her mother.

She looked back to Mark. 'You didn't know?'

'I promise you, Kate. I knew nothing about her. If I had you would have known. You know we don't keep secrets.'

Kate nodded and turned to me. 'Where is she now?'

'She's in social care, or maybe she'll even have been handed over to Lucy's mum by now, but if you want we can give your details to them and you can both go from there and decide what you want to do. I have the details of the social worker who's in charge of Faith's case and I can give you them, if you'd like?'

Mark looked to Kate and she nodded. Mark grabbed hold of Kate's hand and her fingers curled around his. They were in this together. She had dealt with this amazingly well to say she had only just found out her husband had a child.

Aaron pulled out a card from his pocket and handed it to Mark. 'Will you be getting in touch with her?'

Again Mark nodded. He seemed to have lost the power of speech.

'Is there anything we can do for you?'

He shook his head.

'I just need your contact details, Mark,' Aaron's pen hovered over his notebook.

Mark tried to speak but his throat was clogged. He cleared it and tried again, giving Aaron what he needed, then showed us out the door, Kate stayed in the living room. She had a lot of information to process. They both did.

'We'll be in touch with your work, to confirm your location last night, but other than that, we have nothing further we need from you.'

Mark was back to nodding. The anger he had felt at our need to contact his place of work had dissipated.

'Get in touch with us if you have any questions.' I handed him my card.

This was another life that had been affected by the one murder.

29

The doctors' surgery was a lesson in shabby chic. It was clean and tidy but it was old and the furniture needed replacing and was worn in places that were visible and there were scuff marks around the bottoms of the walls. Health posters adorned the walls, giving us lessons in handwashing and checking our breasts as well as timetables for cessation of smoking classes, weight control classes and a grief counselling group. It smelled of furniture polish and disinfectant. One of which was overpowering and caught at the back of my throat. I let out a small cough caused by the tickle and realised I now looked like I belonged in the waiting room with the rest of the patients. Aaron gave me a sideways glance and I shook my head at him.

We were seated in the corner of the waiting room, trying to keep as far away from the sick patients in a holding pattern for the doctors beyond the doors at the side of reception. A woman was holding a child in a nappy. The baby looked to be about eighteen months and the nappy was all she was wearing. That must be one hell of a temperature if she was in a nappy in February and not bundled in knits. An old woman was coughing at regular intervals into her hands then wiping her hands onto her knees. I wasn't sure we were going to get out of here unscathed and neither of us had the time to get ill. We had a case to investigate which was why we were here to talk to the head doctor at the surgery Lucy Anderson used to work at.

Doctor Raahim Basha had agreed to meet us as soon as clinic had closed. It looked as though they were running over schedule. I should have known this would happen from my own minimal visits to the doctors' surgery.

There were two receptionists behind the desk in the waiting room. Both women in their thirties or older and both looked to have been crying, but were putting on a brave face. Make-up was applied neatly and hair was brushed into place. They were professional women but their eyes were red-rimmed. They had looked slightly terrified of me when I introduced myself on arrival. As though murder was contagious. I could see one of them was desperate to ask me a question. She kept looking at me, her mouth opening and closing like that of a goldfish. In the end she decided against it and went with the professional approach and got on with her work.

The young woman with the infant was buzzed through and I got a closer look. The child was glowing red, her cheeks illuminous in her face, her mother pale and anxious. Ten minutes later the old woman was through and a couple of minutes later the door opened and a young man was standing in the open space, smiling.

'DI Robbins, DS Stone?'

We both stood and moved towards the doorway. He held out his hand. 'Doctor Raahim Basha.' I shook his hand. It was firm and cool.

'DI Hannah Robbins and this is my colleague, DS Aaron Stone. Thank you for seeing us on such short notice.'

Aaron nodded his greeting at the doctor and the doctor did the same in return. I think it was a male thing.

The doctor's face was serious. 'It's no trouble at all. Anything that will help in the investigation for Lucy. Please come through to my surgery.' He turned and moved off down the corridor with an expectation for us to follow him, which we duly did. After a few paces he opened a door and ushered us in.

The room looked like any other surgery I had been in. There was a desk, a couple of chairs around it with the usual paraphernalia on it, a blood pressure pump, a prescription pad, a couple of boxes from pharmaceutical companies, tongue suppressors and other such items, a bed in the corner with a paper towel roll running along it. A set of scales at the bottom of the bed with a height tool above it.

There was a faint clinical scent to the room but it didn't have the strength of a hospital. It was lighter, like a memory that this was a health setting.

Doctor Basha seated himself in his chair and indicated we should make ourselves comfortable. Though I never thought of doctors' surgeries as comfortable places I did take a chair and Aaron seated himself at the side of me.

The doctor picked up a pen and tapped his lips with the end of it. 'I was shocked when you broke the news of Lucy's death.' He paused. 'Her murder,' he corrected himself. 'The whole surgery is in pieces. We were late opening the doors this morning as everyone tried to get themselves back into work mode which is why we were a little behind when you came in. The reception staff have taken it particularly hard. They worked with Lucy every day and were close to her.' He paused and looked at me. I hadn't yet asked him a question.

'I'm not sure how we can help you, DI Robbins? Unless you believe her murder is somehow connected to her work?'

I shook my head. 'No, we don't believe it's connected to her work at all. But we do think her actions the day before may have led to her murder, so anything you can tell us about the day before her death would be hugely helpful.'

Doctor Basha leaned back in his chair and tapped at his lips with the pen some more. 'The day before her death?'

I nodded.

'The thing is, Lucy called in sick that day. She wasn't here, so I can't tell you what frame of mind she was in. What I can tell you is that it was most unlike Lucy to not be at work. She never phoned in sick and we were most surprised and hoped that she would be well very soon.'

'You're a doctors' surgery. How do people phone in sick to a doctors' surgery,' I asked.

He laughed. 'The same way they do it anywhere else, DI Robbins. They pick up the phone and tell us they don't feel well.'

'But can't you tell if they're faking or something?'

'Not over the phone we can't and as far as I can remember, she said she had an upset stomach. That's not something we can say much about over the phone other than to keep the fluid intake up, rest and stay off work at least two days.'

It was my turn to laugh. 'They say that but in reality most employers just want you back as soon as you've stopped vomiting.'

He inclined his head. 'That may be the case, but we as doctors can't take that stance.'

'Okay, so what about the day before that, what was she like? Was there anything different about her? For instance, was she nervous about anything? Did it look like anything was worrying her?'

He shook his head. 'She was the same as she always was. Punctual at the start of the day, even though she's a single parent. Busy with the hustle and bustle of the surgery. She kept up with it with no issues as far as I'm aware and to be honest, I would only know there was an issue if there was a real problem. Things tend to tick over quite well for us doctors. The reception staff do a fabulous job for us. I don't have anything to say about her. I really am sorry I can't be of any help but there weren't any signs of her being in any trouble before she phoned in sick.'

I looked to Aaron who made a note in his pocket notebook.

'To be honest, you have been helpful. You have given us a timeline. We know she called you sick and that was when her life started to spiral out of control. We just need to figure out why.' I looked to him. 'Did she say anything? Was she worried about anything at all?'

He shook his head. 'I'm not the person to ask. You need to speak to the girls behind reception. I can take you through if you like. Let them know they're to help you as much as you need.' He rose from his seat. We were being dismissed. It was rare that as police officers we were told what to do, but doctors had a very secure demeanour and were not shy in saying what was what.

'Thank you. We'll find our way out and have a chat with them.' We shook hands again and we left Doctor Basha in his surgery.

The two women were sitting in the now silent waiting room, behind the counter at the computers, working. I let them know what Doctor Basha had said about talking to them about Lucy and the red-rimmed eyes filled with tears.

'I'm sorry. It's been such a shock,' said the one I now knew as Ruth.

'It's fine, please don't worry about it. You were friends, it's bound to be a shock and to upset you.'

'It's come out of nowhere,' said Jill.

'Did it?' asked Aaron.

Jill frowned at him.

'Come out of nowhere?' he clarified. 'Did Lucy say or do anything that would make you think something was amiss?'

'Oh my God, no. Nothing at all. She was perfectly fine until she was ill. That was the only thing that was unusual. She was never ill and she hadn't looked like she was coming down with anything when we last saw her going to pick Faith up. That made me think twice. I was going to phone her, check up on her today if she still wasn't back, but this happened.' She wiped her eyes.

'So you didn't expect her to be off ill?' I asked.

'No, but sickness can come on suddenly,' said Ruth.

The phone started to ring. 'I have to get that, please excuse me.' Ruth leaned over and picked up the phone.

'She never indicated there was a problem.' Jill brushed her hair out of her face. 'This was out of the blue.'

I thanked them both and we left.

'What do you think?' I asked Aaron as he drove us back to the incident room.

'I think something happened between her leaving work the day before she phoned in sick and her getting murdered. A sensible woman with a decent job and a child does not go out and kill the way Lucy did.'

'I think you're right, we just have to figure out what it was that happened. What went wrong for Lucy Anderson.'

30

Martin and I were running late and had to jog down the corridors of the QMC – Queen's Medical Centre – hospital towards the morgue. Jack was waiting for us with the body of Lucy Anderson laid out ready on his table.

'I'm so sorry we're late, Jack.'

'Don't worry about it, young Hannah. It's not as though Lucy is going anywhere. She's more than happy to wait and she's my last one today.'

I let out a sigh of relief.

'Get changed and we'll get on with it.'

Ten minutes later Martin and I were in the morgue with Jack and one of his technicians. He must have been a new one because I didn't know his name.

The smell inside the room was clinical, all sharp and antiseptic, soon to be, I knew, mixed with internal bodily odours and not the types you were used to at home, the real internal odours of a body, the ones that made squeamish people throw up. Ross always wore a smidge of Vicks under his nose when he came but Martin and I, we didn't bother with it.

Martin was here to collect all the exhibits as we went along with the post-mortem.

'How's your day been, young Hannah?' Jack asked as we stood in the room looking down at Lucy.

'It's been busy, Jack. There's a young girl left in the middle of all this.'

'Oh dear, it's not good is it. Poor little mite. I do hope she can get some proper support and for an extended period of time not just for six weeks because six bloody weeks isn't any use to her in these circumstances.'

It was the first time I'd heard Jack curse in any way shape or form. But he was passionate about the NHS and how it was going down the pan with lack of funding at the moment.

'I'm sure she will get all that, for this kind of thing,' Martin reassured him.

'Good, good. Shall we have a look at her mother?'

Lucy lay on the table complete with bag on her head. The bag that had been used to suffocate her, her head still inside, had been bagged again in a police evidence bag to prevent the loss of evidence when she was moved.

'Oh, I worked on the skin and the hand found underneath the car earlier on today, to avoid cross contamination with Lucy here,' he said, still looking down at the body.

'That's great, did you get anything?' I asked.

'I did actually. I managed to get a print and I sent it off to your fingerprint office. I have no idea if they got a match. You will have to let me know if I need to run the DNA on the skin.'

'Where was the skin from? Were you able to tell?'

'Top of the shoulder. The widest part of him.'

I picked up on his comment straight away. 'You're going with him?'

Jack rubbed his chin with his wrist, avoiding contaminating his hands. 'I can't tell from the partial hand what gender it's from, but for me, I'd say it looks like it's a male. But don't hold me to that. It may very well come back to a large-handed lady.' He looked at me, a look that said it all.

'Okay, I get it, don't hold you to it.'

I saw Martin smile with his head down. Jack was particular about his science.

The first thing Jack did was a verbal account of what he saw in front of him. Lucy. This was recorded by the microphone hanging from the ceiling. He talked about the bag, the bruises visible on her arms. He counted and described them and mentioned that she was barefoot when she was brought in. She must have answered the door not expecting to go out or to fight for her life.

The clothing was removed with the help of the technician and handed to Martin to bag up in individual brown paper bags, signing the exhibit labels as he went. After all the clothing was removed, the bags were removed from her head. These were secured by Martin. Everything would go to forensics to be examined for trace evidence and fingerprints and any other evidence that may help ascertain who killed Lucy.

Jack was a methodical pathologist and respectful of his patients.

Finally he removed the bags over her hands and gave these to Martin for evidence.

Next, Jack drew her bruises on a body map. The technician recorded the whole process on video, careful not to get in the way.

The room was well lit and everything on Lucy was stark in contrast to the paleness of her body. She had obviously put up a fight. There were bruises down her arms and legs and some on her body as well as bruising around her neck where he had held the bag tight to cut off the air supply as she fought. The injuries told the story of how hard she had fought for her life, knowing her daughter was one floor above her. She must have been terrified that her daughter might be next or if she would be left to find her mother's body. Fighting was the only option she had and, with these bruises, she must have fought like a tiger.

She had lost.

He had to be a strong male to keep her overpowered the way she fought him.

Once Jack had finished drawing, he walked away and placed the pad and pen on the table at the end of the room.

'Okay, young lady, tell us what happened and don't leave anything out, we want it all. All of your secrets. We're here to help.'

He picked up a small clear plastic bag and a long, thin, metal instrument and picked up one of her hands. Pulled the lighted magnifying glass over the top. He peered down into it and gently and methodically, he scraped the insides of Lucy's nails. After completing one hand he swapped sides and did the other. He signed the exhibit labels for the bags and placed them on the side.

He turned to us. 'Well, that was interesting.'

'What is it?'

'She has skin underneath her nails. It looks as though she scratched your killer. We should be able to identify him.'

31

I gathered everyone in the briefing room and made a quick call to Baxter to let him know that we were going to brief, as he'd requested. I didn't want to get on his bad side if I didn't need to. It seemed as though he had taken whatever Catherine had said to him in his stride. I hoped our working relationship could now continue on an even keel.

The room was noisy. I'd put some money in a mug and told them to order pizzas and a table was stacked with takeaway boxes. The smell of cheese and tomato and meat feasts and garlic and ham and pineapple wafted through the room.

Baxter walked in and wrinkled up his nose. 'Dinner time?' He laughed.

'Want to help yourself to some pizza, Sir?' Ross asked before he stuffed half a slice into his mouth. Cheese dribbled down his chin.

'Don't mind if I do.' He picked up a napkin, pulled away a slice of chicken garlic and sweetcorn, and walked to a spot at the back of the room. 'It's been a productive day then, Hannah?'

I wiped the grease from my mouth before I spoke. 'Yes, Sir. It's been a positive day all round, I'd say.'

'I like it when a case goes well.' He bit into his pizza and cheese stretched between his mouth and the slice in his hand. It was good to see he was as human as the rest of us.

'Okay,' I said, trying to get everyone to settle down and pay attention as we ate. 'Let's get started, then someone can put the kettle on to wash down this grease.'

There was a slight battle of wills about who would be putting the kettle on but they soon quietened down as I glared at them.

'This briefing is to get everyone together to see where we are in the investigation after a full first day. I know it's been a busy one and you've all been tied up. I appreciate the work you've all put in.'

There were grunts of acknowledgement now.

'Aaron and I went to see Faith's grandmother and found out that the father was not on the scene and was not even aware of her birth, so we identified him, a Mark Wallace, and went to give him the news of his fatherhood. He's a married man and was working on an afters shift at the time of Lucy's murder. We've checked it out and he was at work when he said he was. As for what he's going to do about Faith, we're not sure. He's got to talk to his wife and discuss that. I've given them the details of the social worker involved.'

'That's a bolt out the blue for him this afternoon then,' said Ross, picking a piece of stray cheese from his tie.

'It was certainly a shock to the system today. He was somewhat lost for words.'

Martin wiped his mouth with the back of his hand then leaned back into his usual position of his hands behind his head and relaxed. 'That's one bomb to throw into a marriage, an unknown child.'

'Agreed. He's not alone in deciding what he does from here on in, which is going to be even more emotionally difficult for him.' I was tired and my arm was throbbing again. It had been a long day and I was glad that we were nearly through.

'The PM didn't throw up anything unusual. She was suffocated by the plastic bag and she put up one hell of a fight with her attacker. There was massive bruising all around her body. Arms, legs and torso. He must have had to proper hold her down to get that bag to stay in position and be able to suffocate her because she certainly wasn't letting him slide it on and hold it in place quietly.'

'Good for her.' Ross threw a crust down onto a paper towel on his desk. 'It should never be easy for them, they can't just walk into someone's home and take their lives like this.'

'Do we have news on the partial body under the car?' Martin asked.

'As it happens we do,' I said.

Baxter stood up a little straighter. The rest of the team stopped chewing. A couple even got their notebooks out and lifted up pens.

'But first, let me finish up about the PM. I know I said it didn't throw up anything unusual, but it did give us something interesting.'

All faces were turned my way.

'Jack took nail scrapings and clippings. There was skin under her nails. It's highly likely we're going to be able to identify the offender because she put up such a fight. So good for her.'

'That's fantastic.' Pasha was smiling. 'I love a strong woman and she was strong till the end.'

'Yes, she was. And it shouldn't take long to get the DNA results back. I've authorised them to go through as urgent. It's a strange case and I want to get to the bottom of it. As for the body parts, I spoke to Jack, he managed to get a fingerprint. He sent it back to us to see what we could find and the fingerprint bureau emailed while I was out with a match. The young man in question had been arrested for possession of a small quantity of cannabis when he was nineteen. So we have a name for him. Tyler Daniels. He was only cautioned but we still have his details on record which made this possible.'

There were a few quiet nods of heads.

'What do we know about him, Boss?' Martin was sitting more upright. Arms down from head.

'He was twenty-two and his death is already being investigated.'

Ross looked incredulous. 'You mean he's the lad, the hit and run from yesterday morning? In Carlton? Lucy Anderson did that? She drove into him then actually backed over him?'

'It looks that way.'

'But she's—'

'Looks can be deceiving, Ross. We know that more than anyone.'

He grew quiet. I knew I had prompted a difficult memory for him, for all of us.

'So we think someone in Tyler's circle of family or friends found out it was Lucy and went for some payback?' asked Martin.

'I do. It's a strong motive. Bearing in mind she still had parts of him underneath her car. Though how they found out it was her I don't know. Maybe there was a witness that didn't speak to the police but decided to deal with it themselves. Personally.'

There were lots of nods. Surprised faces. The case had taken a turn no one expected.

'Look, go home, get some rest and we'll check out this line of inquiry when we come back tomorrow.'

32

It was five thirty-two am when John Crowley logged onto his laptop at the kitchen table. He didn't want to wake the family, but he had a busy couple of days ahead of him. A huge deal was about to go through and it was going to make all the newspapers. His company would be the biggest grossing business in Nottingham once they acquired Byrnes Construction and the tenth biggest construction company in the UK.

He loved this space in the house. It was one of the largest rooms with huge windows bringing the daylight streaming in, no matter how grey the day. The high gloss surfaces glinted under the constant polishing Trisha gave them. Coming from somewhere small and pokey, this huge six-bedroom property in Ruddington was her dream home and he was also proud of what they had achieved.

He'd taken on his dad's small outfit at the age of twenty-one when his dad had passed away suddenly, and he'd turned it into the behemoth it was today, through hard work, determination and perseverance.

The freshly ground coffee smelled good, he was buzzed, and the coffee would keep him alert for the day ahead.

He went first to his emails and saw what he expected, emails from his solicitor and his business manager, both with last minute messages. They were good guys and he couldn't have done this without them. There was a message from the media department, informing him that more requests had come in through the night. He was glad to see his staff worked as hard as he did and were as dedicated to this acquisition as he was. This was good for all of them. Not just for him and his pocket, but for the whole firm.

He frowned over an email from an unknown sender. It wasn't in his spam folder so it wasn't someone suggesting he increase the size of his penis. He was more than happy with the size of his penis and so was his wife. They had a happy marriage and two great kids, Lizzy, twenty-three, and Blake, nineteen. Both were living at home still and making the most of what he had to offer them. Not that they were spoilt. He made sure they understood the value of money.

John opened the email. The sender's address was just a list of letters and numbers. An anonymous email.

He read it with incredulity and shock overtaking his body and eventually anger taking over.

DEAR JOHN,

PLEASE FORGIVE *my forward use of your first name but after you have read the rest of this message I think you will agree that we are indeed in the territory of the personal.*

I am aware that you have a big couple of days ahead of you and you will not want anything to spoil it for you. I do not want anything to spoil it for you either. I genuinely don't. But, I have a little problem that I need some help with and I think you might be the person who can help me out.

You see, I need you to kill Scott Rhodes and I need this done on a fairly rapid timeline. Do not shy away from this and think it is something awful that I ask of you. Believe me when I say you will be doing the world a favour when you rid it of Rhodes. He does not deserve to be in this wonderful world of ours. He is a contaminated individual.

Why would I think you would do this favour for me? Well, see the images of Lizzy attached. No, they are not real. Your darling daughter is the lady you believe she is. But it was easy enough to superimpose her head onto those images and it will be easy enough to send the images to the press and your family and friends and also distribute them on social media. Just imagine what her life would be like. Would it affect your business dealings today? Would they sell to you if they believed you to be from a tainted family? Not that I believe that will be uppermost in your mind after seeing those images. They are quite disturbing, I understand that. My work on them is exemplary though and it will not be easy to claim that they are not real, so before you start to imagine you can do that, would you really risk your daughter dealing with that torture?

These are the details of the person I need you to kill. You can use any method you wish, though please leave his face intact because I need you to take a photograph once you have killed him and email it to me as soon as you have done it.

Locate and destroy his mobile phone once you have killed him. This is imperative.

I will know if you have gone to the police and the images will be released. I will know if you try to fake the death and the images will be released. I will know if you do not carry out my request and the images will be released.

Thank you for your help in this matter.
All the very best,
PM

THE BLOOD PUMPED through his veins in a heightened rate, his heart pounding in his head. He clenched his fist and slid it across the kitchen table, pushing the laptop off onto the tiles below with a crash.

'Darling. What on earth happened? Are you okay?' Trisha looked at the floor where the laptop lay, broken and dented, and then back at her husband.

John startled, not having heard her walk down the stairs and into the kitchen.

'John, sweetheart, what is it?' she asked again. She wrapped an arm around his. 'Is it the deal?'

John tried to straighten himself up. He couldn't tell Trisha about the email. He looked down at the laptop to see if the screen was still showing it, if it was possible to see the disgusting images. He would need to recover it and close it. He couldn't have Trisha seeing her daughter that way, even if it wasn't Lizzy. It would destroy her. 'I'm sorry, I was reaching for my coffee and my dressing gown got tangled up in it and dragged it off the table.'

He pulled away from her, he didn't want to face her with a lie on his lips. They were always honest with each other. She had been there from the beginning. They had been dating when his father died so she had known him when he was just a boy and not the wealthy man that stood before her today.

The man that was now being blackmailed to kill.

How had life come to this?

Trisha didn't say a word as he collected the broken sections of the laptop from the floor. Was that because she believed him or because he'd been caught in a lie? He didn't dare look her in the face.

He stood with the computer in his hands. Screen dead and all evidence of his blackmailer gone.

John looked at Trisha, fearful of what he would see.

'Shall I top up your coffee and go and get your other laptop for you?'

'I'd love another coffee, thanks, love.' He leaned over and kissed her deeply. She tasted warm and earthy.

She laughed and pushed him away after a moment. 'I haven't even brushed my teeth yet. Get gone with you, Mr Crowley.' She turned away, still laughing and took his mug to the pot.

'I think you taste bloody gorgeous,' he said to her back and he meant it. He still loved her after all this time. He would protect her and every one of his family. He would do anything for them.

Did that include murder?

33

The incident room was quiet. I was the first one in as usual when a job was running. I went to the kitchen to make myself a green tea.

'Hello, stranger.' I turned to see my best friend and our analyst, Evie Small.

'Hey!' I was thrilled to see her. 'Where have you been hiding? I haven't seen you around for a while.' I threw my arms round her in a hug. She wrapped me in a beautiful floral smell with an undertone of vanilla.

I stepped back and she smiled. 'It's so good to see you,' she said as she walked to the cupboards and pulled a mug down from the cupboard and placed it next to mine. 'As the office was so quiet Catherine seconded me to Robbery. She got me released yesterday for this job you have on. I don't know if I can be of any help, but I'm here nonetheless.'

'And I feel better already,' I said, pouring steaming water into the two mugs. 'You look well. The break from us suited you. Or is there other news I need to be aware of?'

Evie's love life never lasted long. The minute a relationship seemed to be going in a serious direction she backed away and they never saw her again. Not that I could say anything. Things were pretty barren for me as far as any love life was concerned.

'I might have started seeing someone. It's only been a couple of weeks, so don't get excited about it.'

She was glowing but I knew better than to make a fuss. If she started to feel pressure even from me she would back away.

'Well, we need to go out one evening and you can tell me all about it.'

She smiled at me. 'Nice save, Hannah. We will do that. It'd be nice to grab a drink with you, it's been too long.'

I picked up my mug and started for the door. 'It has indeed. I've missed you. How come I didn't know you'd been seconded?'

'Because you stick your head in the sand, missus. If you didn't see me you didn't think about me.'

I paused at what she had said. Inhaled the vapours of the fresh green tea. 'Am I a bad friend, Evie?'

She looked at me. 'You're not a bad friend, Hannah. You're just easily distracted, particularly by work. I'm not offended by it. I know if I tell you I need you you'll be there within minutes. So please, don't beat yourself up.'

'I would, you know.'

'I know that, sweetie. That's why I said it. So this job you have running, do you have anything specific you want me to do?'

I started to walk towards my office, Evie followed at my side, her auburn curls bouncing in time to her footsteps. I adored her hair. 'As it happens, we have a tentative lead that might be of interest and that you could give us a hand with.' I opened the door to my office and stepped inside.

'Wow, nothing ever changes does it?' Evie said as she followed me, the gentle floral perfume wafting in after us.

She was looking at my desk, the piles and piles of paperwork lined up all over it. Some of them threatening to teeter off. There was no room on there to move anything. My laptop was sitting squarely in its space at the front where my chair was so I could use it. If anyone moved the laptop, paper would naturally fall into that space.

'I'm not sure what you mean,' I replied, knowing exactly what she meant.

She eyed me over her mug as she took a drink.

'I know where everything is,' I told her. 'Everything has its place and I can put my hand on it at a moment's notice. You know I never lose anything.'

'But if you're ever off long-term sick someone else will have difficulty putting their hands on anything.'

This quietened us both because I had been off semi-long-term sick when I had been injured on duty. Serious damage had been caused and I'd needed surgery to make sure I could still use my arm. Not everyone had come out of that event alive and we were still sensitive to it.

'I'm sorry,' she whispered.

'It's okay.' I walked round to my chair and threw myself into it.

Evie sat down in one of the chairs in front of my desk. 'So, you think I might be able to help with one of your lines of inquiry?' She held up a hand. 'First things first, do you have chocolate biscuits? I can't drink this coffee without chocolate biscuits, you know that.'

I let out a soft sigh, of course I should have had them out the minute we walked in. I rummaged in my drawer and pulled out a near empty packet of chocolate digestives and handed them over.

'Is this all you have?' She looked disgusted.

'You haven't been here,' I reminded her. 'You're the reason I eat so many chocolate biscuits you know. I would be a lot slimmer if it weren't for you.'

She laughed. 'It's not as though you're wobbling through the station is it?'

I pulled a face at her. 'Anyway, do you want to know about this job, or not?'

'I absolutely do.' She stuffed half a biscuit into her mouth and started to chew.

'You do realise some people are just waking up and eating breakfast, don't you?' I raised an eyebrow.

'And you know I'm working and using my brain and it's powered by biscuits.'

It was my turn to laugh. 'Okay. So, let's give this brain of yours something to work on. You heard about the job we have in the office I take it?'

'Yeah, something about a woman killed in her home by suffocation, but you got a bit nosey around her car and found body parts attached underneath.' She scrunched up her nose. She was never one for the more grim side of the job. 'Do I have it about right? Out murder victim may well have killed someone before she herself was taken out?'

'You have a handle on events up to this point. Other than the fact we now know who the person under the car was. His name is Tyler Daniels and it's highly likely that someone who knew him is our suspect for the Lucy Anderson case.'

'And what do you need me for?' She shoved another half a biscuit into her mouth, and waved the pack at me, offering me the last one.

I shook my head at her. 'No, thanks. I had breakfast before I left home this morning.'

'So did I.'

I shook my head at her. 'I need you to dig into Tyler's social media accounts and find us all his friends and family. List them into family, close and not so close, real-life friends and online friends only, if you can do that from searching his pages. We're going to speak to his parents this morning. But it could be anyone.'

'I'll get on that for you and let me know if you need anything else. By the way...'

I looked at her.

She picked the last biscuit out of the packet and waggled it at me. 'You need to buy a new pack of biscuits.'

34

The knock on my door was firm and solid. I looked up to see a uniformed inspector standing in front of me, a pleasant smile in place. I stood from my chair and walked around to greet Inspector Gabriella Kowalski from Roads Policing. We'd met a couple of times in my uniformed past. It was rare that this department ran into Roads Policing in the course of investigations though.

I held out my hand. 'Hi Gabby, how are you?'

She had a wide infectious smile. 'I'm good, thanks. How about you? Keeping busy over here?' She shook my offered hand.

I indicated we should move over to the desk and seated myself in one of the chairs in front of the desk rather than placing it between myself and Gabby. 'Well, the darker side of life is still thriving, I'll just say that, shall I? But what you get to see isn't pretty though.'

Gabby shook her head. 'It's not. People aren't careful when they're driving. They think they're indestructible as they dash about. And let me tell you, we're not bloody indestructible. We're far from indestructible. We're easily crushed and torn apart. Like butter on a hot day.'

She'd painted a graphic picture. I remembered the parts I had found under Lucy's car yesterday. 'I think our worlds might have actually collided, Gabby.'

'So I see. It's all a little strange isn't it?'

'Just a bit. To have two murders connected to each other like this? I've never had it happen before. Yes, I've had murders connected of course, but not in this way, not where one murder victim was the murderer of another murder victim unless it's gang related. This is just a weird one. It's most definitely not gang related.'

'And that's what you think this looks like, Lucy Anderson is a killer?'

'I think we need to look into this between us. The body parts that we recovered from Lucy's vehicle yesterday were examined by the pathologist, Jack Kidner—'

Gabby nodded. 'I know Jack. Good guy. I rate him.'

'Yes, he's a great guy and brilliant pathologist. He managed to get a fingerprint from the partial hand that was pulled from under the car.'

Gabby nodded again.

'The results on the fingerprint check came back to Tyler Daniels, who I believe is your victim from the hit and run?'

Gabby leaned forward in her chair. 'This is fascinating, Hannah. She really had Tyler Daniels under her car?'

'She did. The car is still being examined. It's with forensics at the moment. You can have full access to it, in fact I've already looped your department into the paperwork.'

'Thank you.'

'What I want to know is how far you've got with the investigation. Were you even close to identifying Lucy Anderson? Did any of his family or friends indicate that they knew who had done it or why? What are they like?' I stopped, pulled myself back. 'I'm sorry. That was a lot of questions and you can't answer them all at once.' I acquiesced by tipping my head sideways at her.

She smiled again. Taking it all in her stride. 'It's fine. Let's work through them all, shall we?' She lifted a hand and put three fingers up. 'First of all, how far have we got with the investigation?' She winked at me, 'You know I'm going to want to ask all these questions back at you?' She sounded genuinely happy whereas a lot of cops sounded tired and ground down.

'I know, I know. We can bash it out.'

'Okay then.' She wiggled the fingers she was holding up. 'How far had we got? The short answer is not very far.'

I nodded, not really surprised.

'There was no CCTV in the area of the hit and run and we had no witnesses.'

'No one came forward?' I asked.

'Not a one. Were you expecting someone to have seen it?'

'Well, it would have been a good motive for Lucy's murder if someone in Tyler's crowd had an idea who killed him.'

'We need to place Lucy Anderson in the car. It helps now we know what the car was. We can search for it on CCTV further out from the scene and we know in which direction to search, going back to where Lucy lives. What I want to know is where the child was while Lucy was killing Tyler? Did Lucy's mum have her? Or was she in the car while her mum was running over a twenty-two-year-old lad in Carlton?'

'Urgh,' I shuddered. 'That's a grim thought. It's hard enough to see Lucy as a killer as it is, without seeing her as a mother who allows her four-year-old daughter to sit in the back seat while she commits murder with a vehicle.'

'Maybe the grandmother had her?'

'No, she said she hadn't seen Lucy for four days. And she doesn't have any more family.'

'So where the hell was the little girl while Lucy Anderson was out committing murder?'

At that point I realised I hadn't offered Gabby a drink. I jumped up. 'Can I get you a tea or coffee?'

A gentler smile this time. 'Well, it is cold out there and I did wonder when you were going to offer me your finest.'

'Instant coffee?'

'Instant sounds good. If it's warm it's good with me.'

We stood and walked to the kitchen, passing Ross on the way to the incident room with a tray full of mugs in his hands.

'Hello, Ma'am.' His smile was wide. 'Have you come to see us?'

I looked to Gabby. Cops knew each other no matter where they worked. We often come across each other because we all moved around.

'Hi Ross. Yes, I'm here to see Hannah about the case you're working on. It's interesting to say the least.'

'It's a strange one all right. It's good to see you anyway.'

'And you, Ross. Keep well.' She turned to me. 'I didn't know he was on your team now. He's a good kid.'

'He is. He works well.' We walked into the kitchen and I filled the kettle. 'That was an angle I hadn't thought about until now you know, where the little girl was during Tyler's murder. This case is getting stranger from moment to moment.' I poured the water into the mugs. 'Do you want to pay Faith Anderson a visit with me and we can ask her where she was when she wasn't at school or with her mum at the time Tyler was killed?'

Gabby crossed her arms and leaned back a little. 'I think that's a damn fine idea, Hannah.'

35

John Crowley was standing in his bedroom buttoning up his shirt. Did he really have to go through with this? He looked at Trisha in the en-suite bathroom brushing her teeth. She would never let him do it if she knew about it. Though he hated to think of her distress at seeing the images of Lizzy. Their beautiful Elizabeth. Nothing more than a few disgusting pixels.

How would he do this? He couldn't be covered in blood. It would very probably lead to his arrest. He needed to find a way that was bloodless and that wouldn't lead to him being caught. There was no point in protecting his family, if he was going to bring their world down around their ears by getting arrested.

He'd googled Scott Rhodes, matched the details the email sender had given him and found his social media accounts. He was a high-school teacher. He taught kids for a living. He was one of the good guys in life. Why would someone want a teacher dead? The email implied that Scott Rhodes deserved to die. What could he have done to die and at the hands of a stranger this way? John remembered back to the email, which was seared into his mind. It said Rhodes was contaminated. That was the word that had been used. And what was the connection between the emailer and Rhodes and why couldn't he do this himself? Mind you, why would he if he was capable of getting other people to do it for him?

John knew the advantages of getting people to do menial jobs for him and that was what was happening here. He was being given one of the more menial and difficult tasks. The one the emailer didn't want to dirty his hands with.

Crowley had Rhodes' home address and even his school. He had every detail he needed to carry this out. All he had to do was to make a decision on when and where and how he would do it.

He looked in the mirror, smoothed down the front of his shirt and realised he had decided he was going to get this done. The sooner he did it the sooner it would be in his rear-view mirror.

36

Following a quick briefing in the incident room, Gabby and I jumped in my car and set off for Cheryl Anderson's house. Social care had stated when I phoned them that this was where Faith was currently homed.

'So, we never finished our conversation,' I said. 'We got distracted by realising the girl might be a witness to something. We thought Christmas had come.'

'And it very well may have done,' Gabby said.

'We'll see when we get there. She's only four so I'm not sure how much help she's going to be. But if she does remember something we'll get her straight into a visually recorded soft interview suite. It's worth a try.'

'Sounds like a plan.'

I turned and looked at Gabby. 'Thanks so much for coming over this morning, Gabby.'

'Hey, look what putting our heads together has done so far. Even if nothing pans out with the child, it's shown us that pooling our resources is actually a pretty good idea.'

She was right, though I was hoping that the child would turn out to be helpful.

'So where were we?' Gabby asked.

I manoeuvred around a car that was pulling in to the left. 'You said you hadn't got far with the investigation, there were no witnesses. No CCTV. I also wanted to know if you were even close to identifying Lucy Anderson as the driver?'

'I'll give you the short answer which is no. Nowhere near. We had paint flecks on the body which meant we could tie down the make and model of the vehicle, but that was going to take a couple of days.'

I slammed on the brakes as a shopping trolley rolled in front of us. We jerked forward. Gabby slapped down hard on the dashboard with her palms. A young woman ran out to retrieve the shopping trolley and waved an exuberant apology at us. I lifted a hand in acceptance and set off again.

'As far as family or friends goes, no one indicated they knew who might have done it or why.'

'Did they think of any reason why someone might want to hurt Tyler?'

'Not at all. They were all shocked and hurt and grieving. There was no mention of this must be so-and-so. Or, this is because of this-particular-issue. They all felt he was far too young to be taken from them and they couldn't believe what had happened.'

It didn't take long to get to Cheryl Anderson's home. I'd phoned to prepare her for our visit, told her we'd also like to talk to Faith. She'd sounded surprised but then agreed that yes, Faith was in the house, we could talk to her, but the minute she started to get distressed the conversation would be stopped.

The woman who answered the door was a shell of the woman we had seen only yesterday. Her hair was flat to her head and her skin had a grey sheen. Her eyes were dark and lifeless, red-rimmed, hollowed out. A little how she looked in herself. It was amazing what twenty-four hours could do to a person.

'DI Robbins, do come in.' She couldn't tell me it was good to see me again. These were dreadful circumstances under which to meet police officers.

We stepped into the house. 'Thank you, Cheryl. This is my

colleague, Inspector Gabby Kowalski, she's...' I nearly said she was from Roads Policing but Cheryl was not yet aware of the body parts that had been found underneath Lucy's car or the implication that Lucy had killed someone before she herself had been murdered. 'She's giving me another perspective today,' I went with instead.

Cheryl nodded. 'Faith is in her room. Like I said on the phone, you can speak with her but if you upset her in the slightest then you're not going to be talking to her any further I'm sorry. I do want to catch my daughter's killer but she would prefer me to put her daughter's welfare first and foremost. She adored that child.' Tears sprang to her eyes.

'Please don't worry, Mrs Anderson. We're not here to upset her. We'll be very gentle.'

Cheryl Anderson gave a single nod and went to the bottom of the stairs to fetch the girl then she turned back to us. 'Did you know her father has asked for custody? He wants her. He said because he didn't know he was a father he wasn't given the chance to care for her during her first years, but he wants to now. He's married and his wife is on board with it.'

I didn't know what to say.

'Social care are doing the relevant checks and will make a decision at some point. They've said it won't be quick. They have to do what's in Faith's best interest and it may have to be resolved at court. He told them he won't stop me seeing her. I'm an integral part of her life and he wants to cause as little disruption as possible. I don't know what to do. He's her father but Lucy didn't want it. I should fight him. That's what Lucy would want.'

The tears flowed freely and I could see why her eyes were so dark and red rimmed. I didn't think she had stopped crying since we saw her yesterday.

'I'm sorry, it must be a difficult time for you,' I said. And we were going to make it even more difficult for her when she realised what we were implying when we started to speak with Faith.

'I don't know what to do for the best. Lucy didn't want him in Faith's life at this young age, she'd made that clear. But, legally I don't have a leg to stand on. He wasn't physically abusive, it was just a feeling she had about him. She was able to make that decision while she was alive. But now...' She trailed off and the tears continued. They were a part of her now.

'I'd better straighten my face up.' She wiped a hand across her face, smudging the tears from under her eyes. 'I can't have Faith keep seeing me this way. It's hard enough for her without having to put up with her gran this way.' Now she put up both hands to her face and wiped. The tears were smudged away but she didn't look any better for it.

'How is she?' I asked.

'She's quiet mostly. She's holding it all in. There have been a few tears, but on the whole she hides. Literally, hides in the house somewhere or hides emotionally, in the quietness of the house, it's going to be a long, long journey back for her.'

'I'm so sorry, I'm sure it is. But I imagine social care will be putting the right things in place for her.'

Cheryl gave a quick nod. 'I'll go and fetch her.' Cheryl took a deep breath in. 'Make yourselves comfortable in the room and we'll be down in a minute.' She took two steps up and turned around again. 'Oh dear. I'm not very good today. I should have offered you tea.'

'I'll tell you what,' said Gabby, 'I'll put the kettle on and you bring Faith down when she's ready. How does that sound?'

A small smile broke through on Cheryl's fragile face. 'Thank you. That sounds very kind.' She turned her back to us and continued up the stairs, her shoulders heavy and her feet slow and sluggish.

With drinks made we seated ourselves in the living room and waited for Cheryl to return with Faith.

'Do you want to lead?' asked Gabby.

'I don't mind. Whose part of the investigation is this?' I considered it. This wasn't about who had killed Lucy, it was about Lucy using the car to kill Tyler. 'Actually, this is more about your side of things. It's about Tyler. You can lead. I'll pick up anything you might miss. Sound okay?'

She smiled. 'Sounds good—'

Cheryl walked into the room with a small child clasped in her hand. I hadn't seen Faith because she had already been removed from the scene by the time I arrived yesterday morning. She was a petite little thing. Long dark hair flowing over her shoulders and a pale face with huge eyes staring out at us. We both stood to greet her.

'Hi Faith. This is Gabby,' I pointed to Gabby, and I'm Hannah. We're very pleased to meet you.'

I realised I had jumped in when I was supposed to be allowing Gabby to lead. She should be building the rapport with Faith, not me. I took a physical step back.

The small girl shrugged.

Cheryl stepped in ushering her grandchild to a chair. 'They're lovely to talk to, sweetie.'

I quietly thanked her and handed her a drink which she took and seated herself on the arm of the chair next to Faith.

We all shuffled back to our seats and settled ourselves.

Gabby took the reins. 'Thank you for coming down to see us, Faith.'

Faith stared at her. She hadn't had any choice, her gran had brought her down to see the police officers.

'I'm so sorry about what happened to your mummy,' Gabby continued.

Faith flinched. She might be hiding but she wasn't doing a very good job of hiding from herself or from what had happened. She was going to need a great deal of support and I hoped it was all in place for her.

'You might be glad to know we're not here to talk about that though.'

Cheryl looked to Gabby, surprised. 'You're not?'

I shook my head at her. I hoped she would let this flow without stopping it or interrupting. It was hard for parents and guardians to not speak when their child was being asked questions. They thought they were helping but we really did need the answers to come from the child's mouth and not be prompted by the adult.

'We want to talk about the day before, Faith. Can you remember the day before yesterday?'

Faith nodded.

'Did you go to school?'

'You did go to school, didn't you, sweetheart?'

I looked to Gabby then to Cheryl Anderson. 'Mrs Anderson, if you can allow Faith to answer the questions that would be helpful. Then when it comes to something relevant, we'll know it's definitely Faith's answer.'

'Oh, yes. I'm so sorry. I just want to help her.' A knuckle went into her mouth.

'I know. I understand that desire. It's fine. We're doing fine.' I gave her a smile and she nodded.

I looked back at Faith. Her mouth parted slightly, eyes wide.

'So, school, was it a normal day?' asked Gabby.

'The day before Mummy...' She trailed off and her face was firmly angled towards the floor. Discussing such an emotional subject with a child of Faith's young age was never an easy task. We had our work cut out for us.

'Yes,' Gabby answered quietly. 'The day before that.'

Faith nodded and grabbed hold of the end of her hair, looked at it as though it would hold all of the answers then wrapped it around one of her fingers.

'Mummy took me to school. I want my mummy.'

My heart broke for this little girl who just wanted her life to go back to how it was a couple of days ago but who was now facing a couple of cops who wanted answers from her. She had no understanding of what was happening or why.

There were tears balancing on the rims of Cheryl's eyes. She wrapped a protective arm around her granddaughter's shoulders and pulled her closer. Faith tucked her chin into her chest, her face pale and wan. She was nothing but a tiny dot within the frame of her grandmother.

'And Mummy picked you up as usual did she?' Gabby asked gently.

Faith refused to lift her head up, to recognise that we were both there to talk to her. She leaned in even closer to Cheryl who let a tear slip down her cheek. This was her daughter we were talking about and her granddaughter who was breaking her heart. But these were questions we needed to ask.

Faith shook her head.

No one moved.

She twisted her finger into her hair some more. I looked to Cheryl. I'd asked for her to leave this to us but we needed her help.

Cheryl crouched down still holding the small child in her arms. 'Faith, sweetheart, what do you mean Mummy didn't collect you from school?' She rubbed her free hand down her hair then a finger gently caressed her cheek. Faith stayed staring at the floor.

'Mummy's friend, the man, he took me to his house.'

37

'A man picked you up from school?' Cheryl was in before Gabby could even form the words.

Faith stared up at her gran who was still crouched down at eye level with her. Her eyes widened even more. The strand of hair she had been curling was now tight around her finger and looked as though it was about to cut off the circulation.

'It's okay, sweetheart, we just need to know who he was and what happened,' Cheryl soothed, though from her face I could see she was far from soothed herself. Her eyebrows were drawn over her eyes and she was biting at her lip.

Gabby tried to gain control of the situation. 'You're not in any trouble, Faith. You're doing fine. Let's keep going shall we?'

Faith just spun more hair around her finger.

'So, who was it that picked you up?'

Tears pricked at her eyes and she crossed her legs. She was getting anxious. We couldn't carry on much longer but neither could we stop before we knew that Faith had not been harmed.

'I don't know.'

Cheryl took in a sharp intake of breath and a hand shot to her chest. How would Gabby ask the next question?

'Who did school think he was?' Good call.

'A friend of mummy's. He was a friend of mummy's. She was late so he came. I knew if the teachers said he was mummy's friend then he was because mummy said to always do as the teachers said.'

Cheryl opened her mouth and I shook my head. No matter what she was going to say she could say it to us later not in front of Faith. We didn't want her afraid and to clam up. But from the way Cheryl's face had drained of colour I didn't think Lucy knew any males she would trust to pick Faith up and would usually rely on her mum.

'What did you do with the man?' Gabby pushed on. From school to the time Tyler was hit was several hours.

Faith shook her head and tears started to roll down her face. We were upsetting her. Cheryl looked terrified. She stroked Faith's hair again.

'It's okay, Faith, you're doing really well. You can go back to your room again in a minute. We're nearly done.'

A quick nod.

'We went to his house. He let me watch CBeebies and I had a sleep on his sofa.'

'Then what happened?'

She unravelled her finger from her hair and started all over again with a fresh lock. 'He took me home.'

'Do you know what time it was, Faith?'

She shook her head and bounced on the spot a little. 'Mummy put me straight to bed. She said it was late. I heard her crying before I went to sleep. I don't think she was very well.'

Cheryl was twitching. She couldn't keep still. She rubbed at her head, rubbed at her arms, adjusted her clothing, shook her head multiple times and gnawed on her knuckle.

'You're doing well, Faith. Thank you for talking to us today. Can I ask you one more question?'

Faith nodded again.

'Can you tell me what he looked like?'

Faith shook her head.

Cheryl jumped off the chair now unable to hold herself any longer. 'You know what I want to say.'

'Cheryl, please. Not yet.'

She let out a long breath then turned around and crouched in front of the little girl and hugged her close, putting a hand on the back of her head and pulling her in even tighter.

I looked to Gabby and shook my head. This was a strange set of circumstances. It was certainly something we hadn't expected. What on earth did it mean? Why was Lucy crying when Faith came home? Who was the man? Why did he have Faith and why did he return her? There were now more questions than answers.

With Faith returned to her room upstairs Cheryl was quick to get into it when she came back down.

'I have no idea who this man is. He had Faith!' she shrieked. 'What the hell are you going to do?'

'Look, at this moment in time, we have nothing to say that Lucy didn't organise this. School seemed to think it was legitimate otherwise they would never have let Faith go, so what we'll do is go and speak to school and get to the bottom of it from their end. Plus Faith was returned and Lucy never contacted the police at any point.'

She jumped in. 'I know my daughter. I know my daughter's friends. There are barely any women she would ask to collect Faith, there are certainly no men she would ask to do it. I'm not sure she even has any male friends. She would come to me first and I never heard from her.' Cheryl's voice was rising with every word.

'I do understand that this appears a little unusual,' I started.

'It's more than a little unusual, DI Robbins, it's kidnap.' Where her face had been ghostly pale before it was now reddening at a rapid rate.

Gabby raised a hand to try and calm the situation. 'We will bear this in mind during our investigation. I assure you. In fact, what I want to do is get Faith into a proper interview suite and get what she's said down in an official capacity. All it involves is her talking as she did today, the room she is in is recorded so we don't have to do anything else. How does that sound?'

Cheryl nodded, appeased we were taking this seriously. 'Yes, we can do that. Thank you.'

'It would be very helpful to us so we have to thank you. I do want to promise that we want to get to the bottom of what happened with your daughter and we'll go wherever that takes us.'

'I really don't know what this thing is with this man. Oh, I do wish Lucy had told me if she was having some problems, she knew I would have helped her out with anything.' She swallowed, an attempt to hold back tears this time.

'We'll be in touch to organise a mutually convenient time for Faith's interview,' I said to her, gently extricating ourselves from the situation as I backed out of the house.

'Thank you for your help today,' she said in a calmer place. No doubt about to interrogate Faith herself as soon as we were gone.

In the car Gabby turned to me. 'That was very strange, don't you think?'

'The thing with the bloke who turned up and took her away for the day and then dropped her back off at home? Just a little. What do you make of it?'

'I think it covers the time frame that Tyler was killed. So does that mean it was more premeditated than we first thought? Did Lucy get Faith out of the way so she could kill Tyler? Lucy isn't seeming to be as innocent as she appeared at the start. And maybe she used a male friend and not her mum because mum would ask too many questions, I mean, it's not as though she doesn't want to know what's happening is it? She's a bit of a busybody. She kept Mum out of it on purpose and kept Faith out of the way so she could do the hit and run in the evening. Who knows how long she waited for Tyler to walk past? We need to try to find a link between them and we need to try to identify and locate the man who had Faith so he can tell us more about the arrangement between them and what he knew about the hit and run. What about you?'

'I think you've pretty much covered it. The other option is Tyler was the man who picked Faith up and that's why he ended up underneath her car, but that doesn't make sense because from what Faith says her mum didn't leave her alone once she got home, so it's more likely someone was looking after Faith while Lucy carried the hit and run out. We've opened up a whole line of inquiry for you and your investigation, but nothing so far as ours is concerned. Unless the male in question killed her not long after he dropped Faith off but why? We need to ID him. Hopefully Faith will be able to help us out with the Achieving Best Evidence interview and give us more when we probe deeper.'

'Thanks for today,' Gabby yawned.

'Am I keeping you up?'

'Sorry. I had a late one last night. I should know better when it's a work night.'

'I think I'm getting too old for those kinds of nights. I never recover well.'

'Yeah, tell me about it.' She rubbed a hand through her hair. 'So, we've a lot of work to be doing.'

'Yes, I want to talk to Tyler's parents after we've popped to the school to see if we can get a description of the man who collected Faith and get a feel for if anyone did know who hit him. See if we have a vigilante on our hands.'

38

I pulled the car into a parking space and Gabby and I walked into the school and to the reception desk. I introduced us and asked to speak to the teacher who had allowed Faith Anderson to be collected by a male other than her mother a couple of days ago. The way I said it suggested everything I needed it to convey and the receptionist looked suitably mortified at what was coming. She was too scared to ask if Faith was okay. I knew she hadn't been in school since the event and certainly wasn't at school now so fear was etched onto the receptionist's face.

'Miss, can I phone my mum, I've forgotten my PE kit?' a child shouted at the hassled receptionist from behind us.

'Jayden, go and sit on one of the chairs, I'm busy. I'll sort you out in a minute,' the receptionist snapped as she scrolled through lists on her computer monitor looking for Faith Anderson and whose class she was supposed to be in. Gabby and I waited patiently for the results.

'That'll be Mr Hughes you need to speak with. He's in class at the moment. Can I make you an appointment for after school to speak with him?' she asked.

'No,' I said quietly. 'We need to speak with him right now. We're quite prepared to search the school to speak to him but I'm not sure you need that kind of disruption. The case we're investigating warrants such dramatic actions I'm afraid.'

She gave a curt nod. I got the impression she knew this anyway but was simply going through school procedures. She kept looking from me to Gabby, her mouth moving silently, desperate to ask the question. People hated knowing something bad had happened and not knowing exactly what it was. She picked up a phone and talked into it quietly before placing the receiver back down.

'He'll be out in a moment.'

She leaned forward and looked around us. 'Jayden, come here.'

The boy shuffled forward and the receptionist lifted the phone towards him. 'Call your mother and make it quick, I don't have all day for this. How many times do you need to forget your PE kit before you remember you have it every week?' she snapped at him.

'Sorry, miss.' He apologised and dialled home.

'DI Robbins, Inspector Kowalski?' A deep male voice came from behind us. We turned and saw a male in a rumpled suit and scuffed brown shoes.

'Mr Hughes?'

'Yes.' He held out a hand and we all shook. He turned and led us through to an empty classroom. This was a school that housed children from nursery age up to school leaving age and this was a classroom for older children, the tables and chairs were not squat to the floor as infants generally were. 'What is it I can help you with today? I believe it's something to do with Faith Anderson. I haven't seen her for a couple of days. Her mum phoned in two days ago and said she was sick but we've heard nothing since. Is everything okay?'

Lucy and Faith were my case so we'd decided I would take the lead with the school. 'I'm afraid I have to tell you that Lucy Anderson, Faith's mum, is dead, Faith won't be in school for a while now.'

'She's? Oh my.' His hand went up to his chest and he staggered backwards a little. His other hand feeling for a chair or something to grab hold of. He found the back of a chair and pulled it closer to him where he leaned on it for support. I looked at Gabby and raised my eyebrows. A little dramatic for a teacher of her daughter. Maybe he just wasn't used to death.

'Did you know her well?' He had paled considerably and had in fact turned an odd shade of grey.

'I... erm... Lucy, I mean, Mrs Anderson and I...'

Oh, it was going there.

'You were having a relationship,' offered Gabby.

Hughes shook his head. 'No. Not any more anyway. She broke it off. Told me it wasn't the best thing to do, that she shouldn't be doing it as her daughter was at the school.'

'How long had you been in a relationship?' I asked.

'Not long. A couple of months. I agreed with her. I shouldn't have been involved with her that way. But dead. I can't believe it. What happened?'

'We're not actually here to talk about that, I'm afraid. The day before she died her daughter Faith was picked up from school by a man. What can you tell us about that?'

Hughes looked towards the classroom door. No one was coming to give him the answers.

'That seems like an odd question, Inspector. Has something happened to Faith as well as Lucy?' his voice hitched at the end of the sentence, fear taking his voice control.

'There are questions over whether she should have been released to the male who attended and we want to know the series of events that led up to it.'

He pushed the chair away and looked for the desk, stepped over to it and sat on top. 'We received a text message from Lucy, from Faith's mum, saying her friend was going to pick Faith up as she was running late. It's not so unusual with our working mums to be honest, short notice changes in their plans and we go with them as best we can.' He rubbed his hands together. 'Is Faith okay?'

'Faith is fine.'

He let out a long breath. 'Thank heavens. I was suspicious for a moment when Lucy turned up to collect Faith after we received the message but she assured me that she had got it all wrong and she ran off. When she left I told myself I had allowed my imagination to run away. I don't think I could bear it if anything happened to Faith as well as her mother. Poor child though, what a lot to go through.'

'How did you know it was Lucy who had texted you?' asked Gabby.

'That's easy. It came from Lucy's number straight to the office. I'll be able to show it you on the way out if you'd like?'

'We would, yes, thank you.'

I imagined the receptionist getting her interest piqued even more and having yet no more information forwarded to her.

'Can you describe the male who collected Faith?' I asked.

Hughes rubbed a hand down his trouser leg. 'He was a little taller than me. It was cold so he was wearing a woollen hat, gloves and a scarf that came up to his nose, so I can't give you a lot of information about him I'm afraid.' He rubbed his other palm down his leg. 'I don't know the colour of his hair or if he had a beard or was clean shaven. Oh no. I really have nothing to offer you.'

I shook my head. I couldn't help it.

'I really am sorry, Inspector.'

'Don't worry about it,' Gabby reassured him. 'It was likely he was dressed like that purposefully. Just so you couldn't give us any details.'

Hughes nodded.

'What about Faith?' I asked. 'How did she seem when a stranger picked her up?'

Hughes loosened the tie around his neck slightly and swallowed. 'I... she...' He swallowed again. 'She seemed a little reticent at first but she didn't say anything. She didn't say she didn't know him. She went with him. Yes, I should maybe have picked up on the subtle non-verbals but I didn't. I was surrounded by kids being picked up by parents all vying to get away from me and go home. I was aware that permission had been granted for someone other than Lucy to collect her. Maybe when I saw it was a male I was a little miffed and didn't pay as much attention as I could have. Will I take that guilt to my grave? You bet I will. I'm just so glad that Faith is safe and that it didn't have anything to do with Lucy's death. If this had been related I would never have been able to forgive myself.'

39

He had nothing better to do than line up the next one. It was like playing an online game and it thrilled him. There had been a purpose when he first started but that purpose had been fulfilled. Now he simply enjoyed the feel of moving people to his will and getting the photographs to prove it had been done. Who would have thought people were so malleable?

The next one, well, he was getting ahead of himself a little, the last one hadn't done what he had been tasked with yet. It wasn't easy finding these pawns for his game. People who had a lot to lose. He'd had a great idea for the next one in the game, though it would take a little research to see if someone fitted the bill in the area, but if they did, it would work wonders. He had to do some deep trawling on the internet. Find the right person with the right problem that he could manipulate. If you didn't want to be twisted up in one of his games then you should have your life in order and not have it so you could be coerced this way.

He didn't feel guilty. Not one of the people he had approached was innocent. They showed the world that they were so corrupt they would kill to protect themselves. What kind of person does that? It was a warped kind of world.

40

We decided to drive straight on to Tyler Daniels' parents' address and see them. Gabby knew them as she was the SIO of his case and phoned ahead as I drove, letting them know we were on our way, that she had an update for them. I wished we had an update for Cheryl Anderson but so far we had nothing. Speaking with the Daniels might nudge us in the right direction. Even if it wasn't the grieving parents who'd taken revenge, which I hoped it wasn't, I figured that maybe they had heard something because vigilantes are usually proud of their work and would hopefully have boasted about it.

The Daniels lived in a lovely semi-detached on Manor Crescent.

'This was the road she hit him,' Gabby said. 'He was on his way home after seeing his mates in the pub for an hour after work. His mum and dad didn't hear a thing and a neighbour had to knock on the door and tell them their son was dead on the street outside their house. Can you even imagine that?'

I pulled the car in front of the address she pointed out. 'Shit. If she did this on purpose it was damn cold of her.'

Mr Daniels opened the door and beckoned us in when he saw Gabby.

'Inspector Kowalski, it's good of you to come by and update us in person, do come in.'

I hadn't asked Gabby how much she was going to tell the Daniels but I trusted her judgement on the situation. As with every scenario like this we were offered drinks and we accepted, to be polite. Mrs Daniels was devoid of make-up and her hair hung around her face and hadn't even had a hairbrush put through it. This was two women we had seen today who had lost children. You should never have to bury your children before you go yourself.

Once the drinks were made we sat at the kitchen table. It was one of those homes where the kitchen was the life and soul of the home, though I could sense it wasn't very much of a soul now Tyler was gone.

'What do you have for us, Inspector Kowalski?' Mrs Daniels asked without preamble, eager to know as much as she could about the death of her son.

Gabby coughed into her hand to give herself some time before she started to talk to this couple, who were leaning forward on the edge of their chairs, eager for news on the investigation.

'We have located the vehicle that was involved in the incident with Tyler.'

A loud gasp escaped from Mrs Daniels and her hand shot up to her mouth. Whatever she had been expecting it wasn't this. She hadn't expected the police to have made this much progress yet.

'My God. You have the bastard who did this to our boy?' asked Mr Daniels as he grabbed hold of his wife's arm. She gripped his hand with her free left hand. They were united in their grief.

Gabby paused before she spoke again. How to explain this next bit? 'Not quite,' she said. 'We have the vehicle, but at this time we don't know who was driving it. We need to put someone behind the wheel for sure.'

'And what does the owner of said vehicle say about it? Because I'm damn sure you've asked them.' Mr Daniels face was like stone. Immovable and rigid. His eyes did not move from Gabby as he waited for her explanation. All that mattered in the world to him right now was what Gabby had to say. Investigations were difficult because they couldn't give the answers that the family wanted the most. What a family really wanted was for the event to not have happened and there was no way we could do that for them. Instead they leapt onto an investigation, believing it would make everything feel whole again. Truth was they would never feel whole again and were clasping at straws. I felt for Gabby right now. This was her case and all I could do was be here with her while she manoeuvred her way around Tyler's parents.

'That's a bit difficult because the owner of the vehicle is dead.'

A groan from Mrs Daniels this time. So much information bombarding her. But this was what I was interested in. To see their reaction to this news. At first look it seemed it was news to Mrs Daniels, at least.

'What do you mean he's dead?' asked Timothy Daniels.

I found it interesting that he had presumed that a hit and run driver would be a male. That it couldn't possibly be a female who had done this to his son.

Gabby looked uncomfortable. We should have discussed this on the drive over.

'The owner of the car was killed the night after Tyler was killed, Mr Daniels,' I said. That was my case so I was happy to help Gabby out.

He didn't flinch.

'I don't understand...' He shook his head and grabbed the back of his neck looking genuinely confused.

'Did you hear anything about who might have done this to Tyler?' I asked. 'Because we still have to place a driver behind the wheel and maybe one of your neighbours saw something that they haven't yet managed to tell the police?'

He barked out what was probably a laugh but which lacked any true humour. 'You think if I heard anything that could catch the killer of my son I would sit on the information? I'd have been straight on the blower to Inspector Kowalski to let her know what I had. I wouldn't have been sitting on my arse, no I wouldn't.' He turned to his wife. 'I presume they want to put the same question to you, love.' His voice was more gentle now.

She looked from me to Gabby and back again. 'I... the Inspector... I... yes, of course I'd have said if I'd heard anything. I want this person locked up behind bars not roaming the streets to do this to someone else, to another family.' This time she reached for her husband and she clung on hard.

They did not know anything about Lucy Anderson, I was sure about that. I gave a quick nod to Gabby.

'We'll let you know as soon as we have anything further. But this is a significant lead. We just need to figure out what is going on now. Why the owner of the car is dead and who was behind the wheel the night Tyler was killed. But as you can see, we are making progress.'

They both nodded.

'Thank you,' Mrs Daniels said quietly.

Her husband stood to let us out.

'How did he die?'

I looked at him.

'The guy who owned the car.'

'It's not something we can go into yet, but trust us when we say we are pursuing all angles. We will figure this out for you.'

He gave a curt nod. 'If he was the driver that cut Tyler down then I hope he died a blindingly painful death and knew what was happening up until the last minute. He reversed over my boy, you know, actually reversed over him. What kind of animal does that?'

I didn't have an answer. I was desperate to find one though.

41

Back at St Ann's police station car park I said goodbye to Gabby and thanked her for joining up with me on the investigation and for allowing me to visit the Daniels with her.

'Keep me up-to-date with what you get from the vehicle, won't you?' she said.

'Absolutely, you're looped in on the file now, so all information should also go to you, and let me know if you hear any whispers from your investigation that you feel we need to follow up for our investigation. They're pretty much entangled now.' I thought for a minute. 'Maybe I could send one of my DCs over to your team to work with you, to liaise between the two investigations?'

Gabby threw her car keys up in the air and caught them in her hand again. 'I think that's a great idea. Who would you send?'

'Well, as you know Ross already, how about I send him over?'

'Sounds like a plan, Hannah.'

'I'll get right on it. Thanks again, Gabby. It's been a useful day today.'

She nodded. 'It has. More so for me, I think. Thank you.'

I agreed. We were still no further forward in Lucy Anderson's murder investigation but Gabby had a vehicle. She needed to identify a driver which would mean sitting through hours of CCTV footage to see if they could find the car and then identify a driver from the images. If it turned out to be Lucy they could pretty much close down their investigation as *detected no further action* because the offender was dead.

I walked into the station, grateful for the warmth of the heating. The snow Martin had predicted hadn't materialised yet but it was certainly cold enough.

I wasn't sure if it was going to be as simple as that for Gabby though. It didn't feel right. Having been in Lucy's home, and having met her daughter and mother, Lucy didn't fit the bill as the type of person who would go out and wait for a young man to walk into the road so she could run him over and not just run him over but reverse over him and make sure he was dead. Plus there was all this confusion with the man who took Faith. That was a kink in the chain. Where did he fit into all this? Cheryl was adamant she didn't know him, but Faith had been returned home safe and well with no signs of any improper activity between them. Though she had said that Lucy was upset when she got home. Was that because she had killed a man or was it because of where Faith had been all day? We would know more about what happened with Faith once we had interviewed her. Had the school been derelict in their duties in allowing Faith to go off with the male or had they indeed done all they needed to do in the circumstances. The text message we looked at on the way out looked to be real enough.

'I saw you walk in.' It was Aaron.

I dropped into my chair and let out a breath. 'Hey, everyone been busy here?'

'You know them, they don't stop. How was your day with Gabby Kowalski?'

'It was long and confusing. Honestly, Aaron, the more I think about this case the more confusing it becomes.'

I filled him in on what had happened as we'd talked to Faith and Cheryl, the school and then Tyler's parents.

'So we have an unknown male we have to identify?' he said.

I nodded.

'What part do you think he played in all of this? Can we be sure he was with the child when Tyler was killed?'

'I don't know, Aaron, but the fact that Cheryl doesn't know who he is and is adamant that Lucy wouldn't have had anyone other than her pick Faith up, another female friend at a push, it doesn't feel right. Faith didn't even seem to know who he was. I don't think she'd seen him before. We're going to get her in for a full interview. I'll get Pasha and Martin to do that and we might find out more. We'll get them to set it up for tomorrow. We need to make a start on the inquiries into the unknown male. Maybe he came back after dropping Faith off and killed Lucy? The fact that we know so little unnerves me.'

'I don't see any reason for killing her other than the fact that it's likely she killed Tyler and you're saying they have no idea that Lucy did it? If it's not payback for Tyler, then what is it?'

'It might still be payback, but it's not the parents. Maybe someone else witnessed it and is keeping it to themselves. Or maybe it's another reason altogether. But it's a bit of a coincidence, don't you think, that she kills someone and then she's killed straight after?'

Aaron rubbed his chin. 'Not a lot about this case makes much sense.'

42

John Crowley looked at the phone in his hand in disgust. Why were people so accessible nowadays? He was standing here in the coffee shop with his wife, taking a quick, but well-earned break, as she said, and a new email had come through.

Trisha gave him a look. A look that said what-the-hell-are-you-doing-on-your-phone-you're-supposed-to-be-taking-a-break, kind of look.

'John.' She'd moved from the look to verbal assault. 'You're supposed to be relaxing. Leave your emails for half an hour can't you?'

He really wished he could. That email address from this morning. It was like a magnet, he had to click on it. He couldn't close his email down without opening that one. He had to know what the sender was saying to him this time.

'Where's Lizzy?' he asked.

His wife glared at him, not unkindly, but in a way that said she expected him to do as he was told. 'She's at work, where do you think she is?'

He knew she was at work, he just wanted to make sure. He wanted to know she was safe.

John put his phone down on the table in front of him.

He may have put it down but the contents of the message were seared onto his brain. Every single word of it, down to the punctuation.

'What is it, love? You're not worrying about tomorrow, are you?'

He had practically forgotten about tomorrow. Tomorrow no longer mattered. If it went ahead or not, it was irrelevant. All that he cared about was Lizzy and Trisha.

Dear John,

I see you have not acted on my email yet. I chose you because I thought you cared about your family. This is a time sensitive request. Please hurry the process up or you will be forcing me to do something unseemly.

PM.

There was another two images attached just in case he had forgotten what they looked like.

John was no longer hungry. He pushed the plate away from him. He couldn't admit to Trisha what was really wrong. She would be terrified by the blackmail and horrified by the images of Lizzy. He did not want her to see them.

'I don't know, I feel a little out of sorts. Maybe I'm coming down with something.' He picked up his coffee mug and held it between his hands without taking a drink. Having to do something with his hands managed to hold him together when all he wanted to do was throw the table over and scream to the heavens. How could someone do this to him and to his family?

He would do this. Then he would find the man behind these

emails and he would do exactly the same thing to him as he was about to do to the poor unsuspecting soul he was being set upon. He would do that. He would find him and kill him and tell him face to face who was in charge and pulling the strings, because no one did this to John Crowley and his family.

43

John made his excuses to Trisha as soon as it was possible without getting her Worry Radar pinging. He said he still had a couple of loose ends he wanted to tie up. In reality he had to plan what he was going to do. Scott Rhodes was a married man and John had to find a way to get him alone. He worked in a school and drove from work to home. Maybe John could find a way to get the wife out of the house. He certainly wasn't going to kill both of them. He went to his home office and closed the door. He searched for Scott's social media and found his wife. Once he located her he trawled through her page. It was amazing how many people had open pages, rather than limit their privacy settings. Any Tom, Dick or Idiot could look at their lives this way.

John was lucky, Wendy Rhodes was a busy lady. She went to a book club once a month, a wine tasting club.

She did Pilates four evenings a week and tonight happened to be one of those evenings. The odds were in his favour.

His stomach twisted. Tonight would be it. He was going to actually do it.

John pushed the chair back and leapt up, running from the office into the downstairs toilet. He reached it just in time to throw up. He hadn't eaten much so it was bitter on the back of this throat.

Trisha knocked on the white gloss door. 'John, love. Are you okay?'

John wiped his mouth, washed his hands and then rinsed out his mouth, and washed his hands again.

'John?' Trisha knocked on the door again.

He pushed his shoulders back, unlocked the door and opened it. Trisha was standing before him, eyes filled with concern, her handbag thrown carelessly on the floor. She raised a hand and put it to his cheek. 'What is it, love? I thought you dashed off a bit quick earlier.'

Hiding this from her was nearly as bad as what he was about to do. 'I think I have a bit of stomach flu. Bad timing if ever there was some.' He raised a weak smile.

'So you came home instead of worrying me?'

'You know me so well,' he lied and his stomach twisted again. At least he wasn't lying about how bad his stomach was feeling.

44

Evie opened the wine bottle as I placed the two glasses down on the coffee table.

'It's so good to see you again,' I said. 'I've missed catching up with you. Now, I want to know all about this new man on the scene.'

Evie poured the wine, generous with the bottle. 'It's also good to see you again. I have been a little wrapped up in myself of late.'

'Which is not like you at all. You normally run when it starts to get even the slightest bit serious, what's going on here, Evie? Tell me everything.'

I picked up my wine glass and curled my feet underneath myself. We were in my apartment at Castle Rock. A beautiful apartment block built into the base of the castle itself. I could see it lit up in the evening if I stepped outside.

'It kind of started by accident,' she said as she pulled her own legs up and mimicked my pose.

'Accident?'

She laughed. 'Yes, literally by accident. I ran into the back of him at some traffic lights and from there he had my phone number.' There was a huge grin across her face.

'Evie! What the hell were you doing to run into him at the traffic lights? You were texting, weren't you?' I shook my head.

'No. I was not texting. But, he braked suddenly for a cat. The traffic lights were on green. It was his fault.'

'Were you okay? Why have I never heard about this?' I was annoyed I didn't know my best friend had been involved in a traffic accident.

'Because I was fine. There was nothing to tell you. It was a minor bump. The lights had only just switched to green. We had all been stationary not a minute earlier.'

I let out a breath of relief.

'And it kind of went from there,' she said.

'So does this kind-to-cats man have a name?'

He does and he's called Sam, Sam Quinn.' She couldn't stop grinning.

'And what does he do, this Sam, Sam Quinn?'

He's a professional photographer.'

'A photographer? He's artsy and is kind to animals. There has to be something wrong with him, Evie, I'm not having this.'

She laughed at me and I joined in. I was happy for her. She deserved to be this happy. She never had a decent love life that I could remember.

'What about you?' she asked. 'Has anything exciting happened for you in the past few weeks?'

I shrugged noncommittally.

'If it can happen for me it can damn well happen for you.'

'I don't need a man to feel whole.'

She looked affronted. 'I of all people am not saying that you do. But a bit of company is kind of pleasant as well, you know. You put that damn job of yours above everything. You put in so many hours—'

'That's because the job demands it,' I butted in.

She held up a hand. 'It might demand it sometimes, when a case first kicks off, but not all the time. You give yourself to it willingly and it's not healthy. What is healthy is having a home life as well as a work life. Have you heard of the phrase work life balance, Hannah?'

I had and I presumed I balanced to the best of my ability. It was as though Evie could read my mind as she sat there shaking her head. 'The closest you got was with Ethan and then you backed away—'

'In Evie fashion.'

'I'll let you have that. But, I'd love to see you have more in your life than just the job, Hannah. You're my best friend. I want the best for you.'

It had been a long day and my arm was throbbing again. I held up a hand for Evie to wait a moment and wandered into the kitchen. Rummaged in the kitchen drawer and found my painkillers. Popped a couple with my wine.

'And that's no good for you.' She was stood in the doorway.

'I thought you were in the living room.'

'You hoped I was in the living room. How long are you going to take those for, Hannah?'

I took another gulp of the wine. This conversation had turned and I suddenly wished I was alone as I had been for the past few weeks. It was easier to be on my own.

She stepped a couple of paces closer. 'I don't mean to be a nag. I love you. I care. You know you shouldn't be taking those while you're drinking.'

'It's just one or two, Evie, it's not as though I'm drinking the full bottle on my own.'

She nodded towards my arm. 'Is it still giving you pain?'

'Yeah. It doesn't stop. It's incessant. It throbs deep in my arm as though it's damaged something deep in there.'

She stayed silent for a moment. Then it came. 'You don't think it's deeper than just physical?' She looked at me and held up her spare hand. 'Don't bite my head off. But I'd have thought it might have been easier by now. But I'm not a doctor. Maybe something is damaged deeply but it's not in your arm? I only say it because I care so much, sweetie.'

I placed my glass on the kitchen side. 'I think I need to get some sleep. It's going to be another long day tomorrow.'

Evie took the not so subtle hint and put her half full glass on the side and walked over to me. She wrapped her arms around my shoulders and pulled me close. 'I love you, sweetie. Please take care of yourself. I don't know what I'd do without you.'

45

Scott Rhodes was sitting on the sofa, a pile of school books on the arm waiting to be marked and a couple of books at the side of him already marked and one on his knee which he was supposed to be marking. His mind was elsewhere though. Since he had entered that woman's home and put the bag over her head he had not been able to concentrate properly. He had not been in school, instead feigning migraine, from which he had never suffered. Wendy was worried because he had never been ill with migraine before and he was definitely not himself. He was trying to mark the books but his head wasn't in it. All he could see was the woman as her legs kicked and thrashed and she grappled with him for control of the bag and control of her life. A life he had taken from her.

He put a hand to his head as that image seared into his mind once again and his stomach roiled in response.

'Oh, darling. Do you want me to stay at home with you tonight? I don't have to go to Pilates if you'd rather I stay?' She tapped a finger against her lips.

Scott scratched at his neck. 'It's okay, Wendy. You go to your class and I'll see you later.'

She let out a little sigh. 'I don't like leaving you like this. Why don't you put that marking away though, you're in no state to be doing it. They don't expect it done, not when you're this poorly. I'm so not used to seeing you ill it's rather disconcerting, you know?'

He smiled at her. They were a busy couple who led an active life between them, though not always together, but they were used to going out and getting on with their lives and she was right, she wasn't used to seeing him this way. But he couldn't pull himself out of this and he didn't know how he was going to do it, to get himself into such a place that he could face going back to school and pretending that life was fine and worth carrying on with. 'I know it is. I'm sure it'll be over soon enough.'

'Well,' she said, 'if it's not, I'm making you an appointment at the doctor's.'

They wouldn't do him any good. He understood patient confidentiality, but he didn't think it applied to a confession of murder and the trauma it causes. He nearly laughed. Trauma counselling, caused by the trauma of murdering someone, paid for by the NHS. You couldn't even get trauma counselling when you needed it for legitimate reasons they were so underfunded.

'Okay, if you're sure?' Wendy wrapped her coat around herself and pulled on her woollen hat. It was cold outside this evening.

'I'm sure, I'll see you later.'

She bent down and kissed him on the head. So gently he could feel the love emanate from her. Then she was gone and he was alone with his thoughts and images and feelings. All of them crowding in on him. Burning a hole through his brain. He had no idea how he was going to get through this. If he should even attempt to get through this. Did he deserve to? After all, the reason he had been chosen in the first place was bad enough and now he had made himself so much worse. How could he have done that? How could he have made that choice? How could he have thought that protecting that secret was worth... this? To become this man.

He didn't deserve to carry on with this life any longer. What he had stolen from that woman, that child, he was despicable. He could no longer recognise himself in a mirror.

Was he strong enough to end his own life though, as he had ended the woman's life? How dare he even begin to think he couldn't, not after he had ended hers so easily. Ending his own should be a walk in the park for him.

But how would he do it? He didn't want to hurt Wendy any more than he had already, but there was no way he could live with what he had done. He didn't want her to find him and to live with the trauma of that. He would have to do it away from the house. He pushed the book from his lap onto the not-done pile. He would need to... what? When would he do this, before or after he had marked these damn school books?

He heard a noise in the house.

'Wendy, is that you? I told you, I'm okay.' He was such a liar, but he wasn't going to lay this at her door. She would never find out. Her pain would come when she found out about his death. She would never find out what he had on his computer because he had deleted it but he would remove the hard drive and get rid of it and hope that no evidence ever came back to him for the woman he'd murdered.

Then it was there, something tight around his neck. Thick and rough, pulling his head back against the back of the sofa. Stopping his breath in his chest. He tried to suck air in, arched his back, his hands flew to his neck, the books on the arm of the sofa pushed off and onto the floor.

It was rope, thick rough rope and it was being pulled back hard. It was digging into the skin on his neck and Scott couldn't get his fingers underneath it. His mouth stretched open trying to pull in air, his whole body lifted up off the sofa now, feet planted on the floor as he pushed back with the rope, trying to get some leeway, some tiny bit of air in, his hands scrabbling. His mouth yawning open, his tongue starting to protrude. His brain starting to close down. He couldn't think straight.

What was this? Who was this?

He needed air.

The rope was rough against his throat, against his fingers as he pulled at it. It was being pulled harder and harder and with such anger.

Scott, his hands still clinging to the rope because his reflexes couldn't let go of the fight for life, even while he was losing all thought processes, realised this was his perfect opportunity. His chance to make things right with the world. Though it was horrific that Wendy would come home to find him, he wouldn't have to make the final decision and he wouldn't have to find the guts to go through with it. It was all being done for him. Scott didn't understand how or who or why, but he was grateful all the same and, with tentative fingers still holding on to the rope he gave in. It was painful. The rope, it was large and rough on his neck. Whoever was behind him was pulling hard. He didn't need to. Scott wouldn't fight any more.

He had nothing left in him. The edges were blurred. The middle all grey. The comfortable home he once loved was barely visible. His hands fell to his sides. His body dropped down to the sofa. His tongue protruded from his mouth. The room went black and he no longer needed to gasp for air.

46

I was tired. I hadn't slept much the previous night. It was tempting to finish the bottle of wine that Evie had left but I'd thought better of it and instead finished my glass then took myself to bed. I hoped that things were okay with Evie. She cared for me but I had ended up on the defensive when she was talking last night and I had pushed her away so needed to go and find her this morning and make sure everything was good with us.

First I headed into my office and turned on my laptop and waited for it to load. These were not new laptops and were not new versions of Word either so they were slow to get going. You could go and make yourself a drink while it considered whether it was going to wake up or not this morning.

In fact, while it was thinking about it, I would go and find Evie and clear the air with her.

I pulled the pack of chocolate biscuits out of my bag, went to the kitchen, made a couple of drinks and walked to Evie's office. She was there, back to the door, curls tumbling free around her head.

I knocked once on the open door and walked in. Evie turned and looked at me. I waved the biscuits at her like a white flag of surrender.

'Okay, you can come in.' She smiled at me and took one of the mugs from me as I was balancing two in one hand.

'Thanks, they were starting to burn me.'

'More important to protect the biscuits, you did good, Padawan.'

I smiled in turn. We were okay.

After a quick catch up with Evie I went back to my office and my laptop and checked my emails from the previous afternoon and evening. There was one from forensics that caught my eye. I opened it.

Oh my. It couldn't be this easy, could it? And I couldn't believe I didn't see this last night. We could have had this wrapped up last night. Though what were a few more hours? This was bloody quick. Though Jack had said that there was material under her nails. I printed out the email and stomped down to the incident room which by now was filled with the entire murder inquiry team staff, other than Ross who was with Gabby Kowalski and the Roads Policing team.

'Everyone listen in please.' I called them all to order.

'We have some results from forensics. As I mentioned during our briefing last night, Jack Kidner found some biological material underneath Lucy Anderson's nails during her post-mortem.'

A thrum of noise went around the room as they processed where this was going. Pens were picked up and notebooks opened.

'Forensics have run it for DNA and have found a match, which is a surprise because the guy is a teacher. But, it's possible he didn't disclose the offence to his place of work and it's not a disclosable offence for us to have done it for him.'

'What did he do?' asked Pasha, forever interested in other people.

'Assisting an offender. Something to do with his brother. His brother got into a bit of a brawl with a neighbour and our guy lied to try and protect him. It all came out in the wash and the Inspector on duty was not impressed by the sounds of it so went for our guy as well. I know it's unusual, but that's what you get for interfering.'

'And our guy is?' asked Martin.

'Scott Rhodes of Conway Road, Hucknall. We need to do the

relevant checks on him and then Aaron and I will go out and make the arrest. Martin, if you and Ross start on preparing for the interview, that would be great. Theresa, link him up on HOLMES and see what other actions it throws out please.' They all nodded and made notes.

Ten minutes later we were in a car and on our way to arrest Scott Rhodes. He had no other criminal history other than the assisting an offender, which was pretty minor in the scheme of things. I had phoned the school and got no reply yet. Reception was not yet answering their phones. Whether the teachers were in yet I didn't know so we were trying him at his home address first.

'Are you surprised we have a lead this early?' I asked Aaron as he concentrated on the road.

'Not really. You said she'd put up a fight so it was likely we'd find some of his DNA. He must know we're going to come for him. He can't imagine after a battle like that that he'll walk away from it.'

'It's the wives I feel for. I still feel sorry for Knight's wife, you know.'

'The poisoner?'

'Yeah. He caused such bedlam and the city was in uproar. Fancy having to uproot your life because of your husband's actions.'

'It was a tough case.'

'Do any cases stay with you?' I was curious.

'Not in the way they stay with you, no. I worry about doing my job correctly and that the Asperger's is getting in the way, particularly during an interview, be it a witness or offender, because I don't want to miss a nuanced sentence.'

'Well it's perfect that we interview in pairs because I pick up on the emotional stuff and you're brilliant at the logical stuff. When I'm getting too emotional about a subject you can see the wood for the trees. I couldn't do without you, Aaron. And as we're talking about this, I'm pleased that things seem to have settled down with Baxter. It's as though there has never been a problem with him.'

Aaron nodded. 'I know. And to think how worried I was about it all. This is one of my points. I worry about things. I over worry. Look where that got me. I could have resolved this issue months ago instead I let it drag out when I should have faced it head on.'

'I'm so pleased, Aaron. I don't know what Catherine said to him but she worked wonders, but saying that, he's always been a professional officer so once he was told by a supervising officer to back off and why, that there was a reason for your actions, the ones that seemed to bother him, it made little sense for him to carry on being a twat. He had to fall into line and get on with the job which is what we're all here to do.'

Aaron indicated and we turned right onto Trent Drive and then left into Conway Road. It wasn't long before I saw the emergency vehicles. 'I wonder what's going on there?'

'I'm not sure. We never checked the overnight incidents once you briefed us on this arrest. We were too busy prepping for this. They've obviously had an incident on the street though.' Aaron slowed, checked the numbers on the houses. 'Hannah...'

I was coming to the same conclusion. 'Shit... it's at Rhodes' address.'

Aaron parked as close as he could. Blue and white police incident tape stretched around the semi-detached red-brick house that mirrored the rest of the tidy red-brick houses on the estate. Marked cars and vans blocked the road so we were several houses away. I climbed out the car and stared at the scene. I didn't know how recent the incident was but people were outside their homes in the freezing cold, wrapped up in coats and scarves, with mugs of steaming drinks in their hands, watching events unfold in front of them as though this was some show they had paid to view.

'I hate rubberneckers,' I hissed at Aaron. I pushed my hands into my pockets to try to get warm, the cold air nipping at my fingertips. My breath wafted up in front of me.

'They don't have interesting lives so when something like this happens they can't help themselves.' His own breath spiralled around him as he spoke and looked around at the people staring at the two new arrivals.

We walked up to the uniformed officer guarding the scene. I

rummaged in my pocket and pulled out my warrant card and showed it him. 'DI Robbins, Major Crime,' I said. 'Can you tell me what's happened at this address, please? We wanted to speak to the occupant, Scott Rhodes.'

The cop blinked at me. 'I'm sorry, Ma'am, Scott Rhodes is dead. He was murdered last night.'

47

Dead? Scott Rhodes was dead? 'What the bloody hell is going on?' I said to Aaron.

'I'm sorry, Ma'am.' The uniformed officer furrowed his eyebrows.

I waved my hand at him. 'No, sorry, not you. I was talking to my colleague.'

I took hold of Aaron's arm and turned him away a little until our backs were to the officer. 'Aaron, what the hell?'

Aaron shook his head. 'I don't know, Hannah. This doesn't make sense. Lucy was murdered and we find that before she died she killed someone else. And now we have her killer and—'

'He's been killed,' I finished for him. 'It's as though we're in some kind of weird horror movie not everyday life. How are these people all connected and all dead?'

He shook his head again.

I looked back to the uniformed officer then back to Aaron. 'We should go and speak to the SIO on the case and let them know what we have. That the cases are all linked and see if we can take this case off them. We should also phone Baxter and let him know what's happening. I hate to ask you this but can you phone Baxter and I'll go and talk to the SIO?'

'It's not a problem, Hannah. I told you that on the way over.'

I stepped over to the uniformed officer. 'Who's still on scene?' I asked.

He consulted his scene log. 'The SIO and some CSIs. The body left about an hour ago. The wife is long gone.'

'Can you let me through to see the SIO, please?'

He looked concerned. People who weren't part of the investigation wouldn't usually be allowed through the tape and if he was doing his job properly he shouldn't let me through just because I asked.

'Bear with me one moment would you, Ma'am. I need to check with DI Kapoor.' He bent his head to speak into the radio pinned to his breast and had a brief conversation.

A moment later a very slim tall male wrapped in a wool coat, came striding out of the house, arms swinging freely by his sides. He ducked under the police tape and approached me.

'DI Robbins?' He held out his hand. 'DI Bikram Kapoor.'

I nodded. 'Please, call me Hannah.'

'How can I help you, Hannah?' He shoved his hands in his pockets. He towered over me. I was petite compared to most males I met but Kapoor was blocking whatever sunlight there was as I looked up to him.

'Your victim, Scott Rhodes, we have a bit of an issue.'

'Do tell me more.'

'The reason we turned up today was to arrest him for the murder of Lucy Anderson, the victim of a murder we're investigating from two days ago. And now he's turned up dead. Can I ask how he died?'

He tipped his head to the side. 'I think you'd better come inside and we'll talk.'

I nodded my thanks to the uniformed PC who smiled in response at me. He was professional and knew what he was doing. I appreciated a good cop like that. I looked behind me. Aaron was finishing up his call. I stopped a minute and waited for him. When he finished I indicated he should follow us inside the address. I made the introductions as we went.

The house was warm and welcoming. The heating must be on a timer because Mrs Rhodes most certainly would not have thought to put it on this morning.

We walked from the entrance into the living room. There were students' school books scattered all over, on the sofa and thrown on the floor. Other than that the room looked to be in order. Nothing seemed to be out of place. You might not even know anything had happened in this room, if it wasn't for the presence of a couple of CSIs still in the room, including Doug Howell, the crime scene manager.

I said hello to Doug then turned back to Kapoor and nodded to the sofa. 'This where it happened?'

'It is. He was approached from behind and strangled with a thick piece of rope which was left at the scene. His wife had gone out to Pilates and found him when she returned home. She said he hadn't been feeling well. He'd been sick from school with a migraine and was trying to do some marking but was failing. She told him to stop and go to bed but he was on the sofa when we found him. He hadn't moved from when she left him. She was in a real state last night and is with her sister now. We'll get a statement from her later today.' He looked concerned. 'You say he was your suspect in a murder case?'

'His DNA was found under the fingernails of a woman who was suffocated by a plastic bag. She'd put up a fight and managed to catch her offender. It led us here. But that's not all. This case is beyond strange. Lucy Anderson, our victim, has also been found to have killed someone before she was killed. I'm officially freaked out now and they are words that we don't want to get out to the press.'

'What the fuck? You're serious? About your victim having killed before she was murdered?'

'There's no doubt about it. It was a hit and run. There were body parts underneath her car.'

Kapoor let out a low whistle. 'This is one freaky case.'

'Yes, and because of the links between them all, I was wondering if we could pick this one up off you?'

Kapoor rubbed his cheek. 'I don't normally like to fob a job off, I'm not that kind of guy—'

'You're not fobbing it off, I'm asking for it, I want it. It makes sense for us to take it off you because of how these cases all line up. I don't know what the link is yet, but there has to be one.'

'I get what you're saying though a part of me wants to stay involved because of my interest in the case. I can't see how this can happen. I've never seen anything like it before. But it does make sense for you to take it.'

I looked around the room again. 'What do you have, Doug?'

Doug had been stooped over something in the room. He straightened, put his hands on the back of his hips and wriggled himself back into a comfortable position. 'We might get something off the rope. It was pretty thick and coarse. It might be that as the offender was pulling on it he pulled on his own skin and there might be blood molecules on the rope strands. Other than that, he didn't touch anything that we can see. We've fingerprinted everything and nothing. There are no footprints that we can find. It was straight in and out. Wendy, the wife, said the door was unlocked when she left so he could easily have walked in.'

'So,' Kapoor said, 'if this had have been London where barely anyone leaves their doors unlocked as they do up here, he would have probably been safe?'

I looked at the scene around me. 'It's rare for strangers to walk in and kill in your home this way though. You're more likely to be killed on the street by a stranger and in your own home it's someone you know. Locking the door doesn't usually come into play.'

'You're right, I know, it's just my sister lives in south London and always has her door locked. She would see this as a perfectly valid reason for doing so, no matter what I say to her.'

This was definitely unusual. We had to be hopeful the rope brought us something useful. Before we ended up finding this next killer dead. 'Doug, do you think a woman could have killed Rhodes?'

'With the amount of pressure needed to have been applied, I would say it was not impossible but not likely.'

I looked at Kapoor. 'We need to find this guy before he turns up dead. I don't like the way this case is progressing. Every offender from one murder is then found murdered themselves. I think we're on a ticking clock and I can't understand why.'

48

The photograph was perfect. Scott Rhodes was laid out on his sofa with the rope around his neck and his tongue protruding from his mouth. He was most definitely dead. This was not a set-up photograph. Something he had been worried his subjects would try to do to get out of killing. But it seemed that they hadn't even considered it. They were more than willing to kill. No matter how they fought against it and said it was against their poor sensibilities they still went ahead and killed when they were told to.

The next person was lined up. He had found her. There had been a trail online he could follow and once he pulled the virtual string it all unravelled and now he had control. She was fighting against him though. She was trying. But he had the upper hand and he knew it. She had so much to lose. One question he had not yet asked himself, would he be prepared to carry out his threats if they did stand up to him? He hadn't even considered it before because they all capitulated. Would he do what he said he would? Would he destroy a person that way? He supposed he would. He was doing it anyway. What was to stop him being directly involved in their destruction?

This was all moving so fast. To him this was all just a game. Pieces on a board to just be moved around. Out there in the real world there were actions and consequences. He needed to move quickly. He needed to be ahead of the police. He needed the next person to be killed before the police caught up to them because he didn't want them to be arrested and for them to tell all. To tell them that they were being directed by a third party. Then the hunt would be for him and not for the killer. He couldn't have that. He needed to keep rolling the dice and playing the game.

Time to push the next piece into play – whether they wanted to or not.

49

Selena Glass stared at the email. She had ignored him once and replied to him once and told him no. She would not be forced into such despicable behaviour this way. No matter the consequences. It was disgusting. How could someone believe they had this kind of power? How could someone ask this of another human being?

'Mummy, can we bake this morning?' At three years of age, Zoya was already turning into a master baker and it made Selena smile every time she asked to do it. She and Simon had adopted Zoya from Ethiopia, paying the birth mother and authorities for the process. It wasn't exactly a legal adoption, not within the UK anyway. They'd had to have documents forged for Zoya, a birth certificate being the most important of all, and if the authorities found out then Zoya would be taken from her and she would be arrested and sent to prison for the heinous offence of child trafficking, but Selena didn't see it that way. She saw it as saving a child from an unbearable life. She was giving Zoya a life that was so much better, safer and kinder than any life she would have experienced had she left her where she was. Selena was no child trafficker, not the type you imagine when you say the phrase. She wasn't taking babies from parents who loved them and vanishing with them off in the night so she could make herself hundreds of thousands of pounds. She had paid to save a little baby who needed it. A birth mother who couldn't care for her child but who had loved her enough to wish her a happier and safer life in the UK where there was health care and education, where Zoya would get the best that could be offered and from a couple who would love her as their own. And they did. She thought of Zoya as her own child as though she had birthed her. She couldn't bear to lose her.

She took one last look at the screen of her phone and shoved it in her pocket, determined to ignore it.

'Yes, of course we can bake, sweetheart.' Selena jumped up from her seat, picked Zoya up and spun her around, her little legs kicking out behind her as they spun in a circle. 'What do you want to bake?' she asked as she gently placed her back down on the floor.

'Cupcakes with green goo on the top! Like the ones we did at Halloween.'

Zoya laughed. To Selena it was the most beautiful sound in the world. Nothing could replace it. It was high and musical and it sounded as though it was made for her ears.

'You're sure you don't want to make cupcakes with pretty pink icing?'

'Nope.' Zoya chuckled. 'Green goo.'

'Green goo it is. Mmmm, I can't wait to eat them.'

They both skipped through to the kitchen and started to pull the ingredients out of the cupboards. Zoya pulled the mixing bowl and weighing scales out because she could reach those and then she pulled her little baker's apron over her head.

'Oh my God, sweetheart, you look adorable every time you wear that. Let me take your photograph.'

Selena pulled her phone out of her pocket and Zoya stuck her hip out and placed a hand on it, posing for the photo. Selena woke the phone up and saw she had another email. She ignored it and took the photograph of Zoya.

'Oh wow. Just look at that beautiful girl in that image, Zoy.' Zoya leaned forward and looked at the phone. 'Isn't she beautiful?'

'It's me, Mummy.'

'Really? But she's so beautiful.' Selena grabbed hold of Zoya and snuggled into her neck. 'You're so beautiful, my gorgeous little girl.'

Zoya giggled again and wriggled free. Selena feigned hurt. 'Okay then, wash your hands, sweetie.'

Zoya pulled her step stool in front of the sink and turned the tap on. Selena stared at her phone. Should she open the email? It could be from work. It could be from anyone other than the awful person who was scaring her half to death. She should stop being silly, open the message and get on with baking with her daughter.

She tapped on the app. The new message was from the same unidentifiable email address.

The last message she had sent back had been: 'Leave me alone. Go and harass someone else. I am not impressed by your silly games or your ridiculous threats.'

She supposed she needed to know what his response was.

'Come on, Mummy, you need to wash your hands as well.' Zoya was completely enveloped in soap suds, the smell of jasmine and apple blossom permeating the air between them, sweet and fresh.

'Yes, give me a minute, sweetie, I've got to read this, I'll be right there.'

She tapped on the top unopened email and watched as it opened on the screen. She read the message and her world crumbled down around her.

DEAR SELENA,

THIS IS NOT A SILLY GAME. *As you are well aware my knowledge is correct. Zoya is not your daughter and has not been legitimately adopted. She will be taken from you if it were to become known that she was here illegally, that you brought her here illegally.*

. . .

Let me be clear on one thing. If you do not follow out the instructions in my previous email I will inform the authorities of where Zoya is from and how you came to be her parent. If you no longer wish to be her parent and you wish to see the inside of a jail cell then feel free to ignore this email. I have nothing to lose – but you, I feel, have everything to lose.

If you inform the authorities of these emails then I again have nothing to lose in informing them of Zoya. So you lose either way.

The choice is all yours. But this is not a game. This is real and I intend to carry out my threats if you do not do as I ask.

PM.

Selena looked at Zoya, at the beautiful child, wrapped in soap, playing with the bubbles and loving the small things in life. How could she lose this little girl? How could she have let this happen? This was all her fault. She was the one that had put them in this position, by going there and saving a life. Only she was the one who could get them out of it – by taking a life.

50

I gathered everyone in the incident room as soon as I got back to St Ann's police station, including Baxter and Detective Superintendent Catherine Walker and I had even called Gabby Kowalski and Ross over. This case needed all hands on deck. I had never in my entire career experienced anything like this. In fact, I felt a little out of my depth. Yes, I had practically demanded Kapoor hand over his case so it could be merged with mine, but that was because it made sense, not because I knew what I was doing with it. I needed Baxter and Walker for their experience and seniority. I needed some guidance and it wasn't very often I said that, or even thought it.

'I need everyone to listen in. We have a real problem on our hands with this one and I'm not afraid to say it has me stumped. I want all heads on this. No idea is too stupid. If you have something to say then say it. You won't be shot down, I'm looking for anything.'

Everyone looked concerned. I had never said I needed help this way before.

'Aaron and I went out this morning to arrest Scott Rhodes whose tissue was in the fingernails of Lucy Anderson, who, as you will remember, had the body parts of Tyler Daniels under her car. When we got to Rhodes' house there was another team there, another Major Crime team. Rhodes was murdered in his home last night.'

The room erupted in a wall of noise. Baxter and Walker were already aware as Aaron had phoned it in, so they waited at the back of the room as everyone else took the information in.

'What the hell?'

'Shit.'

'Fuck!'

'What kind of game is this?'

'Are you kidding?'

All of the phrases being thrown about at each other. Shoulders being shrugged. Blank looks. Bemusement.

'Okay, quiet down.' I waited them out. 'Now obviously we have a real problem. Something is going on here, something we have no idea about. Something behind the scenes. This is not just coincidence. Coincidences might exist but not to this extent. I might have fallen for it with one case, for instance Lucy Anderson having Tyler Daniels' body parts under her car. That was strange in itself and was not something I had come across before, but I took it on the chin and followed the evidence. That evidence took us to Scott Rhodes and now Rhodes is dead and I no longer believe in coincidence. I think there's something at play here that we aren't seeing and I want to know what it is.'

The room was silent as they processed what I'd told them.

'The offender left the murder weapon, a length of coarse rope, at the scene. It may be that there is evidence of who he is on that. Though, how much that will help us is another matter altogether. Are we going to find another body, for instance? That's a serious question we have to ask ourselves. My concern is for the killer. From the current timeline, I'm thinking he's going to be dead before tomorrow night is out.'

'What now?' asked Evie.

'That's the thing, I don't know. How do they all know each other and how is this happening? It's like dominoes. One goes down and then in order the rest go down, but there is a specific order to them.

Who is controlling the order they go down in?' I looked at Evie. 'You were looking at Tyler's social media accounts before the DNA came back. Did you find anything of interest, any noise on the murder?'

Evie shook her head. 'No one was talking as though they knew who had been behind it. The people I could access, they were all shocked rather than people with information or an agenda of revenge. I checked Scott Rhodes name against Tyler's social media circle and he was not known. There's no link to him through any of his other friends or associates either. And none to Lucy Anderson. These people don't look like they're connected to each other at all.'

'Okay.' I looked around at the whole team. 'Time to throw the floor open to you lot. Give me your thoughts. Anything you have in your head, throw it out. We need it. Nothing is out of bounds.'

I looked at them. They looked stumped. Ross was tapping a pen against his desk. Gabby looked shocked, scribbling furiously in her notebook. Walker and Baxter looked concerned and waited patiently for the team to get going because once they started they'd wake up and give this a good go.

'So, you think, whoever killed Scott Rhodes is also going to end up dead, probably by the end of tomorrow?' It was Martin. Trying to get his head around it.

'Yes, exactly. If what we have so far is anything to go by. We have three dead and two are the killers of the one before.' A shudder went up my spine just saying that.

'It feels like some kind of game,' said Pasha. 'Like someone is playing a game.'

'Someone?' I queried. 'Who? They all end up dead.'

'Maybe it is a game, and once they have killed, they pass on their details to the next person to come and kill them? Maybe it's one of those weird dark net websites,' said Ross

'Not a bad suggestion,' I agreed. 'But Lucy Anderson fought for her life. Not the action of someone who had agreed to be murdered. And she was a mother and her child was upstairs. I'm not a mother but I'm not sure a mother would agree for that to happen while her child is in the house.'

'They don't know when it's going to happen and maybe it's a reflex that happens with your body that it automatically fights back when the life is being suffocated out of it, the fight to live is strong.'

'Okay, an online game where the participants know what is happening but not when or how?'

'It's a bit out there but it's a possibility,' said Gabby.

'It's very out there,' I agreed. 'I've never heard anything so bizarre. How do we figure out who is the next person to be involved, the one to kill Scott Rhodes' killer?' I asked. 'Because that's the person we need to stop. As well as identifying and arresting Rhodes' killer, we need to protect him.'

'This is a first,' said Martin. Not looking so relaxed this morning.

A phone started ringing somewhere in the room. Pasha took the call and spoke quietly into the handset.

'Any other suggestions?' I asked.

'There's one person in control instead of a game and them all being involved?' Evie looked flushed. It wasn't usual for her to speak in a briefing. She liked to do her thing in her office and keep out of the hubbub of office life.

'With or without their knowledge?'

'Either I suppose, though without is the more likely scenario. I'm not sold on people agreeing to be murdered.'

'What about if it's a suicide site?' Ross piped up again.

'I like that,' said Gabby. 'I could imagine that existing. A mutually beneficial suicide site. Where instead of doing it yourself and maybe bringing shame on your family, you're murdered. But first you have to do the favour for the person in front of you.'

'That makes sense,' I said. 'But how do we find a site like that? I'd have to get computer forensics involved but I'm not sure they could search the dark net and find it. I don't think it works like that. Plus, this is just theory. We have no idea if we are on the right track at all. The idea that one person is behind this could be the right one though. Whichever is right, we need to figure out a way of identifying the next person in the line-up and as far as we can see, there is no pattern, no link between them. So we need to get to Scott Rhodes' killer before his killer is set loose and maybe we can question him and find out what this is all about. So, that's our priority, everyone in here. I want all heads working on this current part of the case, finding Scott Rhodes' killer. It's the only way to stop this train of murders.'

Everyone nodded. I looked at Baxter and Catherine and they both inclined their heads. They had nothing else to add.

51

Selena paced around the kitchen. Zoya was in the living room on the floor doing a couple of jigsaws. She loved jigsaws, puzzles, things that taxed her mind. She was an active clever child and was more than ready for nursery.

The timer on the oven buzzed and Selena jumped out of her skin. The noise seemed extraordinarily loud in her ears today. She rushed to the oven and pushed the button to stop the sound. It was inside her head. Screaming at her. Tearing her very insides apart.

Zoya bounced into the kitchen. 'Are they ready, Mummy?'

Selena's legs wobbled beneath her and she needed to sit down. She leaned on the kitchen counter. 'Yes, they're done, sweetie. Shall we get them out? I'll have to do it though, they'll be too hot for you to touch yet. You'll stay away, won't you? I don't want you to get hurt.'

Zoya nodded solemnly, still bouncing on the balls of her feet on the spot. Her hands clasped tight in front of her.

Selena opened the oven, hot air washing over her, and pulled the cupcakes out. They had risen beautifully. She placed them on the cooling tray and brought Zoya over to look over her work. 'They're fabulous, you gorgeous girl. Just like you.' She hugged her. Holding her close.

She couldn't lose this girl. It didn't matter that she would go to jail. That wasn't the point. What mattered was what would happen to Zoya. Would they send her back to Ethiopia or keep her in the UK? Selena couldn't bear the thought that she would be sent to Ethiopia, a country she had no allegiance to, no understanding of. She was westernised now. She knew the western ways. She would be lost and afraid and alone in Ethiopia. It would appear foreign and scary over there. Even if they gave her back to her birth mother, Zoya wouldn't recognise her. The mother couldn't afford to look after her anyway. The money Selena had given her would be gone. She had needed it to look after the other children she already had. Selena smelled the top of Zoya's head, the scent of her daughter, the soft fragrance of baby powder and shampoo. She inhaled deeply. Everything she adored about this girl of hers was wrapped up in the sweetness of her.

Selena would do anything to protect her and that included doing what the emailer had asked her to do.

But how? How do you kill someone? She had never even considered it before never mind gone through with it. Her world was filled with the good things in life, not the bad and evil in people. She rarely even read the news because it was so depressing.

She needed a way to kill this man and not be too close to him. A gun meant you could stand at a distance but that was ridiculous because she didn't have the means to get a gun.

Why didn't the email come with an instruction manual? He wanted this task doing, he could at least tell her how to do it.

Zoya's fingers crept towards the cupcakes.

Selena laughed at her. Forced because her mind was elsewhere, but she had to be here for her daughter as well. 'They're a little hot for you at the minute, you'll have to wait for them to cool down.'

Zoya started blowing on them. Little spots of spittle landing on the cakes.

'It's a good job there's only me, you and Daddy eating these, munchkin.' She rubbed the top of Zoya's head.

Would she tell Simon about the email? Would she share the

burden? Or would she carry it all alone and go and do it alone and carry the knowledge alone, living the rest of her life, knowing she had done this to save her family? Or should she tell him? How would he react? It had been hard work to talk him into getting Zoya the way they had. It had all been Selena's idea. She had pushed and pushed until he gave in. He had kept her secret because he loved her and now he loved Zoya, but one more secret, it might topple him and their marriage. They might not survive. He was a good man who didn't like doing the wrong thing, or something he perceived to be the wrong thing. If it was against the law, as the Ethiopian adoption was, then he had argued it was wrong and they shouldn't be doing it. He had stressed and worried for weeks and months when they were setting it up. What the hell would he do if she told him she was going to kill a man because someone demanded it of her? He would buckle under the strain.

No, she wouldn't tell him. She would do this alone.

52

'Boss?' It was Pasha, across the room.

'What is it, Pasha?'

'That phone call that came in while you were talking?' Pasha stood and walked over to me. 'It was Cheryl Anderson, Lucy's mum. She wants to talk to you. I said you would call her back.' Pasha handed me a sheet of paper with two phone numbers on it. I looked at her.

'Before you came in Faith's school phoned and the head teacher Tessa Friedman would like you to call her back.'

I walked to my office and picked up the phone, dialled the first number on the paper and was soon put through to Tessa Friedman.

'Ah, hello, DI Robbins. Thank you for getting back to me so promptly.'

'It's my pleasure. How can I help today? Do you have any further information about the male who collected Faith Anderson a few days ago?' I asked.

'Well, that's the thing. I was told about this by Mr Hughes who as you can imagine is very upset by the whole situation. Can you confirm that no harm has come to young Faith?'

'Faith seems to be fine as far as that incident is concerned.'

'Yes. It is rather tragic what happened to her mother. Please pass on our sympathies to whomever is taking care of Faith at this time and let them know we will take good care of her whenever she is fit to return.'

I wondered if there was any point to this phone call or if she just wanted to make sure the school were covered.

'I wanted to let you know that after your visit we have had a review of how our children are collected and that includes how parents who work change their plans. You see, Inspector, it's difficult when you have working mothers and you have to adapt to their needs. But as we've found, the safety of the child is paramount, so we will only be changing pick-up plans with a phone call in future and a password that every parent has to know in order to change their plans and have another party collect their child. Having this password in place should reduce the possibility of such a thing happening again. I know it's far too late for Faith now, but I hope nothing like this happens in our school in the future and I wanted to let you know. The appropriate people have been made aware of the potential problem and the fix.'

'Thank you, Mrs Friedman. That sounds like a sensible plan of action and very prompt as well.'

'Well of course, we're dealing with children, there's no point dilly-dallying around. Thank you for your time, Inspector.'

I thanked her for letting me know and hung up the call. This still didn't help us understand if it was a legitimate pick-up or not, but I liked that the school was taking responsibility.

I dialled the next number and listened to the dial tone. The handset was snatched up as though Cheryl had been sitting by the phone waiting for me to call.

'DI Robbins?'

'Yes, Cheryl. How are you doing today?'

'I'm sorry for calling, I just can't sit on my hands, I needed to know if you had an update for me? I'm sorry if I shouldn't have called.'

She sniffed and I heard her wipe her nose.

'It's fine, Cheryl. I needed to come out to update you today anyway. Are you happy to talk over the phone? Or I can drive over and see you. I'm more than willing to do that for you.' We had a lot to do but it was protocol to update the families of murder victims in person. But as she had phoned me anyway, this was up to her.

'Please tell me now. I can't be sitting here waiting, it'll drive me insane. Please, tell me.'

'I'm sorry, Cheryl. I can only imagine how hard this has been for you.' I picked up a pen on my desk and started to doodle on a piece of paper in front of me.

'We identified someone because of DNA found underneath Lucy's fingernails during her post-mortem...'

There was a large sniffle.

I took an intake of air and continued. 'We went to the address this morning to make an arrest, but I'm afraid he was found dead.'

'He was what?' Her voice rose, high-pitched and scared.

'This case has taken on qualities we're not quite sure about. We're amalgamating the teams involved and are pooling all the resources. We have a little extra work to do to confirm that the person whose DNA was found under Lucy's nails was her killer, but once we confirm that, her case will be classed as detected, no further police action.'

'No further police action?' she mirrored me.

'Yes, we can't take any action against a dead man.'

She mumbled something incoherent.

'Look, I hate to do this to you, but it seems that Lucy was involved in something... similar. There's evidence that she may have killed a person before she herself was killed.'

'NO. I don't believe you. Lucy would not do that. No way.'

'I'm sorry, Cheryl, the evidence is pretty substantive.'

'I don't care what your so-called evidence is. Lucy was not a killer.' She started to sob. 'I don't understand what's happening. I phoned you for some reassurance and I feel one hundred times worse.'

'I'm sorry. I truly am. We're trying to get to the bottom of this. Can

I ask you, was Lucy feeling sad, blue, upset over anything the last couple of weeks?'

'Sad?'

'Yes, was she depressed would you say?'

'No, I wouldn't say she was depressed. She loved her little girl. She enjoyed her part-time job at the doctor's surgery. She had nothing on her plate that would have made her sad.'

'Okay. Thank you. It's an avenue we're looking down. I appreciate your help and I'm sorry for any upset I may have caused.'

Cheryl took a deep intake of breath. 'Just please resolve this, and what happened. My daughter is not a cold-blooded killer. It's not her. There has to be more to it than that. Please? Find out what happened.'

53

Fay Pride was one of the other pathologists on the duty roster for the Queen's Medical Centre forensic post-mortems. They had a similar system to how we were set up, collaborating with five forces, covering the whole area between them: Derbyshire, Leicestershire, Lincolnshire, Northamptonshire and Nottinghamshire.

Fay met me and Martin in the mortuary with the deceased Scott Rhodes. At nearly six foot she towered over me, with short grey hair and glasses.

'Well, you're keeping us busy right now,' she said snapping her gloves on her hands.

The sound echoed in the cold clinical room. The walls and floors were tiled, with the floors slanting towards drains. The tables around the sides of the room were all metal and easy to wipe and keep sterile and clean. There were several post-mortem tables in the room so that more than one could be done at once. But this afternoon it looked like it was just Rhodes.

'It's a strange series of murders, Fay.' I still hadn't managed to get my head around it. 'I'm hoping that something you come up with here will identify the killer so we can get to him before another one pops up and wipes him out.'

'What is it, Whack-a-Mole for murder?' She made a note on a pad at the side of her.

'Something like that. It's frustrating as hell is what it is. Someone is always one step ahead of us though and we need to pick it up.'

'Shall we see what we've got?'

Martin and I stepped closer.

The rope was matched up to the bruising around Rhodes' neck and was confirmed as the murder weapon. It was flagged up to be tested by the forensic science lab for any evidence of the offender.

'Look what we have here.' Fay pointed to a couple of small scratches on Rhodes' forearms near his wrist. 'Did you say he's been involved in a previous murder, this is your Whack-a-Mole murder case?'

'He has, that was why we were at his address in the first place. We were there to arrest him.'

'Well, these scratches may well be defensive wounds. Would you expect any on him?'

The technician took photographs around us.

'We would actually. The evidence that led us to him was DNA under the victim's nails. She scratched him.'

'What I'll do is swab these scratches to see if I can get anything back from your victim. If he's showered or bathed it's not likely, but it's worth a try.'

'Thanks, Fay.'

She was meticulous in examining Rhodes but found nothing further. Everything was hanging on the rope and the swab. Mostly the rope.

We headed back to the office. As soon as we stepped foot inside the incident room we were accosted by Pasha.

'Ma'am, the Digital Investigation Unit have phoned. They want you to phone back as soon as you're in, something to do with the laptop we seized from Rhodes' address this morning. They started work on it straight away as a priority.'

'Okay, thanks, Pasha.' I decided to make the call from the incident room rather than walking to my office.

The call was picked up by a female voice. 'DIU, how can I help?' It was Elizabeth Turner. We'd worked together during the Colin Benn case.

'Hi Elizabeth, it's Hannah Robbins, how are you?'

'I'm good thanks, Ma'am. And you?'

'Good too. Being kept on my toes here. Is it you I need to speak with?'

'It is actually, I thought it might be you so I picked up. It's the laptop your team submitted this morning. I have something you might be interested in.'

I was already interested. 'What is it?'

'Well, you say he was a teacher?'

'Yes, a comprehensive teacher, why? What do you have?'

'Mmmm, that's interesting. Or not.' She tapped some keys and kept me waiting a minute or two. 'Okay, he had a few thousand indecent images on his computer which he deleted a couple of days ago. All of them, all at once. Not one was saved. He deleted his cookies in an attempt to clear everything but I don't think he realises how good we are at our jobs and how computers store things.'

'So, up until a couple of days ago he had an active interest in children, but something happened to make him delete them all, is that what you're saying, Elizabeth?' I tried to put it all together.

'I can only tell you what the computer says. But yes, he had them all, and he did access them pretty regularly, until he didn't for a while and he got rid of them. Something must have triggered that, I'd say. And I thought you'd want to know that.'

'I do, thank you for getting onto it so quickly. I appreciate it.'

'My pleasure. I still have some work to do on this, but I'll do the report as soon as I've finished the full examination. Who knows what else is on here.'

I hung up and found a chair and sank down into it. This was interesting. A couple of days ago was when he'd killed Lucy. At that same time something prompted him to get rid of evidence he was a paedophile. I thought back to the briefing and the theories that had been thrown out.

If it was the suicide club why would he have deleted his images when he was going to kill someone? Why not wait until he had done it and just before he was about to be killed? Yes, he wouldn't like that stuff to be found by his family, but it suggested the possibility that someone else may be involved and that was why he deleted his images. Was he pressured somehow to do what he did? That was something we hadn't considered.

'Can I have everyone's attention please? I know some of you are out taking statements from Rhodes' neighbours, but those that are still here, I need you to listen in. I've had an interesting phone call from the Digital Investigation Unit and I think we need to discuss it.'

Conversations were halted and all eyes turned to me.

I relayed what Elizabeth had said about the images and their being deleted two days ago and I told them about my theory that someone else was involved, that someone had coerced him into doing what he did.

'What if someone found out about the images and threatened to expose him if he didn't do as he was told? It might be the reason he'd delete them all before he commits the murder and not after.'

'That's a wild theory there, Boss.' Martin leaned back and bit on a corner of thumb nail. 'You're saying we have a murderer who isn't actually doing the killing but is doing it by proxy?'

I thought about it. Was that what I was saying? About all of them?

'I think I am, Martin, which means we need to know what the rest of them are hiding. What was Lucy hiding? Or what else might have coerced her into—'

It came to me in a flash. 'Shit!'

Pasha got it at the same time. 'No, Boss. It couldn't have been...'

There were some blank stares.

'Faith was picked up from school by a man she didn't know. She wasn't returned until after Lucy had killed Tyler. What if the man had actually kidnapped Faith? Cheryl was adamant Lucy wouldn't have given Faith to a man, that she didn't know any male that Lucy would trust Faith with. Faith was certain she had never seen him before. She was bloody kidnapped and no one ever even knew. Fuck's sake. Lucy killed because she wanted to get her daughter back. No wonder she was crying when Faith came home that night.' The room was in uproar.

'We need to get the disc out and watch the interview you did with Faith, Pasha. School was hopeless when we went to interview them, though the guy covered his face up because it was cold. It now hangs on Faith's interview. We had no idea how pertinent it was at the time.' I shook my head. 'What did he have on Scott Rhodes and how do we track the next killer? Because it could be anyone. He's not choosing people with the same issues. There's no way for us to track him that way. And I'm certain we're looking for a male killer who's using people as his weapons.'

Pasha stood and walked to the secure exhibit room in the corner of the office to get the visually recorded interview she and Martin did of Faith. Who knew what we might get out of it now we knew what we were dealing with?

54

Pasha pushed the disc into the DVD player and we stood in front of the television and watched as the screen fuzzed. Then the soft interview suite came into view. It's like a living room, carpeted, with a couple of sofas, cuddly toys and other games and a table with a box of tissues between the sofas. There was a large green plant in the corner, all designed to make the space feel less like a police station and more like somewhere to have a comfortable chat. This room saw more distress in a day than any other.

The door opened and in walked the tiny-framed Faith. She was dressed in jeans and a cream jumper with Princess written across the front. Following behind her was Pasha, who towered over the tot of a girl. They both sat. If possible these interviews were done without parents and guardians present. If the child was distressed they could have one, but Faith had been brave and said she would go in alone. She'd been told it wasn't to talk about her mum but about what happened the day before. Cheryl, I knew, was perched outside, very probably biting every nail she had, while Faith was inside the interview room. She would have been desperate to burst inside and envelop the child in her arms and protect her from the world. They had been through so much.

Pasha found Faith a small pink and yellow teddy with flowers for eyes out of a box in the corner and Faith loved it. She alternated between hugging it close to her and flicking its eyes with her finger, fascinated by the flowers.

Martin, though not on the screen, would have been in the monitoring room, watching on a screen, making notes of the interview and keeping track of what was said. He would tell Pasha, through an earpiece, if she had missed a question he thought pertinent.

First of all Pasha made Faith feel comfortable, asking her about her favourite lessons at school and her best friends, and then they went through the rules of the room. That everything she said had to be the truth, that anything she said was okay, it was a safe room. That they would probably repeat things just to make sure they got them right, and if she didn't understand to ask and Pasha would do the same. For such a small girl, Faith went along with it really well.

'I'm impressed with her,' I said to Pasha.

'Yes, she did well. It could have been a lot more difficult.'

I nodded and turned back to the screen.

Pasha asked Faith to tell her about the day she was picked up from school, from the moment she first knew she was being collected to when she got home again.

The first account was as quick as you'd expect, with no detail at all. That a man picked her up from school because her mummy asked him to, they went to his house and she watched television and had something to eat. It was so long she even had a nap and then she went home again.

Pasha told her she had done well. That now they were going to go through it a little slower and was she okay with that?

Faith slumped her shoulders as though she was tired and had done enough work for the day. Pasha smiled at her and told her she was doing a great job telling her about the day and Faith bloomed under Pasha's approval.

'Tell me about the man. When you first saw him, what did you think of him?' Pasha asked.

'I didn't know him.' She hugged the teddy to her chest. 'But my mummy said to go with him and he was a friend. He smiled at me and gave me sweets.'

'What did he look like, Faith?'

Faith twisted in her seat.

'Take your time?' Pasha advised her. 'Remember I only want to know what you can actually remember. Nothing else.'

Faith looked at the teddy's eyes. 'He was tall.'

'Okay, that's good.'

'And he had brown hair.'

This wasn't enough and Pasha would need to try and expand her description. Faith didn't know it, but this was the description of our killer. And tall, to a four-year-old, that could be five foot. This was so hard with such a young child.

'What was his hair like?' Pasha tried.

'Short and brown. Can I see my grandma now?'

'You can soon, sweetie. Just a couple more questions, do you think you can do that?'

Faith nodded. She was so disorientated. Her world tipped upside down. Pasha pushed on knowing her time with the child was nearly up. 'Was there anything about him that made you remember him?'

'He had something weird over his teeth. It looked funny.'

'Can you describe it?' Pasha asked.

Faith put her chin to her chest and puffed out air. She was tired now. 'They were stuck to his teeth, little metal things on all of them. I asked him what it was and he said it was traces.'

'Traces?' Pasha mimicked back to her under her breath. 'Traces?' again. 'Oh! Do you think he might have said braces?'

'I think so.'

'Okay, you're doing great. That's a brilliant detail. Thank you.'

Faith shuffled in her seat and tried to lift herself up again.

'Do you know where you went when he took you to his house?'

She shook her head.

There was something about the word braces that was niggling at me. Why was it niggling at me, why?

'If I get your grandma in do you think you can tell me what the house looked like from the outside?' Pasha said on the screen as my mind raced to make a connection I knew was there somewhere. Pasha was trying, but it was hard interviewing such a small child.

'Oh my God!' I shouted into the room. 'Wallace. Mark Wallace, Faith's dad, he wears braces. Her dad took her that day from school.'

'You mean Faith's dad is the guy behind all this?' said Martin, voicing what I had realised myself.

Shit. 'It would seem so. We need to arrest Mark and stop the next murder before it happens.'

55

Selena Glass was sitting in front of her laptop as Zoya lay on the sofa in front of the television, a green goo cupcake held loose in her hand, green frosting smeared all over her face. She was in her element. It wasn't often that Selena allowed her to lie in front of the television this way, but she had to search the web and she needed some peace to do it. It was a surreal task. She was searching for ways in which she could kill without being caught because there was no way she was going to leave this beautiful little girl of hers. Zoya's life would not be turned upside down.

The problem was, when she typed 'how to get away with murder' into the search engine all that was returned was pages and pages of the television show by the same name. She had to be more creative. What about fire? Fire would kill and it would also destroy evidence of her being there. The only evidence it would leave would be that it was arson and therefore deliberate, and where it started, and by what method, but there would be no fingerprints or DNA involved. She needed to go shopping.

Just thinking about this made her head throb. How could she save a child by killing another person and in such a brutal way? Though she couldn't think of a way that wasn't brutal and wouldn't hurt the man she was directed to kill.

What she couldn't understand was how she had been drawn into this. What had she done to get on this person's radar? How had she been so terrible that this was the way her life was determined to go?

Selena scooped Zoya up, cupcake and all, and walked out of the house into the car, plopping Zoya into the car seat and strapping her in. She turned the heat right up because she hadn't bothered with coats and drove off the driveway. It was only ten minutes to the nearest petrol station where she bought a couple of cans of petrol and a box of matches and a couple of lighters for good measure. She didn't know which would work. The old woman behind the counter looked at her over her glasses.

'Bonfire, we've had a bit of a clear out,' Selena said. 'From the loft.' Stop talking, she told herself. People know you're lying when you keep talking. Liars talk too much. Stop talking.

She left the petrol station shop and clambered back into the car and gazed at Zoya, her beautiful, beautiful Zoya.

Zoya tucked her hand into the bag of sweets and smiled before shoving a handful into her mouth.

'They're nice? Do I get one?'

Zoya held out the bag in her pudgy little hand and Selena reached over and took one out. It was all sticky where Zoya had been putting her fingers in her mouth, then putting them back into the bag. Selena popped the sweet into her mouth, tasting the sugary sweet strawberry-flavoured rush straight away. It was her daughter's dribble coating the sweet, and she didn't care. Everything about that girl was precious.

Selena strapped herself in and pulled away. She could feel the extra weight of the cans in the boot as she turned corners and they shifted position. Their presence was dark like a cloud above her head, waiting to drop something ominous on top of her.

She was strong enough to hold it up though. It was either hold the huge pressure above her or Zoya goes back to Ethiopia and that was not an option.

56

I knocked on the door and Mark answered, barefoot in jeans and a T-shirt, totally not expecting us. 'DI Robbins? This is a surprise. Is something wrong with Faith?'

I shook my head. 'Can we come in please?'

I had taken Aaron with me as well as Martin and Pasha, who were standing around the rear of the property in case he decided to do a runner and leave by the back door. There was also a search team waiting in a van parked down the street. They would enter after the arrest was made and do a Section 32 search of the property. A search of the place where he was arrested.

'Of course, come in, come in.' He stood aside and ushered us into the hallway.

Everything looked the same as before. There was nothing out of place. Nothing to indicate that this man was a stone-cold killer who was coercing other people to do his bidding. I looked at him. He smiled, revealing braces over his teeth, just as Faith had described.

There was no reason to drag this out. 'If we asked Faith to look at a line-up with you in it, would she pick you out as having seen you before, Mark?'

He blanched. The colour draining from him. He licked his lips. 'I'm not sure I understand. What's this about?'

I had what I needed. 'You need to get some shoes on, Mr Wallace, I am arresting you on suspicion of the murders of Tyler Daniels, Lucy Anderson and Scott Rhodes and if we aren't in time, there will be one other to add to that list. Unless of course you talk to us and stop it. Also, you are under arrest for the kidnapping of Faith Anderson. You do not have to say anything, but it may harm your defence if you do not mention when questioned something you later rely on in court, anything you do say may be given in evidence.'

I pulled my handcuffs out my pocket. 'Grab a pair of shoes please, you're coming with us. We're going to be searching the property so you need to give us the key to lock up after we finish.'

Wallace puffed out his chest and blustered. 'You can't run rampant round my house like that. Not without a warrant.'

'I'm afraid we can, Mr Wallace, and we are. Find your shoes or we'll take you barefoot.'

'DI Robbins?' Kate Wallace appeared in the doorway, also barefoot. I had expected her to be at work. No doubt this was one of her mornings off. They had obviously both been relaxing at home before our appearance.

'Kate...' Wallace had nothing to say to his wife, everything was unravelling around him.

Her face was pale, her eyes glued to the handcuffs I had in my hands. 'DI Robbins?' again, she wanted answers.

'How much did you hear?' I asked her.

'I don't understand.' She wrapped her arms around her body. She'd heard it all.

'I'm sorry,' I said to her. 'But we have officers here who are going to search your premises. It's going to be a thorough search and they'll be here a while.'

She turned her attention to Wallace. 'Mark?'

He turned to me.

'Shoes?' I snapped, fed up of waiting for him. Now his face

greyed. He had no control and he did not like it. He pointed to a cupboard under the stairs. 'They're in there.'

I nodded to Aaron who went and pulled out a pair of trainers. Kate stood motionless and watched.

Wallace flushed. 'I don't want them, I want the other pair. Are you really so stupid?'

Aaron threw the trainers down at his feet. 'You're wearing them or you go as you are.' He was not taking any shit.

He bent down and put the trainers on. When he stood I applied the handcuffs to his wrists. He glared at me as I snapped the metal around him.

'Mark? Tell me you didn't do this,' Kate pleaded. 'Tell them this is all a mistake. They have the wrong man, you wouldn't kill the mother of your child. Mark?' her voice was starting to get hysterical now.

Mark stayed silent. He stared at his wife.

I radioed Martin to let him know we had secured Wallace and I let the search team know they were free to enter the house. A minute later there was a quick rap at the door. A group of uniformed officers entered, led by a petite woman with the brightest eyes I had ever seen. She smiled as she entered and her face lit up. 'Ma'am. You all sorted here?'

I returned her smile. 'Yes, we're all wrapped up, just about to leave, thank you. It's all yours. You know what we're looking at. Use a fine-toothed comb, search everywhere. At this point in time we don't know what is and isn't relevant so err on the side of caution.'

A quick nod of acknowledgement and she directed an officer carrying the search bag into the living room.

'You can't do this,' Wallace tried again. Spittle flying from his mouth. 'Not while I'm not here.'

I looked to Kate. She ran both hands through her hair. Her eyes now wild as she looked at the stream of cops walking through her house with blue gloves on ready to tear her house apart to look for items relating to murder. Several murders.

'Can I just ask you where you were on Tuesday?' I asked her. We were about ready to go, but if Wallace really had taken Faith then I needed to know if Kate was involved or if she was somewhere else or if Wallace had taken Faith to another location. The description of the room she had been in had been pretty non-descript, but that was only to be expected from such a young child.

'I was, erm...' she ran another hand through her head and looked to be working out her days. 'I was at work. I went in about ten am and by the time I came home it was nine pm. I did the evening clinic that day which was why I had a late start.'

We could easily corroborate that with her place of employment, but if this was true then it gave Wallace plenty of time to snatch Faith and take her back to her mum in the evening.

'Mark, say something.' She grabbed hold of his arm with her hands.

'Get off me you stupid woman.' He pulled away from her, jolting his arm out of her grasp. She flinched as though she had been punched, pulling her arms back to her body and clutching herself. Her eyes wide, her pallor now grey.

I pushed him forward by his rigid cuffs which were applied to the rear. 'We're going back to the station. Let's go.'

He planted his feet down and wobbled on the spot.

'It's going to be like that, is it?' I grabbed hold of the middle section of the rigid cuffs which was a solid black bar attached to the hard metal of the rings locked around his wrists. I dragged him in the direction I wanted him to move. There was no refusing when the metal of the cuffs dug into his wrists as I moved him sideways. He let out a howl in protest. I pulled some more and his feet sidestepped with me.

'Fucking bitch, you can't do that.'

'There's a lot of things you're telling me I can't do, Mr Wallace, and it seems to me I can and you don't know as much as you like to think you do. So if I were you, I'd get used to the way things are. You're making this more difficult when there's really no need. If I let go, are you going to walk properly to the car?'

He nodded.

Aaron was silent. He knew I could handle Wallace and that any interruption or interference from him would undermine me and make me look as though I couldn't do my job. He was always there when I needed him and that included silently watching while I handled some things alone.

We walked out of the front door. Already there were curtains twitching as people looked to see why police were on the street. Even though ours were plain cars, the van the uniform search team had turned up in was a full-liveried police van. As we walked Wallace out of the door in handcuffs, a door a couple of houses down opened and a heavy-set male stepped out, arms crossed over his chest, a scowl on his face. I guessed he was not a fan of the police but by the way he was looking at Wallace he was jumping to some conclusions of his own about why we were arresting him and they were not the correct ones. I wondered why people did that. Why the most horrific thing was what people presumed of their neighbours if they saw them arrested. Yet when they find out they're a killer they come out the woodwork to say they never saw it coming, they were always a good and quiet neighbour. Yet here was this guy looking as though he could rip Wallace's head off with his bare hands.

I pushed his head down and helped him into the rear of the car. The quicker we were out of here, the better. Wallace was more subdued now. The walk of shame had eaten away at his bravado. It was easy to be brave and loud when you're in your own home. It's not so easy when you're in the street being faced down by everyone, even if most of them are hiding behind their curtains.

Now we had to get Mark Wallace back to the Bridewell custody suite and get him into an interview room. We needed to know who the next killer was before he struck and we had another victim on our hands.

57

I booked Mark Wallace into custody. The Bridewell custody suite was based in the city centre and was a large three-storey block with desks and cells on all the floors. Before the cuts each individual police station had its own custody block so you could work from your own office and have your offender locked up in the same place. There were now only two working custody suites in the whole of Nottinghamshire and every offender went through them. And in the Bridewell you had to sit in the one report-writing room. It wasn't very big and if the place was busy, it was cramped. Plus, you had to remember to take everything you could possibly need with you for the interview.

I liaised with Aaron while Wallace was fingerprinted and photographed and had his DNA taken. The custody suite was not too crowded at the moment and we were getting through the system at a reasonable rate. Some days it could be bedlam and everything slowed down as staff were run off their feet.

'What do you think?' I asked Aaron.

'I don't think he's going to talk to us. He was pretty antagonistic. It was like the minute he knew the game was up he was going to be as much trouble as he could be. Maybe he knows we're still going to find it difficult to pin the rest on him. Even kidnapping Faith is going to be hard because we don't have Lucy telling us that he didn't have permission. And he is her dad, the text did come from her number, so what we need to do is see if there is evidence on his computer of him cloning her phone and sending a text to the school.'

This case was so complicated. There was so much work involved in it.

I grimaced. 'Even though Cheryl is saying Lucy didn't want Mark involved in Faith's life, we have no way to prove that she didn't change her mind. That she didn't tell him about her and this was their first meeting. Though it is an odd first meeting, we just don't have the evidence for our case. We need to find more from the search at his property. I'll phone the search team to see what they have so far.'

Aaron nodded and continued with the interview plan he was writing up.

I put in the call and the PC who had been first through the door at Wallace's address picked up.

'How's it going there?' I asked.

'It's slow, Ma'am. We don't know what we're looking for specifically. I'm going to go out on a limb and say most of the evidence is probably on his computer so we've taken that straight to the Digital Investigation Unit while the search continues, and hope that they can get you something useful.'

'That's good thinking, thank you. Have you given them my details so they know we have someone locked up with this job?'

'Yes, Ma'am. They have everything they need.'

I thanked her, hung up, and relayed the conversation to Aaron. 'Let's see if he's willing to confess to anything and go from there first, shall we?'

I spoke to the custody sergeant at the desk and Wallace was brought out of his cell, where he'd been placed after processing. We walked him to an interview room. A plain square room with a table and four chairs and a CD recording device on the wall.

I placed cardboard cups on the table: coffees, one for me and Wallace, and water for Aaron.

Once the device had been loaded up with brand new discs I started the interview, making the introductions. Wallace had not wanted a solicitor. This was more common than people thought it would be, even with the more serious offences. I reminded him of his right to legal advice and that he could stop the interview at any time to seek that advice. This was an ongoing right while he was under arrest in custody. He was reminded of the reason for his arrest and cautioned again, the caution was explained in full for him.

After the official script had been gone through, I asked him an open question to see what he would say. 'Tell me about the murder of Lucy Anderson.' I started with Lucy because I didn't know if Tyler was an official target but Lucy most definitely was.

Wallace twisted the cup in front of him on the table. 'I don't know what you want me to tell you. I don't know anything about what happened to Lucy.'

'When did you last see her?'

He dropped into silence. You could see him thinking about where to take his answer. The silence lengthened out. No, he didn't have to answer the questions, but he hadn't had legal advice.

I couldn't allow the silence to stretch on any longer, it would seem like oppression.

'What about when you last spoke to Lucy?'

'She asked me to pick Faith up from school, said she'd text the school to let them know and told me what time to drop her home. Also asked me not to tell Faith who I was to her – which I never. You can ask her.'

'When did she ask you this?' I needed to tie him down to specifics so we could disprove it.

'I can't remember.' He scratched his head.

'How did you have the conversation?'

Silence again.

We couldn't prove something we didn't have. He was making this incredibly difficult for us. But it wasn't his job to make it easy, it was our job to find the evidence.

I drank my coffee and watched him over the rim. It was going to be a long evening. We had three murders to question him about and we had to get to the bottom of the latest one before there was another.

58

John Crowley was in his office at work in the city. The screen on his computer was filled with facts and figures of the deal that would be going ahead tomorrow but he couldn't take them in. His world was over. How had he had been pushed into what he had done he would never know. He would never be able to look at Trisha or Lizzy or Blake again. The three people he loved the most and now he could no longer spend time with them or look them in the eye. He was ruined.

A ruined man.

It had been awful.

As he had pulled on the rope he had been able to feel the fight, the physicality of Scott Rhodes, as he struggled to stay alive. He was a living, breathing, strong man, but John had the upper hand because he was behind and above him with a rope around his neck. Not many people would have been able to get out of that.

John had felt Rhodes' muscles flex in terror through the rope. He felt them push against the rope as he pulled back which made him jerk back harder in fear. John didn't want to fight, he wanted it to be over and the more Rhodes fought, the tighter John pulled. His knee in the back of the sofa for leverage. The sheer terror of what he was doing drove him forward because he wanted it to be over and Rhodes was stopping it from being over and John needed it to stop and if he pulled harder it would be done with and he could go home. He pulled and pulled, panic coursing through his veins. The guy didn't stand a chance.

It was as though Rhodes gave up. He stopped fighting. John thought it was the end but it wasn't. Rhodes was still alive, just, but the struggle had gone out of him and he had to keep pulling against a man who had said fair enough, you win. That was even harder than one who was fighting for his life. To take the last breath of a man who stopped fighting you, it was like kicking a puppy. You just don't do it and yet he had. He remembered the images he had been sent of Lizzy and he pulled for that last minute and finished the job. No one was going to do that to his precious family. He would let no one destroy them. Even if it meant that he could no longer spend time with them, at least they were now safe. He envisaged that Rhodes was the person who could hurt them and he finished what he set out to do.

When he felt it was over he let go of the rope and he fled. His brain went blank and all he could think of was getting out of there. He couldn't be found in the room. He had to get out. He had to get away from Rhodes. Away from what he had done. He couldn't believe this was his life. He had actually done this. He was in this world. He backed away from the sofa and he ran.

Now he was consumed by guilt. He had taken a life. He only had an email to go on that Rhodes was worthy of what he had done to him. Now he was no better. What could people say about him? How was he supposed to carry on with his life? How could he face those he loved?

John Crowley placed his head in his hands and he wept. He wept for Scott Rhodes and he wept for himself. Mostly he wept for himself. For what he had become, for what he had done, for where that had left him, for how he couldn't continue his life this way.

59

Selena took Zoya home, made dinner. Cooked for the family as though the world was turning as it always did. Simon walked through the door, kissed her on the cheek as she stood over the hob where the pan bubbled with pasta.

'Mmm, I'm not sure which smells better, you or the bolognaise.' He nuzzled into her neck, his arms around her waist.

'If you know what's good for you, I think you do know the right answer.' She twisted her head and kissed him hard as though she had not seen him for the longest time.

When they pulled apart he nuzzled again. 'You smell so good. Who needs food?'

'That's better.' She smiled, leaned her cheek onto his head.

'Daddy!' Zoya came running into the kitchen. Simon let go of Selena, bent at the knees and picked up his daughter as she ran into his arms, then he stood and she flew into the air, giggling.

'My gorgeous girl, how are you today?' She dropped onto his hip and wrapped her arms tight around his neck.

'Good, we made gooey cakes and bought petrol.'

'You did, did you? You've had a busy day.'

Selena twitched in her skin. There was no way Simon would even think Zoya meant anything other than petrol for the car but hearing her say it out loud, made her legs quake beneath her.

'I need to serve dinner up. I'm going out this evening,' she said, rushing her words, desperate to get it all over with, a band tightening around her chest causing her to gasp as she talked.

'Are you okay?' Simon looked over Zoya at her.

Selena put a hand to her chest. 'Yes, sorry, something caught in my throat. I'll get dinner served.'

Simon placed Zoya onto the floor. 'I'd better get myself cleaned up if Mummy is going to feed us.' He looked at Selena. 'Where are you off to this evening?'

She struggled not to stumble over her words, her tongue too big for her mouth. 'I thought I might go to the gym, I'm feeling a little flabby.'

Simon laughed. Selena knew she had a good physique. 'Internally flabby, I feel unfit. I could do with a little exercise. All of us could do with more exercise than we get, Simon.'

He gave her a look as her tone cut him off. Her fear making her short with him. He nodded. 'Okay, if you're feeling the need, I'll take care of Zoya and you can go and make yourself feel less flabby.' She could see he tried not to laugh again. 'Do I have time for a quick shower, get out of my work clothes and into something more comfortable before you serve dinner?'

Selena nodded, her throat thickening, making talking difficult as she struggled to hold herself together.

He gave her a smile, rumpled the hair on the top of Zoya's head and walked out of the room.

Selena stirred the pan of bolognaise then looked at her watch. It wouldn't be long until she did this. Until she became someone else. She looked down at her beautiful daughter. She would turn into anyone so long as Zoya didn't have to leave the country and go back to Ethiopia. People often said they would die for their children but how many parents would be willing to kill to protect their child?

60

Mark Wallace was in his cell having something to eat so Aaron and I took a walk into the city centre to get a sandwich.

As we walked back towards the Bridewell my phone rang.

'Boss, it's Pasha. We have some results back on the rope.'

'Really? What is it?'

'A DNA profile.' There was a but coming.

'What's the problem, Pasha?' We stopped on the bridge over the River Trent. The wind blew cold through my coat. I pulled on my scarf with my free hand. The water below me was dark and grey as it flowed under the bridge, a canal boat moored at the side bobbing about, silent and alone.

'He's not on our system. We don't know who he is.'

'Damnit.'

'I'm sorry, Boss.' She sounded tired.

'It's not your fault. I'll see if we can get anything else out of Wallace. At least if we catch someone we have their DNA to match it against.'

I could practically hear her nodding on the other side of the phone.

'Is it not going well?' she asked.

'Not as we'd hoped. He says he was asked to pick Faith up from school. He's talking about things that he knows can't be proved now Lucy is dead, and isn't saying anything for the areas of the investigation that might trip him up. He's clever, I'll give him that. But I want to know if he is behind this, why did he do it? Why did he kidnap Faith, why did he want Lucy to kill Tyler? Did he know Tyler? We've still got some work to do, that's clear.'

After I hung up I relayed the call to Aaron.

'So we have DNA but no one to match it to?' he clarified.

'That's about what we have, yep.'

He nodded. Thinking things through. Though I was sure not even Aaron could untangle the mess we currently had.

'If Mark doesn't talk, I'm not sure we have grounds to hold him, Aaron. We know he won't have had permission to take Faith, but can we prove it now Lucy is dead? It's up to Digital Forensics. If they can find anything, on his phone or his computer, on how he contacted school as though it was from Lucy's phone. If we get that we have a chance. But that's all we'll have to go to CPS with. Is it enough?'

Aaron shook his head. 'I don't know. And I don't know if we have enough time to find them. Even if we keep him as long as we can including extensions. We can but try, Hannah.'

61

I knocked on the door and Kate Wallace answered. She was wearing an overlarge cardigan and had her arms wrapped around her body, pretty much the same stance as I'd last seen her. Behind her I could hear the activity of the search team. Quiet conversations and movement as they went about their business as proficiently but as discreetly as they could.

'DI Robbins, I wasn't expecting to see you again today, do you want to come in?' She laughed. It was forced and brittle. 'I'm sure you could probably come in whether I invited you in or not. She stepped to the side.

'Thank you.' I gave her a small smile and stepped into the house.

She closed the door behind me. 'Are you here to speak to your team or here to see me?' She pulled the cardigan tighter around herself.

'You actually. Can we go and sit down?' I indicated the living room beyond.

She walked into the room and I followed. 'How are you bearing up?' I asked her.

'I've phoned into work, let them know I won't be in for my shift today but that I'll be in tomorrow. I have a feeling that whatever is happening I'll need the distraction of work and the comfort of spending time with my colleagues.'

'I think you're right. A lot of people take time off work during a big change in their life like this but then they find they don't quite know what to do with themselves. Going into work sounds like a sensible option.'

'Is it what you would do if you were in this position, DI Robbins?'

The question was barbed. She thought it unlikely that I would ever be in this position. She had no idea of knowing that I had nearly lost my career because of my drug dealing sister, Zoe, a few years ago.

'I think I would,' I replied, mirroring her as she seated herself on the sofa.

She smiled. It was a polite but dead kind of smile. 'How can I help you? What I'd really like is for you to tell me what is happening. I don't understand what has happened today. What has happened to my life. It has just imploded and I'm left standing in the remains of what I thought it was.'

In the corner of the room one of the uniform cops was on his knees quietly going through a set of drawers. Taking everything out, examining it and taking the next item out. Occasionally he would bag an item up.

'You heard the arrest this morning?' I asked her.

'Yes, but I don't understand. Mark isn't a killer.'

'I can't go into too much detail but we do have information that indicates Mark orchestrated the killings.'

Kate shook her head. 'I just can't take this in. Who has he killed? Other than Lucy.' Her voice broke on Lucy's name and tears started to fall. 'He never said a bad word about Lucy. She was his first love. You know, the one you never forget and will always love no matter if you move on. I didn't mind that, he chose me and he loved me.' She went quiet and I left her a moment, I wanted to know what she was thinking and with some space she would speak again. 'At least I thought he loved me until this morning. He was a different man.'

'Kate, I checked with work and I know you were there while Mark abducted Faith. When you came home did you notice anything different in the house or about Mark? Any signs that he'd had a child in the house?'

She rubbed her tears away with the back of her hand. 'You think he brought her to the house?'

'He might have done.'

She looked around the room. Her eyes stopping temporarily on the cop in the corner before she brought her attention back to me. 'I can't remember thinking anything out of the ordinary.' She stopped and thought again. Looked around some more, her attention wandering around the house. 'There might have been more pots in the kitchen than I would have expected for him being on his own. I think I just presumed he was hungry that day. There was nothing else out of place. Oh and the television when I put it on, it was on a children's channel, I had to switch it over to get the news. I thought it odd at the time but assumed he'd been feeling melancholy.'

'What do you mean?'

'We can't have children, DI Robbins. That's why we were both so shocked when you told us he had a child and why I was so open to taking her in. Though if what you are saying is true, you're telling me Mark already knew he had a child and had met her and by force.' She shook her head.

'I'm sorry. You're sure you can't have children?' I knew it was a stupid question as soon as it was out of my mouth.

Kate did me the honour of telling me as such. 'I think I'd know something so personal.'

'I didn't mean... I'm sorry. It's just Mark said you were discussing children. He didn't mention that you couldn't.'

She let out a long sigh. 'It seems that Mark hasn't been truthful about a lot of things, doesn't it. How am I supposed to get back on with my life?'

I hated the effect these crimes had on the people close by. Even the people close to the perpetrators. They rarely knew what was happening and their lives were turned upside down as they reconciled the heinous crimes their loved ones had committed with the person they knew and loved. 'In the way you already talked about. By continuing with life. By going to work. Relying on your colleagues and by having a life and not letting this define you.'

'That's good advice, DI Robbins. But that's where the phrase easier said than done comes in.'

62

Selena Glass watched from the table as Simon placed the plates into the dishwasher.

'You're sure you're not hungry?' he asked for the sixth time that evening. He hated to eat alone. Though Zoya had eaten with him, he classed it as alone if Selena hadn't eaten too.

She was too nervous to eat. 'I can't go to the gym on a full stomach,' she said. 'I'll eat when I get home or grab something on the way back.' She crossed her legs and wrapped a hand around her knees.

Zoya looked up from the picture she was drawing. 'Can I come to the gym with you, Mummy?'

'I don't think it's for little girls, sweetie. Maybe when you're a little older, okay?'

Zoya stuck her bottom lip out.

Simon smiled at her. He knew, or he thought he knew, she wanted an hour out of the house free of being a mummy. But, little did he know how much her priorities had changed this afternoon. How much she wished she could be a stay-at-home mummy and never let the little girl out of her sight. She would have Zoya cling to her leg as much as she needed to if it meant she was safe and Selena didn't have to do what she was about to do.

She stood from the table. 'I'd better get changed.' She hated the lies. She and Simon had been through so much and here she was lying to him. Telling him she was going to one place when the reality was she was going to another. To kill a man.

In the bedroom, she slipped out of her jeans and pulled on her jerseys ready for a couple of hours supposedly jogging and rowing in the gym. Sitting on the bed, she pushed her feet into her trainers and tied the laces. She really wanted to tell Simon what was happening tonight. Let him in on the truth. But he would try to stop her. Even if that meant physically holding her back and preventing her leaving the house. His mind wouldn't think about working through the implications of that move, of stopping her going out and committing the act she had planned. All he would be worrying about would be stopping her murdering an innocent person. It wouldn't be until much, much later that he would understand what it meant, not doing it. Not only what they had lost, but what Zoya had lost, her whole life, being forced to travel back there, to a place she no longer knew or recognised. It wasn't their home.

She made it to the back door. 'Simon.' She looked at him. His hair, that was supposed to be brushed one way but always at the end of the day seemed to want to go the other way. It made him look like a young schoolboy. Even in his early thirties.

He lifted his head from the paper. 'What is it, love? Having a change of heart? Want to snuggle up with me instead? I can raise your heartrate for you if you want me to.' He gave her a cheeky grin.

Oh, how she loved this man. She shook her head at him, a small smile played on her lips. 'Don't wait up for me if you're tired.'

His face dropped. 'How late does this gym stay open?'

'It's not the gym, but you know sometimes the women at these places go for a drink afterwards. I'm just preparing.' In case she couldn't come home. In case she was in shock. In case she was in a police station. There were many possible scenarios.

He stood and strode over to her, wrapped his arms around her shoulders. 'I know you need this. I'll be here waiting for you. And the offer to raise your heartbeat is open-ended.' He winked at her and went back to his paper.

She walked out and closed the door behind her.

It was freezing in the dark night air. She flipped the collar of her jersey jacket all the way up so it touched her ears. Not that it did much good. February was a brutal time of year for the cold weather. She hated the darkness and the cold.

The drive over to John Crowley's seemed to take forever. Her nerves were eating her up from the inside the whole time she was driving. She would do this and then she would go to the gym and have a quick shower before she went home. Simon would be suspicious if she went home not sweaty, but not showered and damp.

And then she was there, outside the glorious five-bedroom detached home that belonged to John Crowley. Whatever he did for a living he had obviously done well. The house was beautiful. It seemed a shame to burn it down. If she could only think that it was the house she was burning and not the man inside. In fact, that would be what she would tell herself. It was just a house. A pile of bricks.

Her brain refused to function. She had no idea what she was doing or why she was doing it any more. She was lost in a world of darkness. No longer knew who she was. Shrouded in an inky shadowy world where her thoughts were not her own and her life belonged to the creatures within the gloom. It was unbelievable that she had been driven to something like this. She was a person who helped and saved people. Just look at what she had done for Zoya, and yet here she was about to do the most heinous crime there was. All this was clogging up her brain cells, she felt disorientated.

Selena parked down the street so her car would not be noticed and picked the two jerrycans out of the boot along with the box of matches. With a baseball cap pulled down over her head and her hair pushed up into the cap she wrapped a scarf around her face, hiding as much as she could. Though there was every possibility that she could be caught, but all that mattered was that Simon didn't know anything about it and Zoya would be safe. Simon would then be able to take care of Zoya. She would take the blame and her loved ones would be safe.

The jerrycans, one in each hand, balanced her out. She tried to be quiet walking up the driveway to the house. The lights were on so she knew he was home. That was all she needed. To light this and go. Her brain was screaming at her to get this done and flee. There had to be a slim chance she could get out of this unscathed and still live her life with her family.

This was just a pile of bricks she reminded herself as she thought of her own family and it slid into her mind that there was someone inside this house right now. It's just a pile of bricks. I'm doing this for Zoya and for Simon.

As she walked up the drive she was suddenly lit up in a vast white glow as the security light came on above her. Two jerrycans in her hands. Her heart started to speed up in her chest. She needed to move and fast. She looked around her. Both sides of the property had a large bush running the length of the drive to block out the neighbours and all the curtains were closed. No one at this moment in time could see her. If she knew anything about security lights and how lazy people were, they would presume it was a stray cat and ignore it unless something else triggered their attention. She needed to be quiet.

Selena looked at the pile of bricks. It spanned the whole of the drive. There was no way around the rear of the premises other than through a large six-foot gate that was attached to the side of the house. She tiptoed as fast as she could to the gate, to get out of the security light that was raining down on her and pushed herself against it and waited for the light to trip back off again.

Her heart felt as though it was going to beat straight out of her chest. She was standing in front of the property with the cans. She had to move and do it quickly. Yes, she was prepared to be caught but she damn well didn't want to be if she could help it. Now not only was her brain feeling fried but her whole body was starting to let her down. She took a deep breath in and pushed the bar on the gate to open it. It didn't budge. It was locked somehow. She couldn't see a chain and padlock, there must be a bolt on the other side of the gate. She needed to get over it. Her brain scrambled in a panic for what she could do. If she only set the fire at the front of the property it would be far too easy for the occupant to escape out the rear. She had to fire up the rear door as well. But she couldn't get back there. If she didn't get it done then she would lose Zoya who would be sent back to Ethiopia. She couldn't allow that to happen. She had to find a way around this.

Her arms were aching from carrying the canisters. She placed them on the floor at the foot of the gate. Could she get over the gate if she stood on one of the cans? It wouldn't offer much of a lift up but maybe enough of a boost that she could hoist herself up and over? After all, as Simon had alluded to earlier, she was reasonably fit and agile and with some effort it might be possible. She'd have to do it carrying the other can in her hand though.

As quietly as she could and now shrouded by shadow she pushed the can sideways right up to the gate and kept it upright so it was tall and gave her more lift. Tentatively she placed a foot on the canister and lifted the other can in her hand. Now she had to try to get over without making a racket and drawing attention to herself. She was shaking as she balanced on the petrol can. Her leg threatening to give out beneath her. She was terrified of what she was doing. Her whole mind and body were running away with her. She had never felt so out of control. Selena tried to take a deep breath in to steady herself but only had the urge to cough when the cold air hit her lungs. She covered her mouth with her spare hand and tears fell down her face. She desperately wanted this to be over. How had she managed to get herself in this position?

She had to get on with it. She wanted to go home and hug her daughter and snuggle up with her husband. She wanted to put all this behind her.

The gate was solid wood and didn't budge as she grabbed hold of the top of it with both hands causing the can she was holding to stick out towards her, the heavy contents off balancing her. With an enormous pull of effort Selena pulled herself up her right leg scrabbling for purchase as she hefted it up towards the top of the gate. Muscles she didn't often use screamed in complaint. Blood pumped loudly in her head. It was lucky she was wearing gloves otherwise with the strength of the grip she was using she would most definitely have splinters in her hands. Her bottom stuck out in the air as her arms and one leg grappled to keep her steady on top of the gate.

She realised as she straddled the wood that she would have to do this all over again to get back to safety. The blood in her head pounded even harder.

Then she was dropping down to the other side. Into a vast back garden that was all manicured lawn and hedges to keep the neighbours from view.

Her heart was thundering in her chest now. Could she really do this? She wanted to run away as fast as her feet would allow. Digging into her pocket she pulled out her phone and pressed the home key causing the screen to light up and show the photo she had of Simon and Zoya laughing together on the floor of their home. Simon had just finished tickling Zoya and she had turned around and attempted to tickle him in return. He had been in hysterics which caused her to laugh as much as when he tickled her. Whether he was laughing because of her tickles, which Selena very much doubted, or whether he was laughing at her adorable attempt, she didn't know. But they were both in stitches and it was one of her favourite photographs of the two of them.

This was why she was doing this.

She could not lose this child and not to a country she did not know or recognise. It was unbearable. A band tightened around her chest at the thought of this happening. She would do everything in her power to stop Zoya being sent away in such a heartless way.

The weight of the canister in her hand reminded her of how she would do that. She was here to carry out the demand of some lunatic that had contacted her. Surveying the rear of the house she found the back door and strode over to it keeping tight to the edge of the house so as to not alert another security light of her existence.

There was no letter box in the door. She would just have to set the door alight rather than pour contents into the house back here and she would have to be quicker getting round to the front to set the front alight so he couldn't escape. If she made this one small to start with then it might give her the time she needed. It might not alert him that it was ablaze. Just a small fire at the base of the door. That was all she needed here.

Oh my God, was she really going to kill this man?

A door opened. 'Hurry up, Teddy, it's cold out here.' Selena's heart nearly stopped in her chest. It was next door through the thick bush at the side of the house.

They were letting their dog out. Teddy was a dog, she could hear him padding about and sniffing along the hedge.

'Teddy, hurry on up. I'm not standing here all night.' The woman was impatient and Teddy was not going to get long to do his business. Selena couldn't say she blamed her now she thought about it. It was cold out here. And now all she could do was cling to the wall of the house and hope the dog wasn't interested and didn't care what was going on in his neighbour's garden. After all, he wasn't here to guard his neighbour's garden.

'What's so damn interesting about next door?'

Shit.

'Get on with your business or you're staying out there.'

Selena held her breath. She didn't dare breathe in case the dog could hear her and alerted the neighbour to her presence. Neighbours were good to each other. Especially in nice estates like this one. She could hear Teddy with his nose pressed close to the bush his interest piqued by something on the other side.

By her being where she shouldn't be.

'Teddy, I'm warning you.'

Teddy moved away from the bush and Selena dared to take a shallow breath. Her hand gripped white and hard around the canister in her hand which felt as though it was seizing up. Her brain felt as though it was seizing up. How could she do this? She could barely function. This was not her and yet here she was, going through the actions like a robot. This was going to destroy her but better that than Zoya be destroyed.

'Good boy, now get inside.' The door closed and all was quiet. Selena sucked in a deep lungful of air. She hadn't realised just how still she had been and how that had included her breathing. Her chest hurt. Her whole body hurt, in revolt for what she was doing. She bent over, put the can on the ground and put her hands on her knees. Tried to level out her breaths. She needed to get herself together. She needed to finish this. She needed to finish this for Zoya.

Picking up the canister again she moved to the rear door, unscrewed the lid and closed her eyes. There was no turning back now. She was here and she was going to do it.

Very gently she tipped the can up and poured a line of liquid along the bottom of the door. The smell of petrol burnt her nose. It was so strong she was sure the smell alone was enough to disturb the occupant. She had to be quick now she had started. She pulled the matches out of her pocket. Her hand was shaking. Her legs were still shaking. She was utterly terrified.

With one strike there was flame and with one throw there was fire. She had done it. The bottom of the door was alight.

She picked up the can and ran for the gate. She had to move quickly now. The chain of events had started and she had to finish them before he escaped or before she was caught. There really was a chance she could do this without getting caught.

The gate loomed up in front of her. She would have to leave the can here. She pushed it up to the gate, stood on it and grabbed the top of the panel gate, pulling hard and twisting her leg up and over. Then she was on the other side. She grabbed the second can. It was a good job she had brought two cans after all.

She stumbled around to the front with the one full jerrycan the weight of it making her limp along unevenly, the can banging against her leg hard. She could feel the bruises raising on her skin as she lurched around to the front. Again clinging to the bricks of the house to avoid the light. Once she was standing in front of the door she used her fingers and pushed open the letter box and poured the contents of the second can through and into the house. The can was difficult to manoeuvre so the liquid poured not just through the letter box but down the front of the door. The smell was overpowering. She definitely needed a shower before she returned home. She probably needed to throw the trainers away. It seemed as though she was getting more fuel on them than she was getting into the house. The canister was unwieldy and she was rushing. She kept tipping until the contents were gone. Nothing stirred inside the house. So far, so good.

Now came the difficult bit, once she lit the match there was no going back, both exits would be blocked by flames. She thought back to Zoya and Ethiopia. How she had felt when she had been over there. The stifling heat, the poverty like nothing she had ever known in her life. She wouldn't send Zoya back to that.

Selena ran her tongue over her lips and nearly coughed as the rough taste of petrol bit into her tongue and lips and the back of her throat. She clamped her mouth shut. She had to carry this out. If she didn't not only would she lose Zoya but she would go to prison. For saving a child from a life not knowing when she would eat, a suitable roof over her head or an education.

Selena struck a match against the box for the second time. It fizzed into bright orange life, she held it in her hands, staring as the flame jumped about on the tiny stick. There was no going back. She threw the match at the door.

Selena staggered backwards as the door flared up with a whoosh in a bright wall of flame remembering she had fuel on her feet. Her heart nearly burst out of her chest at the ferocity. Her hand flew up to her chest to hold it in. The heat burning her face. Another step back and her heel hit something solid. She stumbled, nearly falling onto her arse. It would be mere moments before attention was here. She had to move. She moved faster than she had ever moved in her life. She turned away from the door and she ran down the drive, the security light blaring into life and lighting her way, and ran to her car as fast as her legs would carry her. The heat from the house bore down on her. Whether it was real or imagined, it was brutal. The heat searing, the glow bright in the sky, like a beacon informing the neighbourhood of her presence, of what she had done, of the events unfolding, here at this address, of the tragedy that was happening in the here and now to a man by the name of John Crowley. Trapped in his home unable to escape and doomed to death by suffocation or burning.

She stopped at the corner of the drive and remembered what the man had asked for, what he had demanded. He wanted a photo. It would take her precious moments to take it. Moments that would risk her freedom, but rather her freedom than Selena's. She pulled her phone out of her pocket again and swiped to the camera app, snapped the glowing house and ran to her car.

Selena locked herself in her car and shuddered. She could smell the fire on herself in the enclosed space, the petrol, the acrid and bitter smell at the back of her nose and throat.

She looked at the photograph she had just taken and tears slipped down her face. She was now a killer. She emailed the photo then turned the car over and pushed her foot down on the accelerator. She had to get away, she didn't know where, anywhere but here.

How had she done something so horrific? What an awful way to die. How could she do this to someone? Yes she had to save Zoya, but she couldn't think of a worse way to die than burning. All because she was scared to get any closer to her victim. She didn't have to look him in the eye. She didn't have to physically touch him. She didn't have to give them an explanation or say that she was sorry. She could do it and run.

Because she was scared.

And now she had doomed John Crowley to the worst death imaginable.

63

John Crowley's phone rang. He looked at the screen. Trisha. She would want to know where he was. Why he hadn't yet come home.

How could he face her? He needed to find a way to put on a mask so he could engage with her as he always had done before he returned home to his family. The family he had done this for.

John Crowley rejected the call and looked out of the office window, through the darkness and across the city.

64

Back in the Bridewell, Aaron and I grabbed a couple of cans of pop out of the vending machine. Wallace would be available to interview again in about ten minutes. Because he was here for the long haul it was important that he was given appropriate breaks for meals. We couldn't keep going without feeding him or allowing him a toilet break.

I pulled my phone from my pocket. 'I'll call Digital Forensics, see if they have anything on him yet.'

Aaron yawned. He was a bit pale. I had to remember he was still recovering from a heart attack four months ago.

'Are you okay? Do you need me to get someone else to come over and relieve you?' I asked.

He shook his head. 'No, I'm fine. I'm a little tired, but it's nothing I can't cope with. Mostly it's this shoddy strip lighting in here that's doing it to me. You don't look your best either, you know.'

And I knew if Aaron was telling me that then he damn well meant it and I ran a finger under my eyes, as if I could rub away any dark shadows.

Elizabeth picked up the line in Digital Forensics again. I told her I was calling about the Wallace job. 'How's it going?' I asked.

'It's slow,' she said. 'He has a lot of stuff on his computer and it's stored in all different places. You know we don't examine a computer the same way you go into one at the front end, don't you?'

I nodded then realised she couldn't see me. 'Do you have anything at all yet?'

'He does have some software on here that can send a text message from a phone number that isn't yours. The company that provides the software keeps all the text messages that are sent so that's good news. We've applied for the information from Wallace's account and should hear from them maybe within 24 hours.' I showed Aaron the thumbs up sign and he gave me a big smile. Elizabeth carried on. 'We haven't found anything with Tyler Daniel's name on yet. It doesn't look like his name is on the computer at all.'

'That's strange,' I said.

'Though,' Elizabeth continued, 'he does have a photograph of the accident on his computer. It looks to have been taken on a mobile phone and also looks like it was taken at the time of the accident because there are no blue lights or other people standing around. I would suggest this might be the person who ran over Tyler Daniels.'

I was sitting up straight now. 'Can you—'

'Like I said, computers are complex things and this job itself is complex, there are so many items you need us to look for, but yes, we are going to look for images of the other murders before police arrived at the scene. If so, this might go some way to proving that Mark Wallace is behind the murders.'

I stood up. 'If I was there, Elizabeth Turner, I would kiss you.' My blood was pumping through my veins so hard my pulse was racing in my throat.

Aaron looked up at me. He made a rolling motion with one of his hands, telling me to wind the conversation up so I could tell him what we had. I laughed at him, then bounced on my feet, I was so excited.

I ended the call with Elizabeth and relayed it to Aaron.

'So there's evidence on there that he cloned Lucy's phone and there's a photograph of the murder victim, Tyler Daniels, before anyone else could have taken it but the murderer. Do I have that right?' He was trying to get his head around it.

'As far as I can tell, Elizabeth didn't want to get my hopes up too high. She hadn't finished examining the computer. We have to be careful. I think we're going to have to hold him for an extension to give her time to go through it. It may be that there are photographs of the other victims if there's photographs of the first one.'

My body was fizzing, we were that close to the truth. I could feel it, I could very nearly touch it and I just wanted to put it all together and charge this bastard for what he had done. For the lives he had ruined.

'Shall we go back into interview and ask him about the telephone cloning software thing? And the photographs of Tyler?' Aaron made a couple of notes in his pocket notebook.

'I think it would be rude not to.' I smiled and we walked towards the custody desk and the sergeant to ask for Mark Wallace to be allowed out for interview again.

65

John decided he had hidden out at the office long enough, it was time to go home. Trisha had tried to call him once and had not tried again. She knew if he was busy he would call her back when he had a chance. Instead of calling her he would just see her back at home. He needed to be at home. To feel the comfort of home, the security of home, even if he could be reached with an email. He felt secure when he was wrapped up in a blanket on the sofa in front of the television with Trisha.

When the kids were younger they all used to get blankets and snuggle down in front of a film together, but as they grew older, those days came less and less often and he missed them. But he was glad that he still shared them with Trisha.

It wasn't a long drive home and the car was just starting to warm up as he approached the turning onto his street.

Something felt off. He could see blue rotating in the night above the houses.

An ambulance? Had Trisha had a heart attack? Dear God, no. Please, no not Trisha. Then he caught himself. People always thought the worst, didn't they. It was more likely to be one of the neighbours. Poor Mrs Moore two doors down, she was getting on. She had probably called Trisha instead of the ambulance and Trisha had called the ambulance, that will have been why she was calling him earlier, to tell him where she was if he came home and she wasn't there.

Damn, he wished he had picked up the phone. She would have been annoyed at him for not answering. It was important. At least he was home in time to catch her before she left for the hospital.

He put his foot down and rounded the corner onto their street and the sight that met him took his breath away.

His hands rose from the steering wheel towards his mouth. The car drifted towards a parked car. John didn't notice. His eyes were focused on the fire engine with the spiralling blue lights. The fire engine that was parked right outside what was once his home but was now a blackened shell, smoke rising from the centre.

There were police cars here as well as an ambulance.

There was an ambulance. Did that mean someone got out of there alive?

Trisha.

The car bumped into the parked car and jolted John out of his disorientation.

He turned the engine off and leapt out of the car, started to run towards the wreckage that was his home. Towards where the ambulance was parked. Emergency workers were all over. Like ants in a worker colony.

The rear of the ambulance was open.

'Trisha!' he shouted towards the open van doors. 'Trisha!'

He grabbed the door and hauled himself around it.

'John... I'm so sorry, I tried. I really tried. The doors, they were... I'm sorry, John.' It was George Loftus from next door. His face was blackened. The paramedic was holding a plastic mask over his mouth and nose. George looked devastated.

'Trisha?' John's voice was a low whisper.

George shook his head. 'I'm so sorry, John.' Tears flooded his eyes. 'I really did try. I could hear— I tried. I tried so very hard.' The tears slipped over and fell down his cheeks.

John couldn't take it. He hadn't lost Trisha. Not tonight. Not after what he had done. It wasn't fair. If anyone should have been caught up in this it was him.

John looked around him, erratic, his movements jagged and jerky. He found a police officer. Stumbled over to him. 'It's my fault. All this. It's my fault.'

The officer looked him up and down. 'Who are you, Sir?'

John didn't have the patience. He needed for him to understand. 'It's my house. This is my house. That was my wife.' The officer's stance changed immediately to one of concern. John continued, grief driving him forward. His thoughts fuzzy in his head. 'You have to understand. This is my fault. I should have been inside there. It's because of me, all because of me. They were after killing me and now she's dead. It's all my fault she's dead.'

He looked the police officer in the face. 'I killed her.'

66

Before he would say anything else, John demanded to speak to his son and daughter. He needed to know they were safe and were not also in the house and would not trust what the firefighters were telling him. He had to find out for himself, meanwhile he was being shepherded around by the young cop who he had first approached. Some higher-up cop had decided that it was better John stay with him as he was John's first point of contact with the police.

John found out the cop's name was Addal.

Addal had taken him away to the side, away from the circus of the cars with flashing lights and the away from the bustle of the ambulance staff and firefighters and the cops, all with something to do, and away from the sight of his house which was now a crime scene until they determined otherwise, he had been informed. The lead firefighter had said there was something suspicious about the fire and investigators would be in the building in the morning when it had cooled down.

Being away from the sight of it all didn't mean he was away from it though. It was in the air. A thick layer of smoke hung over them and they breathed it. It smothered them. It clung to their clothes. A reminder of this night that John knew would not be easily washed away. It was dark and thick and acrid. It bit at the back of John's throat and told of the horrors that were unfolding around him.

John pulled his phone out of his pocket and dialled his son. Blake was the least emotional of the two children. He had to make sure his children were alive. It was all he cared about at this moment in time. God help him if they had been at home when the fire had started.

The dial tone started and John gripped the phone tight to his ear. He realised he was holding his breath and tried to let it go but it came out in a juddering shake and his chest hurt with the motion.

There was no answer. His hand started to go numb from gripping the phone.

'Hi Dad.' Blake's drawl was laid back and relaxed.

John's bladder twinged and he nearly let it go. His son was safe. His baby boy was safe and well. He couldn't catch his breath. Breath that was filled with the taste of Trisha's death. The thick black smoke that managed to fill the whole street and tasted dark and charred, it was as though it was alive and searching for places to curl into. He could feel it, it was so thick.

'Dad?'

Oh my God. Blake wasn't inside the house. He was somewhere else and he was alive. John's legs gave way and he stumbled. Addal caught him by his arm and kept him upright.

'Dad, what's going on? You're making me nervous, speak to me, are you okay? Where's Mum? Do you need an ambulance?'

He hadn't opened his mouth. He was so pleased to have heard Blake that he hadn't yet spoken to him and Blake was starting to panic. Wasn't it funny how the first thing everything jumped to was the need for an ambulance? It was what he had done and was now what Blake was doing.

'If you don't answer me I'm hanging up and I'm calling Mum.' Blake's tone was sharp, laced with worry.

'Don't do that, Blake.'

'Why? Dad, what's going on?'

'Do you know where your sister is, Blake?' Please say she's with him, or she's with a friend. Please know where she is and it's not in the house.

'I don't know, Dad, I'm not her keeper. This is your last chance, tell me what it is or I phone Mum.'

And with a calm quietness he didn't feel because his stomach had turned into a hard knot after Blake's comment on Lizzy, John told Blake there had been a fire and he should come home and he would talk to him here. Blake wanted to talk to Trisha. Of course he did. John couldn't tell him about his mother's death over the phone. He didn't want him to drive knowing his mother was dead. He wanted to talk to him face-to-face, to hold him, to be a father to him, but Blake was spiralling up. There was no way not to tell him.

'If she's gone to hospital tell me which one and I'll go straight there.'

John looked at Addal. He didn't know if Trisha had been removed yet or if she was still in the house. He didn't know enough. All he had wanted to do was to phone and make sure his children were safe. He wasn't prepared for this.

'Blake, your mum was in the house. She didn't make it out. I was at the office. I'm so sorry.'

There was an animal wail, deep and primal through the phone into John's ear and he so wished his son was by his side so he could wrap his arms around him and share in the yawning sorrow that engulfed them both. He worried that Blake would be unsafe as he drove to be with his father, and his sister when he found her.

'Blake?'

There was a snuffle on the other end of the line.

'Blake, I need to find Lizzy. I need to know she wasn't in the house with your mum.'

'Oh my God, no, not Lizzy.' He wailed again. This hurt too much for his nineteen-year-old brain to comprehend.

'Do you have someone that can bring you over here, so you don't have to drive yourself?'

Blake mumbled and said that he did.

'I have to go and find Lizzy, Blake. I'll see you when you get here.

They want to take me somewhere, I don't know where, but I'm not leaving until you get here.'

John was dizzy, lightheaded. It was all too much for him. The past couple of days had been too much for him and now this, how was he supposed to deal with this? It was all because of him. He needed to make that clear. But first of all, he had to find Lizzy.

He dialled Lizzy's number.

She picked up straight away.

This time he couldn't stop his legs from giving out from under him. Addal was nowhere near quick enough to catch him and he was on the cold damp ground sobbing into the phone incoherently. He couldn't bear it. His two beautiful children were both safe and secure. His beautiful wife was lost forever, killed in their home because of him. Because of some faceless emailer. Because of actions he had taken. Because of some ridiculous game he had become involved in. He had figured it out. It was a game of sorts that the emailer was playing. He read the news. He knew what had happened and he knew what would happen next. Only Trisha had been the one to get it.

He sobbed for the world that had crumbled around him.

'Dad?' Lizzy's voice was scared.

John could not stop the tears that had started. Addal gently took the phone from his hand and spoke to Lizzy. Broke Lizzy's world apart. She would make her way to her father just as Blake was doing. And John, he would make them understand how this was all his fault and he would pay the price he deserved. The price Trisha had already paid for him.

67

'Mark, you do not have to say anything, but it may harm your defence if you do not mention when questioned, something you later rely on in court, anything you do say, may be given in evidence. Do you understand the caution and how it applies to you today?' I looked Wallace straight in the eye.

Mark Wallace nodded.

'For the recording please.'

'Yes, I understand the caution.'

'You're still under arrest for the offences you were previously arrested for. This is the second interview. You're still entitled to free and independent legal advice. Do you want a solicitor here?'

'Nope.'

'Can I ask why?' I made notes even though the interview was being recorded because I could easily refer back to them.

'I don't need one.'

Fair enough. 'You're happy enough to continue without one?'

'Yes.'

'You can stop the interview at any time should you change your mind.'

Now the preliminaries were over we could start on the interview questions.

'Earlier in the first interview you said that Lucy had asked you to pick Faith up from school as she was going to be late. Do you still stand by that?'

'Of course I do.' He picked up his coffee and tried to have a drink but it was too hot. The milk was powdered stuff so did nothing to cool the hot water down. He put the cardboard beaker back down on the table.

'Had you seen Faith before you saw her that day?'

'Unfortunately not. Which isn't ideal when you're dealing with kids, especially as she's mine, but Lucy trusted me not to tell her. We weren't at that stage. And I didn't tell her, just ask Faith that.'

'Oh, we believe you didn't tell her. What we're wondering about is why you have software on your computer that can send a text message from another phone number that isn't yours, for example, from Lucy's to the school.'

Wallace swallowed. 'I don't think it's illegal to have that software?'

I smiled at him. 'I don't think it is. But we have submitted a request to the company to find out what text messages you have sent via their software and when we get the answers back, I'm sure it'll make very interesting reading indeed.'

'I think I'll have that solicitor now.'

I laughed. 'I thought you might somehow. Of course you can have your solicitor, Mr Wallace. Let's get you back to the Custody Sergeant where you can sort it out.'

As I was standing at the desk with Wallace, waiting to book him back in to the custody of the sergeant, I turned my phone back on. I had six missed calls from Pasha and a text message from her.

Call me as soon as you get this, Boss. Important.

I booked Wallace into custody and called Pasha.

'What is it, Pasha?' I asked as soon as she picked up. 'You seem to have got yourself in a bit of a twist there.'

'Yeah, something else has happened, Boss.'

'Not the next murder?'

'Yes and no.' There was silence on the end of the line.

'What do you mean, yes and no? How can it be yes, but no, Pasha?'

'There was a fire this evening, an arson, a woman was killed. Both doors, the front and rear of the property had petrol poured over them and there was no escape.'

'We decided a woman would be too weak to have killed Scott Rhodes. She would have been too weak to have pulled on that rope and strangled him. What am I missing?'

The noise in the custody suite was getting louder, prisoners shouting, phones ringing, cell doors slamming shut, I pushed a finger in my ear and tried to find a quiet corner.

'The husband is devastated, he's hysterical and is saying it should have been him that was killed, that he was the target because that was how this was due to play out. I think the husband is our killer and was out of the house when it was petrol bombed and so wasn't killed as he was supposed to be and instead his wife has been caught up in it. He's not in a good place. But I think we can talk to him and find out if he's the link we need and close the loop.'

'I want to talk to him. Text me details of where he is and I'll do that now before I go into interview again.'

I made a quick trip to the location and approached the marked police car briskly. I was cold and I was busy, the smell of burning was heavy in the air. Mark Wallace was locked up in custody and we were waiting to go back in to interview to speak to him but Pasha had contacted me to say there was a male here I needed to speak with, that this scene appeared to be the one we had been dreading and the male in the police car would shed some light on the situation for us. She had received a call from the control room inspector who was aware of our job and had forwarded the information promptly.

I leaned down into the space of the open car door and saw the shadow of a man hunched over, hands over his face, great wracking sobs juddering his shoulders. This was not going to be an easy interview.

Aaron was finding the police officer who had taken the first account from John Crowley. We needed to get all the information we could and if this was what we thought it was, we needed to follow procedure and get everything in order if this was going to go to trial. Though at first glance John Crowley was a victim, but I knew this case and I knew he wasn't likely to just be a victim for long.

'Mr Crowley?' I spoke quietly into the car.

He lifted his head, looked puzzled someone was talking to him.

'I'm here.' I spoke again, still standing outside the car.

He turned to look at me. His face was streaked black and red from the air and from crying.

'DI Robbins. Do you mind if I join you?' I asked indicating the inside of the car. I was desperate to get inside. It was cold out here now.

Crowley nodded, mute.

I climbed in the car at the side of him.

'I killed her,' he said before I could get another word out.

'Before we go any further, Mr Crowley, I'm just going to caution you, okay?'

He nodded again.

'You do not have to say anything but it may harm your defence if you do not mention when questioned something you later rely on in court, anything you do say may be given in evidence. Do you understand?'

He nodded again.

'You're not under arrest but you are making some pretty heavy statements so I needed to caution you to cover myself for the rest of the conversation. What do you mean, you killed her? From my brief understanding of the situation you weren't here when the fire went up. I take it we're talking about your wife?'

Again Crowley nodded. 'It's my fault she's dead. They were trying to kill me. I know they were. If it wasn't for me and what I did then they wouldn't have set the fire and she would still be alive. I killed her. With my actions.'

I thought this might be the case. He was talking about actions he had taken. 'What did you do?' I asked. The light was dim in the car, all we had was the street light outside and it wasn't breaking through the darkness inside the car much. Crowley's face was in shadow. He paused, looked down to his feet.

'Would you consent to a DNA test, Mr Crowley?' I asked when it became obvious he wasn't going to respond.

When I thought he wasn't going to reply again he nodded his head. 'I'll do your test, you can find out the truth.'

It was enough for now. Whatever had happened he was grieving for the loss of his wife. I thanked him and told him someone would do the DNA swab this evening. I wanted it doing straight away. If John Crowley was the killer of Scott Rhodes then I wanted to know about it. It would be another piece of the puzzle. If we put a rush on the DNA we could probably get it back in a couple of hours. The rush was necessary because of Wallace's custody clock that was ticking down and any links we could make to Wallace the better.

That poor, poor woman who had been burnt in her home simply for being married to a man who had become involved in something dark and sinister and something, I had a feeling, going by how I think Lucy was dragged into it, had not a lot of choice about what he was doing.

I found Aaron and relayed what had happened with Crowley. 'We really could wrap this up. If this husband is the piece in our puzzle, if there is evidence we can follow, we might be able to charge him with his offence, but also importantly charge Wallace with his part in running the whole thing. He's too smarmy for me.'

I looked at my watch. After arrest we had twenty-four hours to detain an offender before we had to ask a superintendent not connected with the case for a further detention time of twelve hours. Following that, if we required more time to interview the offender, we needed to go to a court to ask for extra time on the custody clock. So far we were ten hours in but it was evening and we were about to head into the period of time where he was eligible for a full eight hours' sleep. The clock was being eaten up.

68

The DNA on John Crowley came back a match to that on the rope used to strangle Scott Rhodes. Pasha and Martin arrested him in his grief-stricken state and brought him into the Bridewell custody suite where Aaron and I were still holed up with the Mark Wallace section of the investigation. Mark was still waiting for a solicitor so I decided to go into the interview of John with Pasha. This way I would know all strands of the job when it was time to go back to speak to Wallace. I would fully understand the case rather than relying on being told third hand what John Crowley had said. And besides, I had spoken to him back at the fire scene. I was interested in following through with him and he knew me. He might be liable to open up to an officer he had met and had talked to, especially in his fragile state. He might be our offender for the Scott Rhodes case but he was still the victim for the fire. We had to step carefully.

I asked the custody sergeant what his drink of choice was and made him the coffee he'd been drinking since he'd arrived and waited at the custody desk while a detention officer collected him from his cell. He walked up to us his shoulders hunched over, his head down, a look of total and utter defeat plastered all over his body.

'John,' I spoke to him. 'I'm DI Hannah Robbins. Do you remember me from the car at the scene of the fire?'

He lifted his head. His eyes were dark, sunken and red rimmed. 'I remember you.' His voice was even and flat. He had given up. The loss of his wife had hit him hard. This would not be an easy interview to do.

'I'm going to be the officer interviewing you today, along with my colleague, DC Pasha Lal.' Pasha gave him a small smile in acknowledgement. He just looked at her. 'Let's get to an interview room and we can get on with it.'

I nodded at the custody sergeant who booked him out of the custody and into the care of us while we had him in interview.

The interview rooms were all alike in the Bridewell. All bland with nothing but a table and four or five chairs and a recording machine. Going around the centre of the wall was a red panic bar alarm for officers in case a detainee kicked off. I had no concerns that this was going to happen in the case of John Crowley. He had nothing in him. We would be lucky to get a conversation out of him never mind a fight.

Once I'd started the recording and introduced everyone, run through all the required starting statements I looked at John. He had not wanted a solicitor and he looked so alone on the opposite side of the table.

Pasha picked up her drink and looked at me as she drank. There really was nothing coming from John.

'You're here for the murder of Scott Rhodes, John,' I started. 'Tell us how you know him.'

Crowley shook his head. 'I don't know him.'

'Are you denying you murdered him?'

'No. I'm saying I don't know him.'

I knew roughly what will have happened but I needed details. We had figured out some of it but we needed to know how it had worked and why these people had done this for Wallace. 'You just walked into a random house and killed a stranger?'

'No.' He wasn't giving any more than he had to. If I asked him yes or no questions then that was what he was going to answer with. I opened up my pocket notebook to the page where I had talked to John in the car. Reminded myself of what he had said to me and repeated it back to him.

'You said when I saw you in the police car it was your fault she's dead. In fact, your exact words were 'They were trying to kill me. I know they were. If it wasn't for me and what I did then they wouldn't have set the fire and she would still be alive. I killed her. With my actions.'

'Tell me what you mean by that, John.'

He slumped forward dropping his elbows onto the table, propping his head up with his hands. Pasha shifted back an inch or two pulling the paper she was making notes on with her. 'I was made to kill that man and I think someone was then sent to kill me. They must have been. It's the only thing I can think of. Look at the timing. Straight after I kill that guy my house is set alight and my beautiful wife...' His words caught, hitched in his throat, '...burned alive in there.' He spat out the last four words. His face swelled as it reddened and he tried to hold back the tears that were threatening to fall. He wanted to finish this interview but emotion was breaking this man in front of us.

I needed to continue. I needed to know what had happened, as difficult as this was for him. He had murdered someone and we needed to deal with that. 'What do you mean you were *made* to kill, John?'

He swallowed, 'I got an email.'

I looked at Pasha. This was it. We were about to learn the truth behind it all. What had been happening. We could soon confront Wallace with it all.

Crowley continued. 'He threatened my family if I didn't kill this bloke called Scott Rhodes for him. He gave me all the details. His name, his address, etc. but left how I was to do it up to me.'

Pasha was scribbling at the side of me. I took a drink of my coffee. This was the break we had needed. 'He threatened to kill your family if you didn't kill for him?' I clarified.

'Would that make it better?' He couldn't have looked any more defeated or lost. He shook his head again. 'No, he didn't threaten to kill them. That's not him is it? He doesn't get his hands dirty does he?'

He was right, John Crowley might not know we had the man responsible in custody, and that we had an idea of what had been happening, but he was right that Mark Wallace did not get his hands dirty by committing the violence himself. He left that to the poor people whose lives he invaded. 'What threat did he make?'

Tears fell from his eyes. These were not the first that had fallen and they would not be the last. 'He threatened to destroy the life of my daughter, Lizzy. He sent me photographs he'd created of her head photoshopped onto pornographic images. He was going to put them out there, in the public domain. Where her friends and family would see them, her employers and future employers. Where she'd see them and have to live with them when I knew they weren't her. I knew they were photoshopped. My daughter has a birthmark on her right shoulder and there was no birthmark on these images. I couldn't let him do that to her. Have you seen the damage these kinds of things can do to a person's life, DI Robbins? Now she's safe but she's lost her mum and she's about to lose her father. All because some maniac wanted to have his fun.'

I could see why he was so devastated. 'So you killed Scott Rhodes?'

'I killed Scott Rhodes.'

'You have to tell me what you did, John. For the recording.'

Very quietly and very slowly John Crowley talked us through the events of the night he walked into the house of Scott Rhodes and wrapped a piece of rope around his neck and pulled the life out of him. He was thorough and logical. We had everything we needed to go to the CPS for a charging decision. We also had somewhere we could go with Mark Wallace. John Crowley's email account. If everything went as it should it would lead us back to Mark Wallace and tie up this job.

69

I immediately directed the SPOC Unit into identifying where the email address that had contacted John Crowley came from. It wasn't a long task and the piece of the puzzle we needed came back within half an hour. The email address, no matter that it was just made up of letters and numbers, and didn't make any sense, was traced back to Mark Wallace. He was the one behind the killings, even though he hadn't laid a hand on anyone.

Very quickly I phoned Elizabeth again. 'I need you to go through Mark Wallace's emails if you haven't got there yet,' I said to her when she picked up. 'I have a feeling these are what is going to convict him.'

'Why do you say that?' she asked.

I told her about Crowley's interview.

'Wow, creepy.'

'Yes,' I agreed. 'So if you can check his emails. See if he contacted Lucy Anderson and Scott Rhodes as well, that would be great. And Elizabeth?'

'Yeah?'

'We need to identify the arson killer. I know they will have been coerced into it as all the others will have been, but we still need to find them. Can you check for other emails to see who he sent after John Crowley please?'

'I'll make his emails my next task and if I find any I'll submit the addresses to SPOC to ID the owners for you if you'd like?'

I smiled down the phone. 'You are worth your weight in gold, Elizabeth.'

'I'll remind you of that next time we have a delay on and you're getting really tetchy with us,' she laughed.

'Me, tetchy?'

'I know, I know. Okay, I'm going to search these emails now.'

'Thanks, Elizabeth.' I hung up the call and ran a hand through my hair. I was drained but thrilled that we were starting to close the loop on this case now.

I turned to Aaron. 'We're still waiting for evidence to come in, but are you ready to go and talk to Wallace again?'

'Let's get it done.'

His solicitor was a baby-faced young lad. Barely looked as though he shaved. It made me feel old that I was even thinking that.

'Why, Mark?' I asked him, holding my drink in my hand. I was tired. It was late and if we didn't get answers soon then we would have to bed him down for the night and go back into interview again in the morning. We would anyway, but I'd like the answers first. We'd come this far.

He stared at me. Hard and flinty. 'I'm that little girl's dad. Faith. Do you know what that's like?'

I didn't speak. I didn't have children. But neither was I willing to discuss my personal life with him.

'She divorced me without telling me she had had a baby. What kind of woman does that? Stays married long enough to be able to put my name on the baby's birth certificate but fucks me off. I don't matter. You can screw me around as much as you like because it suits you.' Spittle was flying out of his mouth his passion was driving him forward.

'Well, no, no she couldn't. She couldn't treat me so badly and get away with it. I wouldn't allow her to get away with it and to live such a wonderful life without me. Once I realised what she had done and where she was, I knew just how to hurt her. She was too kind for her own good. She hated to kill anything. We caught spiders in a glass jar in our house when we were together you know, she refused to stamp on them like normal people. But, as for any crimes, you can't pin anything on me. My DNA isn't at any scene. I haven't touched a single person.' He smirked, looked at his solicitor, tapped his fingers on the table in a slow and steady, quite relaxed motion. 'I didn't kill anyone.'

I smiled at him. 'I think you needed to have done some more research, Mark. You're as liable as the person doing the action.'

His smile stayed plastered on his face. 'I don't know what you're talking about.'

'You set those people on their paths. Without you these deaths won't have happened. We have evidence, Mark. We're going to put you away for a very long time.'

He laughed at me. 'You have nothing. They're all dead.' He cocked his head to the side. 'As far as I know. Any and all evidence is gone with them.'

'Don't be so sure about that.'

EPILOGUE

I battled past the news reporters, pushing and shoving my way through. Cameras clicked and flashed in my face as I moved. There was no clear way around them but through. The weather was milder, it was starting to change, but they'd have been here regardless of warmth. They'd been camped here for weeks. My mood with them was stretched thin. An elbow may have caught one or two of them off-guard as I fought my way towards the house. A microphone was pushed into my face.

'DI Robbins, anything you can tell us today? Do you know how Wallace is going to plead when he gets to court?'

I ignored them and finally I was through the herd and stepped into the house I had come to know well. It was quiet. I remembered my last time here and made my way up the stairs with Aaron. At the top of the stairs stood a uniformed officer with a large pad in his hand. We showed him our ID cards and he let us pass. The officer indicated which room we needed to be in. I turned to Aaron and shook my head, he mirrored my action then we entered the bedroom we were directed to.

Jack Kidner lifted his head up from his examination. 'Ah, young Hannah. A sad state of affairs this.'

I moved into the room. Through the large bedroom window I could hear the gaggle of reporters and photographers beyond, standing, talking, laughing, getting on with their day while they waited for an appropriate photograph of the resident going about their business. But she wouldn't be going about her business again.

I looked at the bed where Kate Wallace lay, her lips blue, her eyes wide and staring. On the bedside table were four empty pill bottles, an empty glass and half a bottle of vodka.

'Not suspicious I take it, Jack?' I asked, thinking of the cop guarding the scene on the stairs.

He shook his head. 'No. It looks like she did this herself. You can ask the vultures outside if anyone has been in here but I doubt it. There's no sign of a struggle. It looks like she came to bed and decided she couldn't take any more. Her husband is a killer and the press are camped on her doorstep. For someone who has never done anything wrong it's a lot to take in. I was called out just to be safe because it's a high profile case.'

I moved to the window and peered out. 'Another life lost to Wallace's games.'

'How's the prep for the trial going? He going away for a long time?' Jack started to pack his kit away.

'He should be. Elizabeth found all the emails on his laptop where he made threats to everyone and where he told them they had to kill the next person in the line and he asks for the photographs. Then there are the very photographs he's asked for. He can't have got them any other way than by someone being at the scene as soon as it happened and before emergency services. It doesn't matter that he didn't admit it. The evidence is there. Including the text message he sent to the school before he abducted Faith.'

I looked down at Kate. 'You know she told me she couldn't have children? She was perfectly willing to take Faith in as soon as she heard her husband had a child and that child had just lost her mother. She was a good woman.'

'How is the girl?' Jack snapped his bag shut.

'She seems to be doing okay with her grandmother. She never

knew her dad so this is passing her by. We caught up with the arsonist, thanks to Wallace's emails. Selena Glass. She has a daughter. According to the emails sent to her by Wallace the child is illegally adopted from Ethiopia. That's a whole other mess, Jack. We've had to get immigration involved. It's going to take years to resolve. She's been removed from the father she knows because of the illegality of it, but because she's been westernised they don't know what to do with her so she's temporarily housed with a foster family. Poor girl. Two children whose lives have been completely screwed up by Wallace.'

'And this poor girl here,' Jack said looking down at Kate.

'We'll find her family and inform them,' I said still looking down at the baying crowd outside. 'She thought she could carry on with her life. She thought she was strong enough.'

Jack walked over to me and patted me on the shoulder. 'I'm not sure any of us know how strong we really are until we're tested, Hannah.'

BOOKS BY THE AUTHOR

Books in the series;

Three Weeks Dead (Prequel novella)
Shallow Waters
Made to be Broken
Fighting Monsters
The Twisted Web
A Deeper Song

Other books by the author;

Dead Blind
Perfect Murder

ABOUT THE AUTHOR

Rebecca Bradley is a retired police detective who lives in the UK with her family and two Cockapoo's Alfie and Lola, who keep her company while she writes. She needs to drink copious amounts of tea to function throughout the day and if she could, she would survive on a diet of tea and cake.

If you enjoyed *Kill For Me* and would be happy to leave a review online that would be much appreciated, as word of mouth is often how other readers find new books.

DI Hannah Robbins will return in A Deeper Song. When you Sign up to the Readers Club mailing list (on her website - rebeccabradleycrime.com) you not only receive a FREE novella, but you will also receive early previews, exclusive extracts and regular giveaways. As well as keeping up to date with new releases.

Please look her up, as she would love to chat.

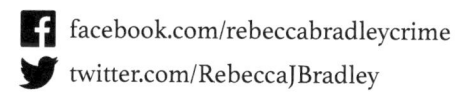

facebook.com/rebeccabradleycrime
twitter.com/RebeccaJBradley

ACKNOWLEDGMENTS

I love writing these books but they can never be written without the support of several other people so with Kill For Me I need to thank the following;

Jane Isaac, my friend, who listens to me complain about where the story is or isn't going and reads early versions and supports me as I need it. I couldn't do it without her. Thank you.

Denyse Kirkby as always for her continued work on Aaron with his Asperger's.

Debi Alper for her structural editing skills and showing me the book is not yet finished.

Helen Baggott for proofreading and Anne O'Hara for a final eye.

Thank you to my launch team for reading and supporting the book as it was released.

As always, my love goes out to my family for the continual support and love as I sit at my desk and write and various hours throughout the day. I couldn't do this without you.

Printed in Great Britain
by Amazon